The Stone Guardians
The Path of Fate

By Katy Mullett

Chapter 1

Slately is a really terrible place to live.

Every child is told what subjects they will be taught in school. Every young adult is assigned a job which they must do until the day they die, no quitting or career switching. You do your assigned job, or you lose everything.

Every adult is told which house they will live in and which district, not that it makes a whole lot of difference, all the houses look the same and what district you stayed in depended on your job.

Dreams are not allowed in Slately.

All the homes are big, bland, and boxy. White brick walls, grey slated roof, black doors, and windows. There is not a burst of colour or nature to be seen, that kind of thing was considered a distraction.

Each person is told who they will marry, how many kids they will have, what they will name their children. Everyone is given a set list of food they are allowed to eat and a list of beverages they can drink.

These citizens have no choice.

However, there is no crime in the city. There are no homeless people nor any rich people. Everyone is equally employed, fed, and have the same size of house. No more, No less.

It may be a boring and depressing way to live, but at least there is no one going hungry.

All the above is not the worst part of this town. No.

There is one thing that makes this place worse than hell.

The Slately Council – these are mysterious people that run the town from afar, no one has ever seen them, no one knows their names. No one even knows where they are!

All they know is if people who look like walking shadows with white masks come to your door, you will never be seen again. These frightening figures were known as The Masquerade.

They always came in the night, silent and precise.

Your partner would go to bed and then be gone in the morning with no sign of a struggle. Nothing would be broken, out of place – There would just be a little white and black striped card, a sign The Masquerade had taken their victim.

You must do what you are told. If you stray from your path, The Masquerade will come.

Again, nobody knew who was in The Masquerade. They did not know where they lived, what they were.

There were many rumours around these mysterious figures. One of which suggested The Masquerade were actually The Council, keeping everyone in place and watching everyone's moves.

There was also a rumour that The Masquerade were not people at all, but souls or maybe beasts enslaved by The Council to keep everyone under control, they moved so silently after all – they couldn't possibly be human.

Yes, Slately is a sad and scary place.

It was the 21$^{st of}$ November.

Huge droplets of rain drummed against the pavements and roads, water roared through the drains and into the system of tunnels below. The water tapped against windowpanes and ran down rooves in small waterfalls. No wind was howling as the heavy clouds covered the morning sun from those below, people walked to work in crowds of black and grey umbrellas. Cars trundled along in lines down roads, all the same model and a dull black. There was no mumbling chatter, no singing, no humming.

Just the sound of rain, footsteps, and the monotone hum of car engines.

This day happened to be a big important one for many citizens.

One of which was Tabitha Murphy.

Tabby blinked her dry eyes open sleepily; golden orbs scanned the white popcorn ceiling groggily as she remembered what day it was. She closed her eyes again with a groan as she pulled a strand of hair out of her mouth, maybe if she just stayed in her cozy bed everything would be ok.

However, she knew she could not.

Today was the adulthood ceremony, a massive formal event where young people coming of age were assigned their careers.

Most people would be overjoyed it was their birthday but not her, not in Slately. This huge life altering event had been hovering over her since she turned fifteen, as it had for most young people.

Tabby was going to be told what the rest of her life held in store for her.

Needless to say, it had been a restless night. Her parents had acted like she was going to die when they said goodnight to her, she had then lay in bed for hours as her brain stressed. She had barely slept a wink; every dream seemed a nightmare.

She had spent many hours trying to predict what work she was going to be assigned, she wanted business. She was happy to do any job as long as it was in the business district.

She did not want agriculture, she did not want entertainment, she did not want law or anything else.

"Tabitha! Get up!" Her mother called up the stairs, her voice anxious and impatient. "You need to get ready!"

"Yeah, I know." Tabby huffed tiredly, finally willing herself to sit up. She rubbed her hands over her tired pale face and shoved her tangled hair back before she finally prepared for the day.

Tabby got herself showered and dressed up in the ceremonial garments – A long black office dress, skin tone flat shoes and opaque tights.

She brushed her long mousey hair lazily; it was naturally thick, wavy and fluffy, but she was not allowed to leave it loose which she was pretty ok with. She tied it back into a neat and tidy ponytail – The Masquerade would have a problem with her if even a single hair was out of place.

Tabby yawned as she strolled down the stairs, the house was buzzing with nerves and activity.

She stood at the bottom debating if she would be able to stomach breakfast through the swirling butterflies, though with all the hustle and bustle she was not sure she was going to get offered any.

Now she felt really guilty for getting up late.

She watched as her mother, dressed in a formal grey dress, rushed past her. Her heels clicked feverishly on the laminate flooring as she hurried to find her purse while securing her watch on her wrist. She was muttering away under her breath and shaking her head as she went, her short bob barely moved from the amount of hairspray keeping it perfect.

Her father was pacing in the living room, he was wearing a smart suit in greys and whites – his black shoes shined so they sparkled. The older man was fiddling with his partnering ring, a known sign he was anxious. His face was stony, his shoulders tight and tense. There was a slight tremour to him, his brown hair was short but messed up from having hands run through it too many times.

Her mother was in the kitchen, she could hear her taking deep breaths and murmuring to herself. She glanced forward at her father, staring sadly at the large back that faced her.

Tabby swallowed as she rubbed her right cheek, she was starting to sweat.

"Tabby?" Tabby looked down to see her little sister, Matilda. "What's going on?"

Matilda was only 7 years old, she had similar but medium mousey hair tied back into a neat bun and was dressed in a puffy white dress. Her small chubby face was pale and wrinkled in concern, her thin mouth was pursed as she waited for an answer.

She was a smart girl, Tabby knew well. If she lied, she would know, if she told the truth she would make her cry. She wasn't sure what to do.

"Um… it's my birthday today." Tabby eventually smiled softly, trying her best to keep her voice light.

"Yeah, I know *that!*" The girl huffed, her wide green tinted eyes betraying her fear. "Why are Mother and Father freaking out?"

"Because today's a special day." Tabby tried to explain gently, "We're going out to a big party and I'm going to be given a job."

"Oh!" Matilda's mouth opened in surprise; her brows then furrowed. "Does that mean you'll be going away?"

Tabby didn't know how to respond.

The kid down the road was assigned to work in the mines and so he was taken away to the mining district. Tabby prayed she was in accounting or business like her parents, that way she could stay here in her home with her family.

"C'mon!" Her father's voice boomed down the hall as he stormed over to the front door. "We can't be late."

"Of course!" Her mother skittered over, neither adult looked at their eldest daughter.

Her mother grabbed Matilda's hand and pulled her out the door behind her, her father held the front door open as he kept his gaze glued to the ground.

"C'mon darling… We have to go." His voice was quiet, serious.

"I know Father…" Tabby nodded, she took a deep breath and walked through the door.

Her future was waiting for her.

Chapter 2

Tabby leaned her head against the cold glass of the car window, she stared out blankly at the rain as her stomach twisted itself into knots. She barely saw the dreary scenery outside as her mind raced through the careers she could end up having, she didn't want this. The car was stuck in a tense, thick silence. Her parents in the front kept their eyes firmly staring out the front window, they were stiffer than boards.

Matilda was sat next to her; she too was staring out of her window. One of her hands was white knuckle gripping her skirt, the other lay flat on the seat between them. It kept twitching and shifting like she didn't know what to do with it.

Tabby hated that she was causing her family so much stress, she wished she could find the words to say to make them all feel better. She had tried to make conversation when they first entered the car but all she received for her efforts were short answers, hums, and silence.

Tabby startled when she felt a small cold hand grip hers, she glanced round to see Matilda staring at her. The younger sister squeezed her hand tightly and gave her a brave smile, even nodding confidently at her.

"Everything will be ok." She spoke up, Tabby saw her parents flinch out the corner of her eye. "You'll get the same job as Mother or Father and then we'll all go home again! Nothing will change!" Tabby couldn't stop her mouth from twitching up into an affectionate smile.

"Maybe you're right," She nodded kindly, "It's not often kids get sent to a different district,"

"I'm always right." Matilda nodded happily; Tabby grinned at her.

"I mean, you still need me." She continued softly, "I'm not about to leave you... besides, who will you torture if I'm gone?"

"Exactly! You have to stay!" Her little sister nodded confidently, seeming to be reassured.

Tabby glanced forward to see her parents had not relaxed any, they continued to pointedly star out the windscreen.

"Guys?" She cocked her head awkwardly, desperate for the silence to end. "What was the ceremony like for you?"

There was a beat of silence as her parents glanced at each other.

"It's... daunting." Her mother finally admitted, "It's very scary but... you're right... it's not often kids get taken away from their birth district... I'm sure you'll be fine."

Her father stayed silent but his grip on the steering wheel softened.

"Yeah..." Tabby nodded quietly, unsure on how to proceed.

The family lapsed back into silence, Tabby sighed and went back to staring out her window.

At least the rain finally seemed to be letting up.

They arrived at the Slately Ceremony Hall; a giant round stone building made precisely for these kinds of important events.

You came here at sixteen to be assigned your career and district. You then came here at 21 to be assigned your life partner and, finally, you came here at 25 to find out if you were allowed children and how many.

The approved names would be sent via letter a week before the baby was due.

Slately Hall was intimidating to say the least, it was as tall as it was wide and there were no windows. Just a front door and a back door though, nobody was permitted to be near the back of the building. Plus, it was close against The Wall, which was just a monstrous and terrifying sight.

The whole town was surrounded by the tallest wall you could ever imagine. The top cannot be seen from the ground for it disappears into the clouds and heavens, nobody really knows just how far up it reaches. What's even stranger is no one knows when it was built, there are no records of it (As far as the public know). It's just always been there.

This huge, towering grey barrier.

A brick cage locking them all away from the outside world. Nobody knew what lay beyond their big city, maybe they were the only humans in the world.

The citizens were told it was to keep something out, but many suspect it is there to keep them in.

It made Tabby feel so small and insignificant.

Tabitha and Matilda stood at the foot of the wall and stared up as the cloud finally broke overhead, they were still holding hands.

"It makes me feel dizzy." Matilda breathed as she finally stepped back and looked away, blinking rapidly. "I don't like it."

"Yeah, it does the same to me." Tabby shook her head, turning to face her little sister. "Hey, it's not gonna be long now."

"Are you scared?" Matilda asked quietly, she glanced around worriedly for their parents.

"A little," Tabby admitted shakily but gave her a smile. "But it won't take long... soon it'll all be over. Besides... maybe this will be the start of something great?"

She tried to sound convincingly positive, her sister didn't seem to pick up on this.

"Ok." Matilda nodded shyly; her hand gripped hers tightly.

The two sisters simply stood together, both wondering if they would see the other again after today. They were both deep in their thoughts as they reminisced about good times spent together, both still clinging to the others' hand.

Neither noticed their parents coming over until the couple were right beside them, both kids looked up at the adults and deflated at the defeated expressions on their faces.

"It's time to head in." Their father nodded, his voice quiet and strained.

The four headed towards the large black doors as they were being opened, they joined the many other families in line. There was a fearful buzz all around, there was dull chatter and the sound of quiet crying.

Families were going to be torn apart today.

The Murphy's entered the luxurious black and white themed hallway, one of The Masquerade stood before them.

"Tabitha Murphy, continue forward until you see the door marked with your name. Family are to go right and sit in their assigned seats." The being commanded in a gravelly voice; Tabby swallowed at how unhuman it sounded.

"Ok Tabitha." Her mother breathed as she gave her a quick hug. "Whatever happens... I love you so much!"

"I love you too." Tabby whispered as she hugged her back.

"Be brave sweetheart." Her father nodded firmly, his shining eyes betraying his brave exterior. "Behave yourself, don't get into any trouble... Just keep your head down and do your best."

Tabby nodded back, unable to speak. She looked down at Matilda, she was just looking up at her with a tear-streaked face.

"See you soon?" She whimpered quietly,

"Of course." Tabby smiled, trying to be brave for her.

She watched as her family disappeared through the curtain to take their seats, she took a deep breath to steady herself. She glanced briefly at the guard before heading down the corridor as instructed, her vision blurred as she tried to read the names.

She was so busy trying to find her room and stressing out that she crashed into someone, sending them both to the ground.

"I am so sorry!" Tabby immediately groveled, "I was trying to find my door and I wasn't looking where I was going I-"

Her mouth snapped shut with a click when she saw the boy in front of her.

The boy was slightly taller, he had blonde hair that was cut long at the top and brushed back tidily with short shaven sides. However, a few of the longer strands seemed to keep falling out of place and into those dark blue eyes – he had a handsome face thanks to the broad jaw, high cheek bones and clear warm olive skin.

Tabby knew the boy and immediately grinned brightly.

"Alfie?" She looked up into the familiar face, Alfie was rubbing his lower back when his head snapped up.

"Tabby!?" He grinned happily back, "Hey! I hoped we'd meet again!"

The two stood up and smiled at one another fondly, both seemed to be reminiscing. Tabby couldn't resist, she gave her friend a big hug. She was just so happy to see a friendly face during one of the most stressful moments of her young life.

They pulled apart as Alfie blushed.

"So, today's the day?" Alfie crossed his arms self-consciously. "I guess you want to stay in business?"

"Yeah... definitely." Tabby nodded with a sheepish smile. "You do too, right?"

"I guess?" Alfie looked to the side distractedly, keeping an eye out for guards.

There was a moment of awkward shuffling as they both tried to find something to say.

"How long has it been?" Alfie asked with a shake of his head, his long blonde hair fell into his eyes at the motion. He quickly swept it out of the way.

"I think..." Tabby hummed, "We finished school not long after we hit fifteen... so... a little under a year?"

"Really?" Alfie frowned thoughtfully, his small red nose wrinkling. "Yeah... I guess so? Man... it feels way longer!"

"Yeah, it does... probably because we used to spend every day together." Tabby nodded with a knowing smirk. "What did you do during your transition time?"

"Same as you I'd guess, taking those dumb tests, filling out the forms in preparation for today and going to work with my mother to get some experience." The boy shrugged easily.

The two friends suddenly seemed to remember where they were. Their joy and excitement fizzled out, they took a step away from each other as their faces fell.

"We should probably get moving." Alfie blushed again as he gave Tabby a shy smile. "Good luck."

"You too." Tabby nodded, returning the smile softly.

Both friends silently found their doors together, they were next-door to each other.

They glanced at one another, both seemingly wanting to say something to the other but neither able to. They couldn't help but wonder if they'd ever see each other again, they shared one last fond smile before heading in.

It was a small room painted pristine white, it had a mirror, a second door that led to the stage, a bench, and a speaker. Tabby sat down stiffly as she waited, she felt terribly sweaty yet cold. Her knee bounced as she chewed her thumb nail, she felt like her entire body was prickling and tingling.

She could hardly breath, her chest felt like it was going to burst. The room wasn't helping. Tabby had never been claustrophobic but the tiny cupboard she was sitting in seemed to be getting smaller and smaller, she wondered what would happen if she fainted and missed her cue.

She then hit her thigh, why was her brain coming up with that garbage now?

"Welcome to the Adulthood Ceremony. Where boys become men and girls become women." A falsely happy feminine voice announced, Tabby tensed as she listened.

"Today, children that have come of age will be assigned their careers and their districts. I will call out their names one by one, the candidate will be given their career and be immediately escorted to their new home." The voice explained, sounding too positive for such an awful situation. *"In the event the candidate is returning to the same district they were born in, they, along with their family, will be escorted home."*

Tabby took deep breaths, she needed to stay calm.

"All family members must stay seated at all times unless collected by staff. All family members must stay silent during proceedings. Any disruptive behaviour will be dealt with by staff." Tabby knew what that meant, it meant The Masquerade would take people away if they tried to fight. *"All candidates must follow instructions. Any disruptive behaviour will be dealt with by staff."*

She took another deep breath as she stood up and paced the tiny space.

"Thank you. Good luck to all candidates and enjoy the ceremony."

There was a beat of intense silence that seemed to last forever.

Then the first name was called.

Tabby counted the seconds and realised it was only ten minutes until the next name was called.

It was deathly silent out there.

The fifth name to be called must have gotten an awful career, Tabby could hear yelling and crying. She could hear them being shushed and warned.

It sounded like the family managed to calm down but the poor boy outside was taken away by The Masquerade.

Tabby gulped, she needed to keep her cool. She did not want to be the next one to disappear.

"Alfred Knotts" The voice called; Tabby gasped as her head shot up. "Alfie… Good luck… Please stay calm…" Tabby begged under her breath, she waited anxiously for any sign of upset from outside but before she knew it another name was called.

She couldn't help but wonder if she would see her friend again, she also wondered what career the boy had been given. She imagined there were a few jobs Alfie would be good at… unfortunately business was not one that came to mind. Tabby figured it was pretty likely her childhood friend had been separated from his mother.

"Tabitha Murphy"

Tabby gasped and shot to her feet in fear when she realised her name had been called. She suddenly felt extremely sick, her heart pounded fearfully against her ribs as she felt her breath leave her body. She stiffened as the door slid open and she was blinded by the stage lights.

She swallowed before walking out onto the wide wooden platform, her eyes scanned the crowd but there were so many people! The lights were so bright, the audience so dark – Tabby couldn't see her family in the sea of blurry silhouettes.

She so desperately wanted to cry as she walked over to the center of the stage.

There, a huge screen stood at the back, ready to announce her fate before the whole auditorium. Attached to it was a strange machine, there was a handprint shape on it – it explained what she needed to do.

Tabby lifted her shaky sweaty hand, she wiped it on her skirt, closed her eyes and placed it on the cold glass.

Chapter 3

Tabby squeezed her eyes shut as the glass warmed up and an electric whirring and buzzing filled her ears. She swallowed thickly as the world around her seemed to stop, she could hear and feel her own breathing. For a moment she could trick herself into thinking she was alone in the room, that there weren't hundreds of eyes on her, and no one would be gossiping about what happened to her tomorrow.

She slowly opened her eyes as the screen cycled through various colours, she chanced a glance out into the audience to see the crowd watching with morbid fascination. She still couldn't find her family but was glad no one was actually looking at her.

She looked back over to the screen as time seemed to slow.

She needed it to be pale blue.

Pale blue meant business and she could stay home with her parents and Matilda. Pale blue meant returning to her bedroom in the house she grew up in, it meant she would sleep in her own familiar bed tonight.

She didn't want orange for food, didn't want red for education or green for health care. She didn't want brown for agriculture, and she didn't want purple for production and delivery.

She didn't know what the other colours were for, there were so many districts it was hard to keep track – especially when some of the districts were just slightly different shades of the same colour. Education was an apple red, but Butchering was a slightly darker blood red – two industries you didn't want to get mixed up!

She frowned and glanced over as one of The Masquerade seemed to step forward, clearly, they knew something she didn't.

Was it supposed to take this long?

She looked back up at the screen, her back to the crowd.

The colours slowed.

Red.

Yellow.

Orange.

Green.

Pale Blue.

Tabby begged it to stop there but it seemed she wasn't heard.

Black.

The audience gasped and dissolved into quiet murmurs – They were quick to fall silent though when The Mask looked out at them in warning.

Tabby blinked once, then twice more as her brain caught up.

The screen was black.

She removed her hand from the scanner slowly, unsure if she had somehow managed to break it.

There were no black, gray or white districts, this she knew for a fact! So, what was going on?

She looked out into the crowd to see subtle shakes of the head, it appeared they didn't know either. She then looked over at The Masquerade guard that stood at the side.

"D-Did I break it?" Tabby asked, trying to sound brave. There was a choked gasp from the crowd, candidates aren't really supposed to talk.

The white masked being simply shook their head and beckoned her to exit the stage.

Tabby glanced back up at the black screen uncertainly before cautiously shuffling towards the guard.

The Mask simply stood aside and motioned for her to continue forward down the long hall; Tabby swallowed but did as she was told.

It was then another name was called.

She shuffled alone down the silent hallway towards the back of the building. Her brain raced as she tried to think up what all of this meant, did it mean she didn't have a career? Did it mean she was bad? Did it mean she was going to join The Masquerade?

There was only one thing Tabby knew for sure.

She was never going to see her family again.

She felt her eyes sting with tears, she wished she had found them in the crowd. She just wanted to see them one last time, she wanted to mouth a 'sorry' and an 'I love you' to her little sister.

She never got the chance.

Now she was being taken who knows where!

Of all the things she thought could go wrong today, this never even entered her mind.

Of course she had imagined a hundred other scenarios last night; tripping over, fainting, farting, throwing up and dropping dead in front of everyone – all very embarrassing things she'd never recover from.

But never imagined she would just straight up not get a career.

It was very annoying really, life always had a way of kicking her down even when her expectations were already incredibly low.

Turns out – things can always get worse! Who knew?

She shook her head as her train of thought switched rails.

What could black mean?

Suddenly, Tabby felt very sick and dizzy. Black was often a representative colour of death.

Was she going to be killed?

No, that's not fair! She hadn't done anything! She hadn't broken any rules, she was always well behaved and quiet.

Did they just have too many citizens that they have to kill some of them?

Maybe she was going to be the one killing people?

She wondered if she'd actually be able to do something like that, if there was no choice in the matter.

Tabby hesitated as she arrived at the back door, another member of The Masquerade was standing there.

"Um... my colour was black? What does that mean?" She asked nervously, "Am I going to be killed?"

The Mask simply looked at her and opened the door, it led the girl outside.

"Can you please tell me what black means?" Tabby tried again as she stumbled after the silent being.

She was led to a line of vans, all intended to ship kids to their new districts. Each van matched the colour of the district and had a symbol of a white mask on the side, Tabby could see a smaller black van on the end.

Another mask stood outside it and watched as the two approached.

"The Council were correct. Another two have been chosen." The new Mask greeted.

"Yes. It has been five years; I believe it is getting more frequent." The leader Mask agreed, they then turned around and headed back to the back door to lead another teen to their designated transport.

The Mask in charge of the black van opened the double door, it twitched its head to tell Tabby to climb in.

"What does black mean?" Tabby begged as she shuffled closer, "Am I going to die? If I am, can you at least tell me why? Or let me say goodbye to my family?"

She was met with silence.

Tabby sighed miserably and stepped into the van with her head bowed, she sat on the bench and flinched when the doors slammed shut.

"Tabby?" Tabby's head snapped up to see Alfie sitting on the bench across from her, they were the only two in the van.

"Alfie!?" Tabby gasped, feeling oddly relieved. Something about the boy always made her feel a bit more confident, she wasn't sure why. Maybe there was just something comforting about having someone taller and stockier nearby.

Though, she knew Alfie was soft and sweet. The most gentle and quiet boy Tabby knew, always in the background and always there to support rather than lead.

Tabby figured that was why they had ended up spending so much time together growing up, they were similar in that regard. Both just wanted to stay out of trouble.

Yet, trouble seemed to have found them.

"You got black too?" Alfie asked quietly as the engine jumped to life, both kids gripped their seats when they felt the van pull away.

"Yeah... Do you know what it means?" Tabby asked hopefully.

"No... No idea... I didn't know there was a black district..." Alfie bowed his head as he bit his bottom lip, "I don't know where we're going..."

Tabby watched the boy sadly.

"At least I got to wave my mother goodbye." Alfie sighed quietly, more to himself than to Tabby.

"I couldn't see my family... I didn't get to say goodbye..." Tabby admitted, her voice cracking slightly. Alfie's head shot up, his brow creased in sympathy.

"Oh... Tabby, I'm so sorry." His soft eyes stared straight into Tabby's soul.

For some reason, Tabby couldn't help but give the boy a soft smile. She felt strangely ok despite everything.

"It's ok..." She nodded, leaning forward towards the tall male. "I have to admit... I'm glad we're going through this together... It's nice to have a friendly face by your side."

Alfie seemed to look pleasantly surprised at that, he blushed and cocked his head to the side with a proud smirk.

"I knew it! I knew you liked me!" Alfie chuckled happily, Tabby gaped at him.

"What!? Of course, I like you! You're the only friend I have!" She insisted in offense, "How could you think I didn't like you? We only spent loads of time together nearly every day!"

"I mean… I dunno…" Alfie squirmed in his seat uncomfortably. "You were always so quiet around me and everyone else, we talked yeah… but I kinda thought maybe you were just putting up with me because you hated everyone else more."

Tabby winced, she was sad to think the only friend she had thought she was just putting up with him.

"Yeah… I just didn't like the other kids… They were all stuck up and we were both so similar… I don't know…" Tabby shrugged. "I just didn't know how to talk to you with all those guys nearby."

"So… Just to be clear, we are friends?" Alfie asked awkwardly, not looking at Tabby.

"Yeah… If you wanna be?" Tabby cringed as Alfie nodded a bit too quickly.

The two lapsed into an embarrassed silence at the vulnerability.

"Well… I guess it's nice to be discovering my new life with a… my friend…" Alfie blushed, glancing at Tabby.

"Yeah… I agree." Tabby smiled kindly, Alfie matched it with one of his own.

"We're losers huh?" Alfie smirked weakly, making Tabby chuckle.

"Oh yeah." She nodded, "Total losers."

They smirked for a moment as they listened to the deep, grating hum of the engine.

"I always kinda figured I wasn't going to get to stay in business… I was always horrible with numbers…" Alfie admitted with a sigh as he leaned back against the wall, seeming to have relaxed a bit.

"What did you think you were gonna end up doing?" Tabby asked, she wasn't quite ready to release her death grip on the bench yet.

"I don't know… I liked to think I would end up somewhere like agriculture… I always liked plants and you just don't see them anywhere else…" Alfie admitted, "I wanna grow food for the city, felt it was worthwhile y'know?"

"Yeah… I guess…" Tabby nodded gently, she looked down at her feet in thought.

"What did you wanna do if you had to leave business?" The boy asked in interest, clearly wanting to keep the conversation going so they didn't need to think about their current predicament.

"I never knew, there was never a career that particularly interested me." Tabby shrugged, "Kinda figured it was out of my control so… I just didn't think about it."

"Makes sense." Alfie nodded in understanding, "I think a lot of kids are like that."

Tabby nodded. She knew other kids were like her in their thinking, why bother dreaming of a job when you didn't get to pick. You were always better off not caring, you had to do the role you were assigned so it was best to avoid disappointment.

Still, she hated that all her peers had to learn to give up. There were such ambitious children in her class and the teachers were forced to stamp those sparks out, warning them not to get too caught up in dreams for they often did not come true.

It wasn't fair to treat young people like that. Then again, there was nothing fair about Slately.

Both teens yelped as the van went over a speedbump. Alfie groaned and rubbed the back of his head where it had hit the van wall behind him, Tabby smirked weakly as she willed her heartbeat to slow down.

"Well… The Masquerade don't make good drivers." Tabby joked, Alfie chuckled and glanced up at her.

"No, they don't… nearly knocked me out!" He griped humorously, "Really the icing on the cake."

Tabby laughed softly, she then stood and carefully sat herself beside her friend. Alfie watched her curiously, a small smile on his face.

"There is no black district." Tabby murmured to Alfie, not daring to look at him. "The districts are always a colour, never black, white or grey."

Alfie stiffened beside her.

"What are you saying?" He asked nervously.

"I'm saying... We're not getting a district... we could be going anywhere, and I don't know what's waiting for us when we get out of this stupid van." Tabby admitted sadly, "But... I don't think it's good."

"We've been travelling for a while... we've gotta be at least halfway across town by now..." Alfie hummed, "We're definitely going somewhere specific."

"I just wish I knew what this stupid colour meant." Tabby sighed as she deflated and lay against the wall, Alfie glanced over to her.

"Maybe we're getting taken to the other side of The Wall?" The tall boy suggested fearfully, "Maybe we're getting kicked out of town and left to fend for ourselves!"

"Maybe..." Tabby frowned, "Or maybe they're just gonna kill us... that takes less effort."

Alfie squeaked before clearing his throat sheepishly.

"I wonder if we're gonna get to meet The Council?" He sat up thoughtfully, Tabby raised an eyebrow as she looked over at the boy.

"You want to meet the Council?" She asked skeptically.

"Um... Maybe they're nice?" Alfie didn't sound convinced.

"They literally control everyone with the threat of death... how could they possibly be nice?" Tabby snorted, "If we are seeing them, I don't think it's a good thing."

There were a couple minutes of anxious silence. Alfie slowly turned to look down at her, his face soft and serious.

"Hey… Tabby?" He began quietly.

"Yeah?" Tabby asked, giving the boy her full attention.

"… Do… Do you ever think about what's on the other side of The Wall?" He asked, looking straight at his friend. Tabby frowned thoughtfully, her eyes glancing between Alfie's eyes and lips.

"I mean… Not aloud, that's the kinda thing that makes people disappear." She admitted finally, "But, yeah… I do."

"What do you think's out there?" Alfie asked in wonder.

"I honestly don't know… I hope… I hope there's more people, cities without walls… Maybe lots of grass and trees and stuff…" Tabby shrugged slowly, her mind trying to conjure up such an image. All she could imagine was the same concrete gray walls that had always surrounded them.

"I hope so too… That sounds nice." Alfie agreed happily.

He turned back to lean against the wall seemingly satisfied with Tabby's answer, the girl in question was now lost in her thoughts. She wondered if they really were about to be kicked out of their city and out into… whatever lay outside. Was there anything out there? Or was Slately the only place that existed?

Somehow, that thought was more terrifying than the possibility of being removed from the city.

Chapter 4

The two friends were stuck in that cold bumpy van for far longer than they could take, time seemed to drag terribly as their nerves only grew with the anticipation – Tabby's cheek was red raw from her rubbing it without noticing. They almost felt like the van would never stop, it would just keep going and going until it drove off the edge of the world. The two had been restlessly standing, sitting, shifting, moving and sighing, unable to calm down and stay still. Which is why they both shot to their feet when they felt the van park and the engine cut out.

They heard The Mask get out of the van but walk away, leaving them trapped.

Alfie stepped in front of Tabby, partially blocking her view of the door. She could see her taller friend was tense and trying to look brave, she hoped it wasn't for her sake.

"It left?" Tabby whispered, not daring to speak any louder.

Alfie gave a nod, his brave stance was faltering.

Tabby placed a gentle hand on the stiff shoulder, Alfie glanced at her before stepping back to join her side. Tabby was glad to see the boy wasn't as tense anymore.

"I wonder where we are…" Alfie whispered, his eyes glued to the door. "Should we try to escape?"

"No, I don't think we'd get very far." Tabby huffed sourly, "We'd best just wait it out… If we run they'll just find us again and then we're screwed."

"Point taken." Alfie nodded in agreement. "No use running."

They both strained to try and hear the sounds outside for any indication of where they were, it was deathly silent.

Both teens jumped when they heard multiple footsteps stomping towards the van, Tabby couldn't help but step back warily as she heard them come closer to the door. Alfie sucked in a scared breath and held it, wide eyes darting around fearfully.

The door was opened with a toe-curling shriek, Tabby was ashamed that in her fear her hand shot forward and grabbed Alfie's wrist.

The boy in question had stepped forward at the gesture, putting himself between his friend and whatever was outside.

Four members of The Masquerade stood before them, this meant they had been stomping purposely to scare them.

"Assholes." Tabby muttered under her breath.

Two of The Masks stepped forward and dragged Alfie out, the last two grabbed Tabby.

Both teens were led through the grey concrete car park with their guards keeping a hold of their arms, they couldn't help but glance around at their new surroundings.

Both gasped as they realised where they were going.

Straight ahead was The Wall looming over them threateningly.

There was a huge iron door with more Masks on guard, they stepped forward to open it as the prisoners came forward.

They were all silent.

Alfie was breathing heavily up front while Tabby was swallowing dryly in an attempt not to cry, her stinging eyes told her it wasn't working as well as she had hoped.

They were led into a large stone entrance hall with two large twisting staircases and four doors, two doors led to the left and two to the right. Tabby guessed the wall was like a catacomb with multiple chambers and sections.

The two were dragged through the first door on the right which immediately led to a complicated hallway, there was a set of stairs going up, one going down and a long, seemingly endless corridor stretching ahead with rows of doors on the left.

Tabby gulped loudly as she heard Alfie gasp beside her - they literally couldn't see the end of the hallway.

They were then dragged down the narrow stairs, this led to a dark and filthy basement.

The floor was an off white with a range of colourful stains on it, most alarmingly blood. There was a row of rusty metal shower heads and drains at the back and gross looking brown towels, there was also a small iron closet in the left corner. Bare lightbulbs hung from the ceiling casting a cold and threatening glow over the dingy room.

The two kids were led to the centre of the room and placed side by side.

"Strip." One of The Masks ordered harshly.

It took a moment for the friends to realise what they meant.

"St-Strip?" Tabby squeaked, her face burning red and her stomach dropping in dread.

"Like… Naked?" Alfie asked, clearly equally as embarrassed and uncomfortable.

"Strip off all garments. Now." The Mask snapped impatiently, the two friends flinched and looked at one another in dismay.

"What're you gonna do to us?" Tabby asked in terror as she began toeing off her shoes, Alfie was doing the same.

There was no response.

Tabby and Alfie slowly and despondently stripped until there was not a piece of clothing on them, they pointedly did not look at each other. They felt embarrassed, scared and vulnerable – not knowing how it could get any worse. Tabby chewed her lip as she watched The Masquerade gather up the discarded clothes, she could hear Alfie breathing deeply in an attempt to stay calm. She self consciously covered up with her hands.

"Step under the shower heads." One of The Masks commanded before it joined the others in disposing of the clothing.

Both friends turned and hobbled over to the showers, Tabby studied the wall trying to figure out how to turn it on but there didn't seem to be any buttons or taps.

"Hey, how do we turn them on?" Alfie turned and asked tensely. Tabby gasped and subsequently choked as ice cold water shot out from the shower head above, she heard Alfie swear loudly in a similar manner.

Tabby coughed and spluttered as she stepped back, she skidded on the water and fell heavily. She sat up as she tried to catch her breath, now she was cold, naked and aching.

"Tabby! You ok?" Alfie asked uneasily, trying looking over at his friend but still ready in case she needed help.

"Yeah, I'm good." Tabby grated as she forced herself up, she stood back under the shower.

Eventually the icy streams were stopped and they were able to start drying themselves with their towels, Tabby held her breath as she rubbed her freezing skin with the tatty fabric. She didn't want to smell it, she'd rather pretend it was clean.

Once dry, the two friends walked forward to stand before The Masquerade again. Both were shivering terribly and had red noses and blue lips, they desperately wanted their clothes back.

Two of The Masks stepped forward to reveal they were each holding a pair of clothes, they handed them to the two before stepping back into line.

"Get dressed, then come up the stairs." One commanded, the friends watched as the four guards left the room.

"Uniforms?" Alfie pondered through chattering teeth as he separated the underwear from the other garments.

Tabby unfolded the fabric and cocked her head at it, it was very strange!

Their uniforms were block colour baggy jumpsuits, they also each had a belt of black leather which had loops for holding something and pouches. Tabby's was a rusty brown/orange colour while Alfie's was a royal blue. Both were also given sturdy, thick, black combat boots.

"Are we... painters?" Alfie questioned curiously once they were both dressed and studying each other's clothes. "Workmen maybe?"

"Plumbers?" Tabby suggested unsure, "Well... We know one thing!"

"Yeah? And what's that?" Alfie asked in surprise, Tabby gave him a wide grin.

"We're not getting executed!" She nodded knowingly, "They wouldn't give us these clothes if they were just gonna shoot us!" Alfie smirked and nodded in agreement.

They stood for a moment, it was all finally starting to sink in. They were in The Wall, the very thing that kept the city contained. The terrifying looming structure that nobody knew what was inside. They were never going to see their families again, this was their life now.

Tabby startled as Alfie stepped towards her tenderly.

"C'mon, we'd better get moving." Alfie nodded softly, "They won't wait forever."

Tabby sighed, her eyes scanned her friend's face and she felt concerned when she saw Alfie's lips were trembling.

Her heart ached. Her little sister's lips did the same thing when she wanted to cry but tried to hold it in.

"Hey... Don't be scared, ok?" Tabby spoke up in a timid voice, she was never very good at the whole comfort thing. "We're a team now, we're gonna get through this together."

Alfie gave her a weak smile as he rubbed his nose with the back of his shaking hand, he chuckled wetly.

"Thanks... I'm glad I'm not alone or with some stranger..." Alfie admitted, keeping his voice quiet. "Still... I'm pretty scared, I just have this bad feeling deep in my gut..."

Tabby's frown deepened uneasily but she never got the chance to ask, Alfie marched forward towards the exit all while dragging the smaller girl with him. Poor Tabby stumbled and hurried to walk in step with him, they didn't want to look weak or cowardly in front of their enemies.

After they made it to the top of the stairs they were once again dragged away through a series of doors, stairs and corridors.

Tabby's head spun and she had long since given up trying to remember their route, she was now the one in front but she could hear Alfie's steps behind her.

Eventually they made it to a sealed black metal door.

Tabby and Alfie watched in fear as one of their guards entered in a long pin number into the panel on the right, they now wondered if they were simply just prisoners now and there was no career ahead of them.

The guards stepped back, blocking both escape routes down the corridor. They had let go of the two friends and were now looking at them expectantly, nobody moved for a minute.

Tabby and Alfie shared frightened looks, were they expected to just walk through the door without knowing what was on the other side?

"Wh-What now?" Tabby asked apprehensively, looking at the guards.

One simply gestured with its head toward the door, indicating for them to go through.

Alfie stepped forward towards the door and lifted his hand.

Tabby looked around, trying to figure if there was some way for them to escape. This seemed to make The Masquerade angry, one of the guards behind Tabby marched forward and grabbed the back of her jumpsuit. It dragged her backwards roughly and shook her, Tabby squeaked as her oxygen was cut off.

Alfie looked round with wide eyes; he hadn't seen why they attacked his friend.

"You. Open the door and get in." The guard snarled, shaking Tabby again. "There are worse places we can take you."

Alfie decided he really didn't want to know what the worse place was, he made eye contact with Tabby and reassured her with a nod. He then faced the door and reached out towards the handle.

Chapter 5

Alfie gripped the door handle tightly as he willed himself to just push it open, his mind buzzed knowing Tabby was vulnerable behind him. Were they going to let his friend join him or had they already decided she was going to be taken away? Alfie took a deep breath. The two friends were terrified to step through and face their reality, but they knew it was inevitable.

"C'mon cowards! It's rude to loiter!" A smooth male voice called from the other side, it was light and somehow reassuring – especially when it was gently shushed by a deep baritone voice.

"Alfie, it's ok." Tabby spoke softly, this did the trick. Alfie finally forced the door open.

The door swung a lot easier than expected, it slammed deafeningly against the wall making those inside jump.

Alfie stared at the open doorway in shock, his hand still floating where the handle once was.

He was shaken from his shock by Tabby's yelp as the poor girl was dragged past him and through the doorway by the guard holding her, Alfie stepped forward to help but two guards grabbed his arms and forced him forward.

They were dragged unceremoniously into the room.

The two looked up as a group of people strolled towards them.

There were two men and two women, they looked utterly bizarre! They were each wearing similar jumpsuits, all of them had the exact same shoes and belt but they had various weapons and equipment attached via the loops and holders.

The first man was huge! He looked to be in his early thirties with a scruffy beard and reddish ginger hair in a clumsy buzzcut, he was incredibly tall and had wide muscular shoulders. Everything about him was strong, solid and scary. His jumpsuit was a wine red, he had wrapped knuckles and a collection of knuckle dusters attached to his belt. Strangely, his brown eyes were soft and gentle, and he wore a calm expression on his weathered face.

The second man was also tall, but he was thin and spindly. He looked like a single hug would snap him in half! He also seemed to be in his thirties, but he had warm mocha hair and dazzling purple eyes, a colour the two friends had never seen before! He had red cheeks and a button nose and seemed to wear a permanent grin. He wore a turquoise jumpsuit complete with various fob watches, tattered notebooks, hundreds of different coloured pens, and a pistol – he wore a pair of what looked like metal goggles upon his head giving him a mad scientist vibe.

The first woman was clearly in her twenties, she was tall and curvy with dark brown – almost russet skin. Her wild thick curly black hair was in two buns atop her head, they were not equal in the slightest – one was too far to the side while the other was too far back. Her dark eyes were accentuated with thick purple eyeliner that flicked out from the corners, she had dark purple lipstick on her full lips. She wore a kind smile, her cheeks had deep happy dimples. Her nails were incredibly long and sharp at the end of her thin fingers, which in turn were decorated with a variety of rings, she had various writings and drawing all over her arms. Her dull purple jumpsuit had its arms pushed up and the trousers rolled up from the bottom to reveal a bit of shin above her scuffed boots, she had nothing on her belt though it looked like the pouches were filled with screwed up pieces of ripped paper, pebbles and crystals.

The last member was another girl in her twenties, she was short with light blonde hair in a neat bob. She wore no makeup; her eyes were a light greyish blue under long eyelashes and her cheeks and nose were dotted with light freckles. She wore a pastel green jumpsuit, but the sleeves were way too long, on her belt was first aid equipment along with healthy snacks and herbs. Her nails were tidy, she wore no rings, but she had a woven string bracelet on one wrist, around her neck was a bright rose quartz crystal dangling by a string.

These people were not like the ones outside in the city. They were so unique, vibrant and alarming to the two friends.

The largest one stepped forward, he looked straight at the guards without a hint of fear.

"We'll take it from here, thank you." He nodded firmly, "You don't need to drag them around like that."

Tabby and Alfie were thrown to the floor and landed in a heap with an audible grunt, they both looked up as the guards left to see the giant glaring at their retreating backs. The man shook his head before looking down at the two with a kind smile.

He stepped forward and gently helped the two to their feet before stepping back to join the group, there was a moment of awkward staring.

"Um… Hello?" Tabby stuttered as she smiled awkwardly and gave a little wave, the purple girl immediately cooed at her.

"Aww look at them! They're so nervous!" She giggled softly, "You don't need to be afraid! You guys are the luckiest kids ever!"

Alfie and Tabby shared a quick look.

"Welcome, Alfie and Tabby to The Stone Guardians." The man in turquoise waved his arms in a grand gesture.

Tabby and Alfie blinked stupidly as their brains struggled to process what they had just heard.

"How did you know our names?" Alfie choked out.

"Uh…" The man chuckled sheepishly as he finally noticed the others glaring at him.

"Oculus! Why are you like this!?" The girl in purple huffed, "For goodness' sake!"

"You've confused them." The huge man nodded, his voice was incredibly deep and quiet.

"You did the same thing to us." The girl in green smiled humorously, her voice was high and soft.

The peculiar four continued to argue as Alfie turned to Tabby, they both had wide confused eyes.

"Do… Do you understand what's going on?" Alfie asked, shaking his head in disbelief.

"Not even a little bit." Tabby watched the adults as they squabbled.

All noise stopped as the four finally faced Tabby and Alfie again, they all had gentle smiles on their faces.

"Come with us." The muscular man nodded softly, "We will explain everything."

With that the four crossed the large stone room to a little seating area filled with mismatched plush chairs and couches.

The two hesitated briefly before shuffling across the room.

The main room was wide yet cozy. The floor and walls were made of grey stone but warm lights made it less cold looking, there were also faded mismatched rugs littering the floor. On the right side of the room was a cozy seating area complete with lots of plush chairs and sofas and a stone fireplace. Every chair and couch were covered with patchy cushions and tatty blankets. There was also a single door with the picture of a bed on it.

On the left of the room was a large wooden table with eight seats around it, there was a book or two lying on it. There was a stone arch which led to a small narrow kitchen. In the back of the room was a pair of double doors.

Tabby and Alfie sat together on the couch in front of the four, they were uncomfortable under all the eyes.

"My name is Oculus." The man in turquoise smiled, "My large friend here is Hercules, this is Nova and, finally, we have Vera."

He pointed to the man in red then the girl in purple and finally the girl in green.

"Hercules and I were the first to come here around fifteen years ago? then Nova and Vera joined us just five years ago… and now we have you two." Oculus continued calmly. "We are the Stone Guardians."

There was a beat of silence as Oculus allowed that information to sink in.

"Our duty is to protect the wall and the city from any threats outside." Nova took over explaining. "We are all picked because we're… different from the others."

"Different?" Tabby asked in confusion. "How? Alfie and I aren't different!"

"You are, you just don't know it yet." Oculus smirked secretively, "We have abilities." Hercules nodded, he then looked slightly pained and mortified as he continued. "I have the strength of stone. I can break boulders to dust and snap tree trunks in half, I can bend and manipulate metal and any other strong materials… Oculus… this sounds a bit threatening?"

Alfie audibly gulped as he and Tabby glanced at said man.

"You did great! Way better than in rehearsal! Anyway, I am a seer and prophet." Oculus grinned mischievously after giving Hercules a thumbs up, "I know the past, present, future and all paths an action can cause…"

"He's exaggerating." Nova rolled her eyes, "He doesn't know *everything*, in fact, he often knows absolutely nothing useful in the slightest."

"Do you know what our so-called abilities are?" Tabby asked sceptically.

"I do." Oculus nodded, clearly proud.

"Ok…" Tabby leaned forward with a suspicious frown, "Then what are they?"

"Patience, you will learn in time." Oculus tapped the side of his nose smugly, "I don't want to spoil the fun!"

"I am a witch!" Nova announced excitedly, giddily wiggling in her seat. "By that I mean I have magic!"

She then clicked her fingers and a flame appeared on the tip of her index finger, she giggled ecstatically as the friends shuffled back in surprise.

Unfortunately, she ruined her trick by sneezing and sending the flame flying across the room, it sizzled out when it hit Alfie's arm leaving a small blistering burn.

Alfie grit his teeth against the pain as Tabby fussed, her hands hovering over her friend's wound uncertainly.

"Nova!" Hercules growled, "We've told you a thousand times! No fire inside!"

"I know I know!" Nova huffed miserably, "I just got excited!"

Vera strolled forward and knelt before Alfie, the two friends watched her warily as she reached her small hands towards the injured arm.

"Relax." She soothed, "My ability is healing, just watch."

She placed a gentle finger atop the wound, Alfie hissed but soon sighed in relief as the burning was replaced with a soothing coolness. Tabby watched in fascination as Vera's hands glowed green, she swore she could smell mint and eucalyptus in the air. She removed her hand to reveal healed skin, she smiled gently and sat back down.

"Th-Thank you…" Alfie stuttered gratefully and slightly shocked.

"No problem." Vera nodded.

"And uh… I'm sorry!" Nova gave a sheepish grin, "I guess I got a little over excited… It's just been a while since we met new people!"

"It has just been the four of us for so long…" Oculus nodded, looking between his friends warmly. "When I saw you two arriving in a vision, we all got so excited!"

"Welcome to the family." Hercules chuckled.

The four stared at the two friends waiting for their response, they deflated as the silence stretched on.

Poor Tabby and Alfie were wide eyed, pale, shaky and exhausted. They were completely overwhelmed by all the anticipation, fear and emotions they had been through that day. They leaned against each other, seemingly needing the reassurance of a warm grounding weight.

"Oh…" Nova's face crumpled sadly. "That's right… You guys have been through so much today… I remember it too well…"

She stood and hurried over, she then pulled the two into a warm hug. She smelled faintly of lavender.

"It's gonna be ok… I promise you're safe now…" She hummed soothingly as she squeezed the two tightly. "We're gonna take good care of you and you'll be feeling right at home in no time…"

Tabby's eyes stung as she buried her face into her neck, feeling emotional at the first bit of comfort she had received all day. She noted Alfie's hand on her back, she then sniffled as Vera joined the hug, then followed by Oculus and finally Hercules.

They understood the pain and fear they had been through that day, they could remember how awful it was.

Tabby and Alfie were oddly grateful for the kind but awkward gesture.

It didn't last long before they all separated again and sat back down, the four adults watched the two with kind smiles.

Alfie could feel Tabby trembling against his shoulder, he knew the girl was still feeling overwhelmed and sad.

"Your names don't sound like something The Council would approve?" Alfie spoke to give Tabby a moment to calm down.

"Oh, they're not the names they gave us." Nova waved them off. Oculus rose to his feet and dramatically swept his arm to gesture to his fellow teammates.

"We have changed our names to break through the chains of servitude!" He announced proudly, "Once you two have figured out your abilities, you will do the same!"

Tabby scoffed quietly as Nova grabbed the tall man and pulled him back down into his seat.

"Oculus basically named all of us." She shrugged nonchalantly, "He's a real baby when you try to name yourself."

"I am not!" The man in question squawked, looking at Nova in shock.

"You sulked for, like, a month when Vera named herself." Nova pointed out, "Hercules and I were fine with the names you chose but she had every right to turn you down, Vera's way nicer than what you wanted."

"Vera is a boring old lady's name!" Oculus snapped back moodily, "Eir is interesting!"

Vera smiled soothingly at Oculus, she even reached over and patted his hand.

"I liked it enough but... I don't know... I guess I just felt I suited Vera more." She chuckled apologetically, Oculus softened and sighed.

"Vera is a beautiful name." He nodded with a small smile,

"So, uh..." Alfie began with a cough, he felt kind of awkward after that. He then thought back to what was said earlier. "You said your... our job was to protect the city and The Wall from whatever's outside?"

"Yup!" Nova nodded excitedly, "Best job in the world! You guys will never have to see that depressing city again!"

"You'll love what's out there." Vera agreed softly, "It's all so different and refreshing... it's the closest thing to freedom you get around here."

"Oh... I guess that is pretty cool..." Alfie smiled shyly, truthfully he was terrified at the thought. "So, what's out there? Why does the city *need* protecting?"

The four looked at one another, seemingly trying to decide whether or not to reveal the information.

"You have been through a lot today." Hercules eventually spoke up, "There will be time to discuss all of that later, we don't want to overwhelm you."

"You guys have magic." Tabby deadpanned shakily, "We're already overwhelmed!"

"Abilities." Oculus frowned, Tabby glanced at him.

"What?" She asked.

"We have *abilities*... Only Nova has actual magic." Oculus looked sheepish as he explained, Tabby blinked at him blankly.

"Vera just healed a burn with nothing but her finger." Tabby pointed out, "How is that not magic?"

"Because magic is flexible." Nova piped up happily, "Magic can bend to my will and do different things! There is healing magic, but it comes at a bigger cost for me than it does for Vera."

"Cost?" Alfie cocked his head to the side in interest.

"Well yeah?" Nova giggled, "Abilities are the same as doing anything else! You can only run for so long and you can only use your abilities so much!"

"Our abilities are channelled through our energy, if you use too much it basically exhausts you." Oculus explained easily, "If you continue using it once you're out of energy it starts channelling through your body which can then cause permanent damage or... death."

"What happened to not overwhelming them?" Hercules huffed in annoyance; he was ignored.

"So, I just get tired when I heal people too much, Nova's magic would transfer the injury in part to herself." Vera shrugged, "So she only heals if it's desperate."

"Can you heal yourself?" Tabby asked Vera curiously.

"No, it doesn't work like that. I can only heal others." Vera smiled, happy the two teens were interested in learning more.

"Guys-" Hercules tried again.

"I don't really have that kind of problem!" Oculus grinned as he stood, he danced around elegantly. "I get my visions randomly! I could probably look if I wish but I try not to, life's no fun when you know what's coming next."

"Seriously-" Hercules growled, his fists clenching.

"Why do you know our abilities then?" Tabby asked accusingly, Alfie nodded.

"It was all in one vision!" Oculus threw up in hands in defence. "Don't shoot the messenger!"

"HEY!" Hercules bellowed making everyone jump, they all looked at the huge man towering over them. "I know this is all very exciting but let's try not to tell them everything now! It's too much! They have lost their homes and families; they've been through so much fear and pain. Let the poor kids settle in and rest."

Oculus, Nova and Vera bowed their heads in shame, Alfie smirked weakly at them.

Tabby looked up at Hercules and found that she actually quite liked him.

"You lost family too huh?" Tabby asked softly, Hercules sighed and sat down.

"Yes. These three were only children so don't understand the pain of leaving behind a younger sibling... do you two?" He asked, seemingly hoping someone could finally understand.

"I don't but…" Alfie glanced sadly at Tabby.

"I have a little sister." Tabby told the large man sadly, "Matilda… She made me promise I'd come home… I didn't even get to say goodbye."

"I am sorry for your loss." Hercules nodded slowly, there was a solemn silence.

"What were your siblings like?" Tabby asked quietly.

"I had two younger brothers… they were twins and only six when I left… I have no idea what has become of them." Hercules explained, keeping his head bowed to hide his face. "Erik and Adam, they were good kids. Smart, strong. I hope they are still together."

Tabby nodded empathetically, she didn't know what to say.

"Come. You two must be exhausted, we'll show you to the sleeping quarters and you two can get some sleep." Hercules stood, leaving no room for argument.

"What? It's not that late!" Nova whined, Oculus nudged her.

"The kids are going to bed! Not us!" He shushed her, Nova laughed in relief as Alfie and Tabby stood and followed Hercules across the room and to the door with the bed sign on it.

Hercules opened the door and guided them in.

It was a large dark room with eight identical single beds with privacy curtains around them, four lined along each wall.

Each bed had a bedside table beside it. They could see the first bed had a damaged nightstand with a thick book lying on it, it had clearly been read to death. The second bedside table had a pile of tattered notebooks and scattered pens on it, there was also a small clock shaped like a cloud. The third had burn marks and scattered rings, the fourth had a crystal, a simple candle and a box of matches.

"You two get your own side of the room." Hercules chuckled as he motioned to the left, the friends saw two of the beds had covers and pillows ready on them. "Get some sleep, tomorrow we can put in an order with The Masquerade for anything you'll need. We'll guide you through."

With that the two friends were left alone.

Alfie took the first bed closest to the door and Tabby took the second.

They got ready in exhausted silence, Tabby settled under her covers and smiled when she heard Alfie lie down under his own.

She slipped out of bed when she heard the other snoring, Tabby quietly pushed her bed closer to her friend's. She felt anxious about sleeping in a new place in a room full of new people, she would feel better being close to her friend so they could look after each other. She just hoped Alfie wouldn't mind.

Chapter 6

Tabby came to slowly, her brow creased at the unfamiliar scent. She wasn't at home or in her own bed. She shifted, debating whether or not to open her still tired eyes, but felt herself pinned down by a warm, large arm.

She blinked her eyes open to see two bare beds in front of her, she frowned in confusion. She then flipped on her back to get a better look at the room, her heart and stomach dropped when all the memories came rushing back from the day before.

She let out a sigh and pushed the back of her head into her plush pillow, she closed her eyes tightly. She didn't want to get up, she didn't want to move. She had no energy or motivation to do anything but lie in her cozy bed, she wasn't with her family so what was the point?

The arm still lying across her twitched and there was a breath on her cheek.

Tabby's eyelids flew open, and she looked over in confusion.

Her eyes fell on messy blonde hair. Alfie.

The nervous girl had pushed their beds together last night to give them both a sense of comfort, Tabby was now quite embarrassed. Strangely, she didn't feel uncomfortable being this close to Alfie. In a way, it felt right. It was comforting and warm, safe.

Tabby thought for a moment, her eyes scanning over the long golden locks. She realised it was strange to watch someone sleep, would Alfie think she was a creep?

Her face heated up in embarrassment, she quickly looked up at the ceiling but her eyes kept glancing over against her will. Would her friend freak out when he discovered Tabby had slept next to him without consent?

Part of her figured it would be ok, they had grown up together after all. She had always liked Alfie. The boy was gentle, caring and pretty smart. He always stood up for the smaller weaker kids, he had stood up for Tabby quite a few times. She always found herself admiring him while in class, watching his soft and careful movements and the way he kept everyone out of trouble. She looked up to him as if he were her brother, someone she could count on to have her back.

They spent a lot of time together when they were young. Tabby never felt she had to say anything to the boy, she simply enjoyed being by his side.

It wasn't a romantic thing.

Besides, it was rare to even be coupled up with anyone, only a small handful of individuals with "Strong Genes" are chosen so they can pass these on to their children they're forced into having.

Tabby flinched in shock as Alfie moved his heavy head to look at her.

She watched as everything slowly dawned on him, he drew back his arm quickly as if burned.

Tabby hated that she flinched at the sudden movement.

"Uh… Sorry!" Alfie croaked, his voice cracking with sleep.

"It's ok… My fault… I pushed the beds together… Sorry…" Tabby chuckled awkwardly, "Um… did you sleep ok?"

"Yeah…" Alfie nodded easily. "And don't worry about it, it's cool."

There was a moment of silence.

"Um… thanks…" Tabby nodded before coughing, "I'm gonna… y'know… get ready…"

She didn't move out of bed instead, she sat up and frowned down at her covers. Alfie slowly shuffled so he was sitting beside her, he kept glancing at her but not saying anything.

They sat together in silence for a moment.

"How are you holding up?" Alfie finally asked, looking over at his friend sympathetically.

"I miss my little sister." Tabby admitted, her voice quiet with emotion. "I wish I could've just said goodbye, I hope she's ok…"

"She will be." Alfie tried to reassure.

"Are you scared?" Tabby asked nervously as she fiddled with her covers. "I mean… we just slept in a room with four adults we don't know who have… abilities or powers or whatever… we're stuck with them."

"Honestly? It's not them I'm afraid of." The boy admitted, bowing his head. "They said our job was protecting the city, that we had to go outside The Wall! That's… that's terrifying, I can't even imagine what's out there!"

Tabby swallowed as she nodded.

"Yeah…" She gulped. She flinched when she felt Alfie bump her shoulder.

"At least it's you and me?" He smiled gently, Tabby nodded.

"You and me… Yeah." Tabby smirked. "We're gonna be ok."

Tabby slipped out and began moving her bed back to where it was, Alfie hurried to help.

"Let me know if you want to move it back." He smiled fondly, "I'll give you a hand, it's kind of heavy for you to push on your own."

Tabby smiled up at him gratefully, glad Alfie understood.

Once the two friends were finally ready for the day, they headed out into the main area. They gaped in shock at the pure chaos unfolding before them, weren't these guys supposed to be big mature adults?

The kitchen was very much aflame and, weirdly, it had nothing to do with Nova. Whatever was in the pan was now charcoal, painted black by the orange flame that fluttered out of it. Thick black smoke billowed around as Hercules stood there flapping a small towel – it seemed to just be making it worse.

Oculus was no help whatsoever. He stood, just out of the way of the choking smog, and seemed to be on a rant about how he saw this coming, and he warned Hercules, but nobody ever listens to him. Which, incidentally, was true in this moment.

Hercules was too busy freaking out to hear a word.

Nova was far away from the smoke and was waving her hands in the air, above her was a huge ball of water swirling around.

"Move! Move!" She kept shrieking to no avail.

Vera was sat on a plush seat painting her nails and ignoring the whole thing.

"Get outta the way!" Nova screamed, getting frustrated at not being listened to by either of the men.

The two teens watched as she stomped her foot angrily before hurling the ball of water straight at the kitchen, judging by her shocked expression she threw it much harder than she intended to.

Hercules and Oculus were knocked over with a huge splash.

"Oh my-! I'm so sorry!" Nova yelped as she ran forward to help.

Tabby and Alfie glanced over at Vera.

"This happens almost every morning." She explained calmly, "Nobody here is any use in the kitchen."

"None of you know how to cook? How have you stayed alive for so long?" Alfie asked in shock.

"We know how... it just usually ends up burnt." Vera smiled in amusement.

Tabby smirked as she watched Alfie shake his head in disgust, the boy looked horrified at all that had happened.

They walked over to the kitchen. Nova had just finished using her magic to fix and dry everything, Hercules and Oculus were silent and shamefully watching.

"Morning!" Nova greeted as her stomach grumbled. "Breakfast won't be long now!"

"I'll cook." Alfie huffed as he stormed into the kitchen, Tabby smiled knowingly as the four adults watched in amazement.

It took a while for Alfie to find anything but before they knew it, six plates of bacon and eggs lay on the dining table. Smelling delicious and cooked to perfection.

"I used to cook for myself." Alfie shrugged in way of explanation as the four adults stared at him in wonder, Tabby chuckled and dug in hungrily.

"Huh…" Hercules hummed as he chewed on a piece of bacon. "So that's what it's supposed to taste like… I'd forgotten."

"This is the best food I have ever tasted!" Nova moaned as she chewed noisily, "Maybe super cooking is his ability!

"That's not a thing." Oculus rolled his eyes,

"Is this really the first non-burnt meal you've had since coming here?" Tabby asked amused, she then laughed at all the confident nodding she received.

"I guess I'm the chef now then?" Alfie smirked wryly; he also received his answer in nods.

Everything fell quiet as the group ate their food.

Tabby zoned out for a bit as she thought about the previous day. She was brought back by Alfie bumping his knee against her own, she looked over to see concerned blue eyes looking at her. She gave her friend a small smile and bumped his knee back.

She was still anxious, sad and scared but this morning had really shown how human these people were. Yesterday, they had seemed like big, confident beings but this morning had shown they were just like herself and Alfie.

Alfie was also helping; she hoped her own presence was doing the same.

It wasn't long until Tabby and Alfie were once again sat down in the sitting area, this time Hercules was standing over them like a stern lecturer. Oculus, Nova and Vera had all been banished to the sleeping quarters.

Hercules was holding a notepad, it looked tiny in his giant hand. Tabby watched in awe as he wrote something down, it seemed miraculous the thin pencil didn't break between his fingers.

"Ok you two. I think it's time I gave you an induction of sorts." He nodded slowly, his deep voice was relaxing.

"Ok?" Alfie leaned forward to show he was listening.

"First. We are unable to leave our... home. We may only leave when the alarm goes off, this means we are needed outside for patrol or to defend the city." Hercules began, his voice was strong but there was a strange expression on his face. Almost like he didn't want to tell them all this, he seemed uncomfortable. "If the alarm goes over the next two days, you two will stay behind while we deal with it. You need a couple days to settle in, get everything you need and to get prepared... We start training tomorrow, just basic defence and attack."

Alfie and Tabby shared a worried look but kept silent, Hercules watched them warily before continuing.

"We get fresh clothes delivered every two days; The Masquerade then take away our old garments." Hercules thought for a moment, "There's not much else really... Oh! Uh... We need to know if you want anything? Like... I don't know..."

Hercules grunted, struggling to explain what he wanted to say.

"I mean… Oculus has taken liberty of ordering you weapons and stuff that will help with your abilities when you unlock them… I probably should have checked what he asked for *before* he handed it over but… well… He knows the future better than I do; we just have to trust he was sensible." The large man rolled his eyes, "So if you want anything… hobby wise? Like… Oculus has notebooks for his thoughts, Vera has a meditation candle… so anything to keep you sane… You can also order anything else like rings, nail polish or whatever. I don't think it's important, but Nova would kill me if she thought I left that out."

There was a beat of silence.

"That's it. Just… say what you want, and I'll show you how to order stuff." He finished lamely, his eyes glanced between the two waiting for some sort of response.

Alfie and Tabby were looking at each other, each wondering what they should ask for.

"Um… Could I get a sketch pad and charcoal?" Alfie asked timidly, "I like to draw…"

"Sure, I'll write that down… we'll see what you get…" Hercules nodded as he slowly wrote on the paper, he looked up expectantly. "Tabby?"

Tabby bit her lip and scratched at her knees, she didn't know what to ask for. She wasn't one for sticking at hobbies, more of a 'love something for a month then find something new' kind of guy.

She began to sweat at the eyes on her, she had been silent for too long really. Most people just know what they enjoy.

Truth was, she never really had time for hobbies growing up. Her father and mother worked so when she wasn't at lessons she was at home looking after her sister, she always wanted her to hang out with her and play.

She had many hobbies.

Which led Tabby to an idea.

Matilda had always loved it on those quiet afternoons when the two of them would just sit down on the living room floor with piles of colourful paper and fold. Matilda was much better at origami than Tabby, she could make all sorts and she did try to teach her but her fingers were just too clumsy.

The only thing she could make were little paper stars.

Matilda thought they were cute so was content on folding her masterful creations while she just littered the floor with an array of colourful stars, it annoyed their parents to no end.

"Tabby?" Hercules' soft voice broke Tabby out of her thoughts, she blinked a couple times and looked up to see both males looking at her in concern.

"Oh... uh... Could I get strips of origami paper?" Tabby asked meekly, "And... maybe a couple of big jars?"

"Of course." Hercules gave her a reassuring smile, "I look forward to seeing what you can make."

"Nothing special... Matilda was always better at it than me." Tabby admitted quietly. Hercules nodded in understanding.

"So... we order what we need by writing it down on paper, folding it in half... then pushing it under the door." The large man explained as he led them over to the front door.

Hercules knelt and slipped it under the locked door.

"There. Tomorrow you should have your things and whatever weird items Oculus has ordered for you." He nodded proudly. "Not so hard, right?"

The two smiled and followed him back into their home.

When they arrived Oculus and Nova were relaxing on the couches and Vera was sitting cross legged on the floor.

"Yoga?" Vera asked, looking up as the three entered.

"Yes. It's time for our daily yoga." Hercules nodded as he headed over to join the other three.

"You guys do yoga together every day?" Alfie asked, cocking his head.

"Yup!" Oculus yawned as he forced himself to stand up. "It's tedious but it's something to do."

"It's good for your mind, body and soul." Nova smiled as she stretched in preparation, Vera seemed to be getting ready to lead them all.

"Will you be joining us?" She asked lightly, the two friends glanced at one another.

Tabby smiled politely as she took a deep breath.

"No thank you... I will tomorrow but I think I just need today to sort of let myself rest." She admitted nervously. "I'm still pretty tired after yesterday."

"Yeah, me too." Alfie nodded, seemingly relieved he wasn't alone in his exhaustion.

"That's ok!" Nova grinned, "Just go relax! You'll be right as rain in no time!"

"If it helps," Oculus smirked mischievously, "You're doing so much better than the two girls did. Nova kept yelling at us to stay away from her, telling us to go to hell and stomping her feet like a child."

"Hey!" Nova snapped, glaring at the tall man.

"And I honestly thought Vera was a mute for the first month or so, she never said a word!" Oculus continued.

"Maybe not to you." Hercules shrugged smugly. "Nova and I would chat to her pretty frequently."

"What!?" Oculus gaped dramatically at the quiet girl, "Why couldn't you speak to me!?"

"Three guesses." Nova huffed in amusement, Oculus pouted childishly.

Tabby and Alfie chuckled before heading off to the sleeping quarters, they wanted to be away from all the weirdness for a while.

It was all just so different from the world they knew. Growing up, everything was grey and quiet. There were no choices, no opinions and certainly no idle chit chat! Everything had to have a purpose or you were guilted into thinking you were wasting time.

They both always figured it would continue like that once they were assigned their careers. Yet here they were! Surrounded by noise and light and colour, the few people they spent time with had big personalities and no sense of wasting time! They were just living and existing without any fear, it seemed that way at least.

It was all such a shock to the system and it was taking time for the two friends to adjust, they still felt vaguely like they were lost in a dream.

If it was all a dream, they couldn't decide whether or not they wanted to wake up.

Chapter 7

The last couple of days had been the most frustrating yet interesting days of Tabby and Alfie's young lives. This strange place they had found themselves in was nothing but a beacon of bright colours and noise, so much noise! It was dizzying and confusing. They were starting to relax into this new environment, enough to at least make their headaches go away and to get decent sleep.

That's all you can ask for really.

They were still adjusting to these strange people.

Hercules was quiet most of the time. He was by far the easiest to get along with and the kindest. His large presence was strangely relaxing and comforting, he was a good listener and he seemed to be very in tune with his environment and those that surrounded him. He continuously checked in on the two, making sure they were ok and healthy. He was very sweet, and the teens found they really appreciated and trusted him.

Vera was also very quiet and sweet. She was thoughtful and seemed to just know what everyone was feeling, she was always calm, slow and smiling. She had a bad habit of just suddenly appearing, her footsteps were too soft and she often made the five jump when she miraculously appeared beside them. She mostly kept to herself so Tabby wasn't entirely sure how to speak to her, though she spent a lot of time with Alfie when he was cooking. Those two were getting on incredibly well.

Tabby adored Nova and spent a lot of time with her. She was cool, friendly and just so much fun to be around! She was one of those people who could just talk to anyone about anything, she had so many interesting stories too! She seemed to really take to the two teens, she watched over them and went out of her way to make them feel part of the team. She also loved showing off her magic tricks to them much to Hercules' dismay. She was also a big hugger! She took any opportunity to hug one of her teammates, Tabby wasn't used to being cuddled so she found she quite enjoyed it. Oculus was a weirdo. There was really no other way to describe him! He often just said random things that made no sense to anyone, then he'd just laugh and go back to whatever he was doing. He often zoned out or sat scribbling away into one of his many notebooks. He was oddly intimidating, he had an air around him as if he knew everything and it seemed he honestly did. He had a terrible ego and a wicked sense of humour but he was nice enough and always grinning away.

The second day had started well. Tabby and Alfie received their order of art supplies and origami strips with jars.

Then Oculus' order arrived and Hercules yelled at the poor man. Alfie received leather arm guards and gloves. For his belt he received a small blade and a knuckle duster. Better than nothing but gave no real clue as to what his ability was, he appreciated it none the less.

Tabby was handed leather fingerless gloves, a pair of daggers and a bag of beef jerky.

This was why Hercules yelled at Oculus.

"What!? She'll need it!" Oculus had insisted with a cheeky smile, Tabby had laughed and wondered what it meant.

They also had their first day of yoga which both teens found they quite enjoyed, especially as every time everyone bent down Oculus would blow a raspberry and make Nova, Tabby and Alfie howl with laughter.

After the yoga session, Tabby found herself cornered by Nova and Vera. They looked excited as they checked they were alone.

"So, welcome to the sisterhood." Nova giggled ecstatically.

"The… what?" Tabby asked with a hint of excitement at the tone.

"We girls have to stick together." Vera whispered in amusement, "So, Nova and I made our own little sisterhood – we got you these when we found out you were coming."

Tabby was handed a silver ring and a carnelian crystal on a string.

"The ring is optional." Nova shrugged, "I added that just in case you wanted one."

"We each have a crystal, the boys don't believe in them but we think they have positive energy to them." Vera nodded knowingly.

"They look cool if nothing else." Nova chuckled. "I keep mine in my pouch with a few others, Vera wears hers around her neck."

And so, Tabby placed the ring on her middle finger of her left hand, then wore the crystal around her neck – Nova helped her tie it so the string didn't hang down so far.

The three women shared a smile, they would need each other if they were going to put up with three men.

The two teens had a small lesson on basic defence and fighting. Hercules admitted it wasn't going to be enough and really, they'd learn more when they were in a fight that really mattered. This scared both quite a bit, they didn't want to be unprepared but nobody would tell them what was out there or what was going to happen.

This fear was only made worse when the alarm rang deafeningly, and Tabby and Alfie were left behind.

The four adults dashed off like they were excited, whooping and hyping each other up as they went.

Tabby and Alfie had waited impatiently for them to return.

When they did, they were covered in filth and were completely exhausted, they didn't say a word about what they did. Just continued on as if they never left.

It was bizarre and jarring but the two didn't know what to do, they too just pretended nothing happened.

Which now brought them to today, their fourth day with their new... roommates?

And today was the strangest yet but not in the good way.

When Tabby and Alfie came out of the sleeping quarters there was a thick tension in the air, it was also silent bar some whispering coming from the sitting area.

When the two cautiously approached, they were alarmed to find Oculus sitting on the ground with a nosebleed, his eyes were closed, and his mouth turned down in pain and misery – there was a faint tremble running through his thin body. Hercules knelt beside him with his heavy hand upon the shaking shoulder, he was silent but oddly comforting.

Nova and Vera were standing nearby and whispering worriedly to each other, Vera was shaking her head and seemed upset while Nova looked borderline panicked.

It was jarring to see these normally happy and energetic people suddenly becoming so serious. It was even more jarring that none of them had even noticed the two kids, they had all been so focused on them since they arrived.

"Oculus?" Tabby questioned as she came closer, Alfie not far behind.

Both teens startled as everyone looked at them in surprise.

"No! Look out!" Oculus groaned, he scrunched his eyes shut and shook his head in distress.

"Alfie, Tabby." Nova smiled softly as she came towards them, "It's ok, Oculus just needs a minute."

"What happened?" Alfie asked, glancing between Oculus and Nova.

"He's having a vision." Hercules explained quietly, his eyes not leaving the distressed man's face.

"A vision?" Alfie frowned,

"Does this happen every time he uses his ability?" Tabby asked in horror.

"No, not every time!" Nova shook her head, she fiddled with her hair awkwardly. "Just when the visions are particularly... um... important?"

"So... What's the vision?" Tabby asked curiously, glancing down at Oculus in search of answers.

"He cannot say." Hercules finally looked up at the two teens, "Though... from what we can gather... It's not long until you discover your abilities."

"And... that's a bad thing?" Alfie asked, noting the grave expression on the large man's face.

"No." Vera insisted, stepping forward to reassure the teens. "It's a wonderful thing! It's just that... well... Our abilities usually only show themselves when we are, or believe we are, in danger?"

Tabby and Alfie blinked as Vera's statement sank in.

"So... We're gonna die?" Tabby cocked her head.

"No! But... you might get hurt... or just a little scared or whatever! Maybe one of us will get hurt instead which then makes you discover your powers!" Nova insisted with a vague wave of her hand. "You'll be fine in the long run! Sometimes they just show themselves when they're ready! That's what happened to Oculus."

The two teens weren't convinced, they had a bad feeling about their future.

"You don't actually know what happens then? You don't know what makes our so-called abilities show themselves?" Tabby summed up in frustration.

"I understand it must be tiresome." Hercules began but frowned when he saw Tabby's eye roll.

"Try infuriating!" Tabby huffed grumpily. "How do you know we've even got abilities? How do you know we don't die? Can't we have *some* details? It is *our* future after all!"

"No..." Oculus shuddered from the floor, his tired eyes looking up at the two. "You will be safe with us... you do have abilities, useful ones... I wish I could tell you but... It could ruin everything..."

"Knowing the future is dangerous." Vera agreed gently. "If you know something's gonna happen then you'll never stop thinking about it and questioning every move and decision! It could then change your fate!"

"Trust me... better this way..." Oculus nodded tiredly.

Tabby and Alfie sighed but dropped the subject, they could see their friend was exhausted and they didn't want to tire him anymore.

Instead, Tabby sat beside Oculus and allowed the man to pass out against her. Alfie and Vera shuffled off to the kitchen to make a hearty breakfast for once Oculus woke up, Hercules and Nova cleaned up Oculus' face and sat around nearby to keep an eye on things.

"Sorry about this..." Nova apologised as she looked at Tabby empathetically.

"It's ok." Tabby smiled softly before frowning in thought, "So you said Oculus doesn't always get hurt by his visions?"

"No, he's usually a real ass about them!" Nova giggled, "He'd skip around telling us that he'd seen something and that he was so excited to see our reactions when it happened!"

"He just about exploded when he saw the vision of you two joining us." Hercules smirked at the memory, "I've never seen him so excited."

"Rude." Nova huffed, "He wasn't excited to see me and Vera?"

"Nah, he was disappointed we were gonna have *two* girls staying with us." Hercules shrugged with a wry smile, "Said he didn't want to deal with dramatic teenage girls."

Nova gasped in offense and sent a useless glare at the unconscious man.

"Right, you and Oculus were on your own for a while huh?" Tabby hummed thoughtfully.

"Yes. Met in the van and have been together in here since." Hercules nodded slowly, "I have known him since we were both sixteen."

"Man, you guys have been in this business for a while... What was Oculus like when you first met him?" Tabby asked curiously, Nova smirked and looked over at Hercules who seemed to be thinking very hard.

"To be honest, we didn't have much to do with each other at first." Hercules admitted, "We stayed away from each other for the first month, acted as if the other wasn't there... Then the alarm went off and The Masquerade threw us out into the wilderness with this huge-... with a beast and... suddenly we both knew why we were here. We became like brothers after that day."

"Adorable, right?" Nova grinned at Tabby, she chuckled lightly.

"Maybe you and Alfie will become like siblings too." Hercules smiled proudly, Tabby blushed.

"We're all a big family!" Nova nodded then smirked mischievously, "But I think Alfie's already your brother, right?"

"Wh-What!?" Tabby spluttered as she stared at Nova, Hercules raised an eyebrow in interest.

Nova's grin only grew bigger as she leaned forward.

"What!?" She cackled joyfully, "It's adorable that you think you've kept it secret, you two are so lucky!"

"Kept what secret?" Hercules asked, glancing between the two.

"Isn't it obvious?" Nova smirked, everyone glanced at her. "Tabby and Alfie are related!"

"Don't be stupid." Oculus groaned as he slowly opened his eyes, giving Nova an exhausted glare. "They're not related in the slightest, don't you know anything about biology?"

Nova blinked blankly.

"They were born on the same day and share no similar characteristics – they can't be related." He rolled his eyes, Nova deflated slightly.

"Cousins?" She squeaked in embarrassment.

"Tabby and Alfie?" Hercules asked before thinking carefully, "Huh... Now that you say it... they are very close... I could see them being cousins."

"Tabby, please." Oculus begged, "Make them shut up! I'm losing braincells just listening to this!"

"Can we stop talking about this?" Tabby hushed quietly, "Alfie and I are not related! We just grew up across the road from each other."

"Go away now please." Oculus waved the two off lazily, "Tabby can stay, she has a brain."

Nova snickered as she and Hercules stood up and left to see what was happening in the kitchen, they hoped food would be served soon - Oculus would need a good meal to regain his energy.

Tabby sighed quietly, she flinched when she felt Oculus finally raise his head off her shoulder. The man groaned as he sat up and stretched his back, he then looked at Tabby with a soft smile.

"I'm not supposed to have favourites..." He began in an amused but hushed voice, "But... I think you're in the lead."

"Um... how?" Tabby chuckled, watching the other.

"Well… I've seen your ability and I think it's pretty interesting."
Oculus nodded almost excitedly. "You remind me of myself when I
was your age. Smart, quiet and sensible… you'll lose that as you
become more comfortable with all of us… but, I think you're going
to be a great asset to the team."

Tabby gaped as Oculus forced himself to his feet, the man shuffled
away gingerly leaving the sixteen-year-old to think about his
confession.

Tabby bit her lip to try and hide her pleased smile, she took a deep
breath before jumping up. She felt light and happy, she was
flattered by Oculus' compliment – she even had a skip in her step
now.

Oculus felt much better after eating. In fact, he was back to his
annoying self!

"Nova… I know what you look like in the future!" He grinned evilly
as Nova tried to ignore him.

Their morning yoga could never go smoothly.

"I do!" Oculus insisted as he continued, "I know…"

"But you can't tell me, so I don't care." Nova rolled her eyes in
boredom.

"I know… just… y'know…" Oculus had a wicked grin upon his face,
"I'm gonna miss your pretty hair."

Nova gasped and rose up from the downward dog position she was
doing to look round at Oculus, Oculus stood up straight and hid his
smile with a serious expression.

"No!" She looked at him in fear, "I do not go bald!… Do I?"

"Everyone rise gently and slowly." Vera instructed, Hercules, Tabby
and Alfie followed her lead.

"You know… Your forehead is pretty big." Oculus teased, "Probably
not long now."

"No!" Nova's hands flew to her hair in alarm. "Oculus! Please tell
me you're joking!"

"Nothing wrong with being bald." Oculus shrugged, enjoying his taunt.

"No but… It's cold not having hair." Nova curled her strands around her finger sadly, Oculus laughed at her.

"Stop." Hercules warned, "Nova, he's just trying to scare you." Nova looked at Oculus who was now looking bored and slightly upset with Hercules.

"I was just about to convince her to shave it." He huffed moodily, "Now we'll never get to see what she looks like with no hair!"

"You were lying!" Nova growled, purple mist swirled around her hands as she lifted them threateningly. "You're gonna pay!"

Oculus yelped and ran as balls of purple flew at him leaving chalky splatters on the floor, Nova was quick to dash after him.

"I guess we're finished for today." Vera sighed as she watched the two run around.

"Thank you, Vera." Hercules nodded kindly, Vera simply smiled at him.

"Nova!" Oculus whined as Nova used her magic to lift him into the air, "C'mon! It was just a joke!"

"Yeah?" Nova smirked, Tabby and Alfie winced at the evil expression. "Well, knock knock."

Oculus yelped as he was flipped upside down and shaken causing his notebooks to fall out of his belt along with a flurry of paper. Nova cackled happily as Oculus grovelled.

"I'm sorry!" He begged, "Please put me down!"

Nova seemed to think about it before nodded in satisfaction. Slowly, Oculus was lifted so he was the right side up and gently placed onto his feet in the middle of the papery mess. The man immediately knelt down and gathered his things all while grumbling about Nova being no fun, Alfie stepped forward to help him.

Tabby grinned as Nova swung an arm around her shoulder.

"You'd think he'd learn." She smirked over at the young girl, "Mr I-can-see-everything."

Oculus stuck his tongue out immaturely making the two teens laugh, Nova rolled her eyes humorously.

The fun was ruined when the alarm suddenly rang out, everyone looked over at Alfie and Tabby.

It was time for their first adventure outside of The Wall.

Chapter 8

It was incredibly tense as everyone stood for a moment as the bell rang incessantly, all four adults were looking at the two youngest with worried and grave expressions. It was as if time had stopped just for a moment as the seriousness of the situation dawned on Tabby and Alfie.

Tabby looked down to her friend, Alfie was still knelt on the floor with a piece of paper in his hand. The boy looked back at Tabby with a similar expression of fear.

It was then time seemed to finally speed up.

Hercules stormed forward as Oculus hurried to scrape up all his paper and notebooks, Hercules was quick to help him. Both were stiff as they worked on the mess, it was important Oculus had his information on him for all excursions.

Nova's arm around Tabby's shoulder pulled her tightly against her side, Vera hurried forward and helped Alfie to his feet. She then dragged him over to join Nova and Tabby.

"This is it." Nova nodded with strained grin. "Maybe we'll find out about your abilities today! How exciting!"

Tabby did not feel excited. In fact, she suddenly felt a bit sick.

Alfie was chewing his thumbnail as he watched Hercules and Oculus stand.

"Everyone, go get ready, get everything you need." Hercules nodded, "Then meet back here. Quickly!"

Everyone ran off to the sleeping quarters to grab their equipment. Alfie tugged on his leather arm guards and gloves shakily. He then grabbed his blade and knuckle dusters and shoved them in his belt.

Tabby shoved her fingerless gloves on and grabbed her daggers. She hesitated as she eyed up the beef jerky packet, debating whether or not to take it.

Oculus had said she would need it. He wouldn't give Tabby something harmful.

She huffed and shoved it in her belt with the daggers before following the others back out into the main area.

"Follow me." Hercules commanded. "Nova, Vera and I will do most of the fighting. I want Tabby and Alfie to watch for now and learn, make sure you both observe closely but stay a safe distance away."

"What about me?" Oculus asked, cocking his head to the side.

"You will stay with the kids and keep them safe." Hercules nodded sternly.

"Great." The other man huffed sourly, "I'm on babysitting duty."

Tabby and Alfie were too scared to be offended.

Hercules led his team to the exit and guided them out into a dark narrow stone passageway, it was a straight but steep decline.

It was deathly silent bar their footsteps echoing around them, Tabby looked up to see there were holes to the right revealing bright sunlight and blue skies.

Alfie was just behind her and followed her gaze, there was a look of wonder on his face.

"Do you hear that?" Alfie asked Tabby breathily,

"The wind?" Tabby asked as she listened to the breeze outside.

"No!" Alfie huffed, "The rustling! The- The... the whistling noises!"

Tabby frowned as she listened closely, she gasped when she suddenly realised, she could hear it too.

"Woah, it's noisy out there." The girl gasped.

"The rustling noises are trees; you likely will never have seen any since you're from the business district. The whistling is from animals called birds, they live outside the wall and are completely harmless." Nova explained gently, "They fly in the sky... but they never fly over the wall for some reason, I've never even seen them land near it."

"Birds..." Tabby frowned thoughtfully, "Like... chickens?"

They had only learned about animals that they could eat or get produce from.

"Yeah, chickens are a species of bird." Nova nodded, no hint of judgement in her voice. "They're not so good with the flying though, they're also bigger than most the birds out there."

Silence fell over them again as they continued their decline. Eventually they arrived at a huge iron door, a cool breeze whistled through the crack at the bottom.

Hercules gave the teens a smile, the others looked happy for them too.

"Alfie, Tabby." Hercules nodded as he put his hands on the door. "Welcome to the whole world."

He pushed the doors open and stepped back so the teens could see the sight beyond, it took a moment for their eyes to adjust to the bright sunlight. Once they did the two gasped in delighted shock, their jaws falling as they gazed beyond.

Outside were rolling emerald hills, soft grass dotted with colourful flowers fluttering in the breeze making the ground look like an ocean. There were various bushes and shrubberies, a contrasting dark green to the bright blades. Huge towering pine trees lined the horizon casting large shadows as they stretched up towards the blue sky dotted with puffy white clouds.

"I never knew the sky could look so huge…" Tabby breathed as her eyes darted around trying to see everything. She felt so exposed without walls surrounding her, but strangely – it wasn't a bad feeling.

It felt like she was free for the first time in her life.

"You should see it at night." Nova whispered, swinging her arms by her side as she tried to contain her giddiness. "Because there's no light out here you can see the stars and the galaxies!"

"Wow…" Alfie smiled before taking a deep breath of the fresh fragrant air.

Tabby looked down at the grass, her feet were still firmly planted on the stone floor of the wall. She jumped as she saw Alfie step forward and out into the open world, she was quick to follow and stand by his side.

"It's so… big." Alfie shook his head in disbelief. "I can't believe this has been out here all this time… Nobody in there even knows."

"It's beautiful." Tabby agreed wistfully, gazing up at the bright blue above. "I mean… look at that sky! Doesn't it just look brighter somehow when there aren't grey buildings framing it?"

A strong breeze hit the two making them stumble slightly and laugh.

Tabby then crouched down and lay her open palm down on the lush grass. She gasped with a grin, she then sat crossed legged and ran both hands through the strands in delight and amazement.

"Tabby? What're you doing?" Alfie asked curiously as he looked down at his friend.

"I thought the grass would be soft but it's… kinda cold and smooth instead!" Tabby explained. "Is this really what it's like? I've only ever seen it in our schoolbooks!"

Alfie sat beside her and cautiously ran his own hand across the plants, he chuckled as they tickled him.

"I never would've guessed it would feel like this..." Alfie agreed breathlessly. "Even the dirt underneath feels hard instead of soft like it looks!"

Tabby nodded, both flinched when the girl accidently plucked a blade from the dirt. She held it out in shock.

"You can pick the grass?" she gasped. "Huh..."

Alfie stared in amazement.

"Cool." He grinned.

Tabby suddenly sent Alfie a wicked grin, one that always made the poor boy groan in dread. She reached forward and plucked a small white flower along with some of it's stem, she then placed it lightly in Alfie's hair.

"Now you look pretty!" She nudged him as her eyes twinkled playfully, Alfie rolled his eyes but his subtle smile betrayed him.

It was then something else caught their eye.

A sparkling pond to the far left, it was surrounded by more flowers and bushes littered with berries.

Both teens leapt to their feet and rushed off to explore it, they fell to their knees next to it.

"Eww... it's all dirty!" Tabby frowned in disgust; she didn't like the smell.

"Tabby! Look!" Alfie gasped as he pointed, Tabby followed his finger to see small creatures wiggling around in the murk.

"Woah... Fish!" Tabby leaned forward more to get a closer look, Alfie grabbed her arm absentmindedly just in case she lost her balance. "They're not big enough to eat though."

Alfie shook his head.

They watched the creatures swim around in their home with fascination, they had never seen anything like it before.

They stood together with big grins, they then turned round to see the four adults watching them from just behind.

Nova was emotional with tears in her eyes and a watery smile, the others were simply pleased that the teens were discovering nature. "This is the world that was so cruelly kept from you." Hercules nodded gently. "There is more than just Slately… This is Emerelda. Just one region among four on Portus Naturea."

"Wait… so there's more?" Tabby asked in wonder, "More places like Slately?"

"I hope not!" Nova laughed almost bitterly.

"We don't know. We just know there are more people out there, we've found all sorts of artifacts!" Oculus explained giddily, "We found a tablet not far from here which explained our world and the regions! Unfortunately… it was destroyed the same time Nova discovered her powers."

Nova blushed as both teens listened in fascination.

"Our region is called 'Emerelda' because it is forever lush and green. There are three others: 'Blossoming', 'Bronze Forest' and 'The White Rocks'. 'Blossoming' is full of flowers, water and plants, 'Bronze Forest' is a kingdom made up entirely of towering toadstools and trees which have leaves of gold, rust and copper!" Oculus explained excitedly. "Then 'The White Rocks' is a barren and harsh wasteland filled with frozen rain and icy stone."

"At least… that's what we gathered from the tablet." Vera interrupted pointedly, her eyes apologetic. "We don't actually know… But we have a theory that Slately isn't supposed to exist. We think The Council built it for a reason, but we just don't know why."

"It looks different from the rest of the region, it has its own weather, it looks as if it's just been dumped here…" Oculus summed up as he shook his head, "Something just doesn't add up."

Tabby and Alfie looked at one another thoughtfully, they could understand how they came up with that idea. Slately just looked so wrong and ugly compared to the rest of the region.

It was then a mighty howl came from the trees beyond, the six looked out to the horizon.

"Here comes trouble." Hercules frowned, donning a serious tone. "Alfie, Tabby and Oculus – stay near The Wall. Nova, Vera you two are with me."

The two women nodded in determination.

Oculus huffed before leading the teens to lean against the wall while the others stepped out into the wide-open space, plenty of room for the upcoming battle.

"What are they gonna fight?" Alfie looked to Oculus in worry, "It sounded big!"

"I dunno... the howl kinda sounded like... just a wolf honestly." Oculus stretched his arms out casually, "We scare off a lot of wolves... they're kind of a pain."

It was then they heard the heavy thumping of something large running towards the city, everyone looked forward as the red speck got bigger and bigger.

"What the... that thing's huge!" Alfie gasped as the beast came closer.

"Huh... That's new..." Oculus looked surprised, worried and utterly intrigued.

"What is that thing!?" Nova squealed fearfully.

The monster slowed when it saw its opponents, instead choosing to now approach them warily.

The creature was the colour of fresh blood, it was nearly as tall as the surrounding pine trees, and it was incredibly thick and muscular. It walked on two legs with the body of a man though it had the face of a demon with its yellow eyes, thick black mane, two curling horns protruding from its skull, sharp teeth, and claws – it even had tusks pointing out from its lower jaw! It towered far above the group and dragged its metal club threateningly; it was naked bar a scrap of clothing wrapped around its waist.

Oculus flipped through one of his tattered notebooks hurriedly, he stopped and read the text carefully before looking up at the creature once more.

"Um… It's an Oni!" Oculus informed them, studying the creature warily. "It's a kind of yokai or… demon… It um… well it eats people so… avoid that… It carries an iron kanabō club so… don't get hit?"

"Very helpful!" Nova snapped sarcastically, "Thanks a lot!"

"But… demons are just myths, aren't they?" Tabby asked in alarm, her eyes not leaving the beast before her.

"The only reason you think all those creatures are myths is because the council are hiding them from you!" Oculus grit his teeth, "All those 'mythological' creatures? They exist! They're real!"

Tabby coughed as she let out a very high-pitched squeak.

Alfie was completely silent as he watched in horror.

"Oni." Hercules yelled authoritatively, "If you turn around and go, you can leave unharmed."

There was another loud howl, only the beast didn't open its mouth. It licked its lips as it eyed the group hungrily.

"Th-That howl… it was its stomach!?" Nova gasped before looking up sympathetically. "You hungry big guy?"

The beast began to drool.

Hercules opened his mouth to command the beast to leave once again but didn't get a chance to say a word, he leapt to the side as the large, clawed hand swiped the spot he had been standing - Scattering grass and dirt as it left a deep trench.

The Oni growled in frustration and stomped towards the women next.

"Oculus! Weaknesses?" Hercules called over as he diverted the beast away from the girls and The Wall.

Oculus shrugged cluelessly.

"No idea! Let me know if you find some!" He replied unhelpfully.

"Why is it you always know the names of the stupid things but never how to beat them!?" Nova snapped as she rose into the air using her magic.

"Oh, I'm sorry??" Oculus snarked back with his hands on his hips. "And what exactly do you know about it? Nothing. Nada. Stop complaining!"

The Oni stomped over towards Nova and tried to swat her out of the air as if she were a particularly annoying fly.

"I'm not so sure there's much I can do!" Vera called out as she ran to avoid the ginormous foot. "Maybe I should switch with Oculus?"

It was then Oculus fell to his knees with a groan, his hands shot to his head and gripped his hair tightly.

"No..." He moaned in pain, "Not now!"

Alfie knelt beside the man in worry.

"Another vision?" he asked awkwardly.

"Yeah- OWWW!" Oculus howled; his nose began to bleed again.

"OCULUS IS HAVING A VISION AGAIN!" Tabby yelled over to the others as she watched the colour drain from the man's face.

"Not good." Hercules grunted as he grabbed the red foot and pulled it, his super strength managing to unbalance the yokai and cause it to tumble backwards.

Tabby glanced at Oculus and Alfie, she then looked over at Vera who was stuck dodging and hoping she could at least be a distraction. She knew what she had to do; she wasn't so sure how good an idea it was though.

"Alfie?" Tabby called over; her friend looked up at her. "Look after him!"

"Wha-?" Alfie frowned, he gasped as Tabby ran towards the fight. "Tabby! Get back here!"

"Vera!" Tabby panted as she joined the woman's side. "Switch?"

Vera shook her head worriedly.

"But Tabby-" She tried. Tabby smiled reassuringly.

"I at least have weapons…" She shrugged nervously. "Maybe you can help Oculus then I can switch with him?"

Vera sighed begrudgingly; Tabby was right.

"Ok… be careful!" She nodded before hurrying to the two by The Wall.

Tabby ran forward and managed to pull Nova away from the fist coming towards her.

"Tabby!" She yelped, she patted her on the head. "Don't die."

She then ran off to attack with a bolt of lightning, Tabby smirked and took a deep breath.

She jumped into the fray.

Chapter 9

Tabby yelped as she pulled her daggers out of her belt and ran around the Oni, she could see Hercules was on the beast's back - making it dizzy and angry as it spun around trying to reach him. Nova was out of the way and floating in the air, using her magic to wrap a rope around the creature's legs. The Oni was not stupid though, it simply kept lifting each leg as if it were marching which prevented the rope from securing both appendages.

If Tabby was honest, she had no clue what she was doing. She had no belief she could do any damage to the monster, she also figured she was going to get stepped on any minute.

Especially seeing as it kept stomping and Nova was not getting the hint!

"Nova!" Tabby groaned as she once again fell over from the tremor running through the ground. "It's not working! Please stop so I don't get squashed!"

"Urgh!" Nova growled as she made the rope disappear, she was clearly getting frustrated with their lack of progress.

Tabby took her chance now that the feet were still, she ran forward and stabbed her daggers into the beast's foot and dragged them along as she ran. The Oni bellowed and stumbled away in pain and anger.

"Well done, Tabby!" Hercules praised proudly, waving to the girl from his perch.

Tabby grinned secretly to herself, she was happy to receive some praise.

"Actually... it's feet seem to be pretty sensitive..." Nova noted as she noticed the beast was careful to not drag its skin against the grass below. "I wonder..."

She then reached forward, focusing on the ground below the demon.

The grass hardened and pointed straight up like nails.

The Oni screeched as it stumbled around, stepping on the painful grass below. It howled as it tripped and fell backwards sending Hercules tumbling away, Nova was able to make the grass soft again for him just in time.

"Hercules!" Nova and Tabby yelled in alarm.

Meanwhile, Alfie and Vera were knelt beside Oculus and watching the battle in worry. Poor Oculus was groaning and twitching away on the ground as he endured his vision.

"C'mon Oculus... We need you..." Vera whined as her head flitted back and forth; her hand clasped his as she tried her best to lower the pain.

Alfie was barely paying attention. His eyes were fixed on tiny Tabby darting around under the yokai, he was waiting for any sign of his friend needing help.

"Tabby... No..." Oculus murmured looking sick, this finally got Alfie's attention.

"Vera!" Nova called over, "Hercules needs healing!"

Vera looked over to see Hercules holding his shoulder, she hissed through her teeth.

"Coming!" Vera nodded, she then turned to Alfie. "Stay here and look after him!"

Alfie watched as she ran away to help their leader, he then focused his attention back to Oculus. The man was saying his friend's name over and over while shaking his head in distress.

"Oculus?" He questioned quietly when the man finally stilled.

Oculus blinked his purple eyes open groggily, they fell on Alfie's face. The man then frowned in confusion, Alfie waited patiently for him to get his bearings.

Suddenly, Oculus sat up and gasped. His eyes searched the battle ahead and landed on Tabby, the seer looked terrified and seemed to be wondering what to do.

"Oculus?" Alfie repeated firmly. "Are you ok?"

Oculus looked at Alfie with wide eyes and shook his head.

"Tabby... she's in trouble!" Oculus insisted hurriedly, "I saw her! I saw..."

Alfie watched as his teammate seemed to battle with himself.

"Tell me." He insisted, forcing his face in front of the other's so he'd have to look him in the eye.

"I saw Tabby lying on the ground... she was hurt, her eyes were closed and it didn't look like she was awake... there was a shadow of a foot coming closer..." Oculus explained quickly, seeming distressed.

"But she can't die?" Alfie pointed out unsure, "You already saw what her ability was!"

"Yes, but the future can change!" Oculus stressed impatiently, "Maybe she wasn't supposed to take part in this battle! Maybe this path ends with only you on the team!"

Alfie shook his head in denial.

"No... No, she'll be ok!" Alfie nodded, patting Oculus on the arm in an attempt to reassure him – the seer gave him an irate look.

"Hercules isn't gonna let her get hurt! Neither is Nova!"

Both males looked over to see Hercules still out of action with Vera by his side. Nova was now perched on the Oni's head and was trying to make him fall asleep to give them all a break, Tabby was still dashing around the mountainous feet, stabbing and slashing with her daggers whenever she was able to get close.

The Oni screamed furiously, it shook its head sending Nova flying through the air. Tabby ran to try and help her out only to be stopped by a giant hand wrapping around her and lifting her into the sky.

"Tabby!" Alfie howled in alarm.

Everyone watched in horror as one of their youngest recruits was lifted to the beast's eye level, she was completely defenceless.

Alfie could see Hercules and Vera hurriedly trying to think up a plan together, Nova was throwing spells at the beast's legs while shrieking Tabby's name in pure unbridled panic.

Tabby struggled in vain against the tight grip, she whimpered at the warm sweaty hand around her. It was dizzying being lifted so unexpectedly and abruptly – she felt completely dazed.

She froze when she was ogled at by a pair of bright yellow orbs and a heavy scowl. She gulped as she felt the hot breath on her face, she didn't even dare blink.

The beast seemed to study her for an agonising moment, it looked inquisitive yet aggravated. Tabby couldn't do anything, she was trapped.

"I know you're hungry…" Tabby whimpered, her face ashen. "But I'm really not worth eating! Look at me! I'm more of a toothpick than anything else!"

The Oni cocked its head curiously, it appeared to be listening to her.

"If you just put me down and get away from The Wall, you won't get hurt anymore!" Tabby promised hopefully.

The yokai was still focused on her and Tabby had to wonder if it really understood what she was saying.

The two gazed into each other's eyes, both wary yet interested in the other.

For a moment, it seemed the demon was going to put the girl down.

The Oni's stomach let out another loud wail and this seemed to make the creature's mind up for him.

The big beast glanced around, looking for something. He then squeezed his fist making Tabby wheeze helplessly, she couldn't draw her breath back in. The Oni then plodded over to the wall and began slamming the poor girl against the sharp stone, cutting her face and the beast's own knuckles.

"Stop!" Nova screamed as she continued attacking the monster desperately.

Hercules and Vera were on their feet watching in horror, knowing there was nothing they could do to help. Oculus had his eyes shut, unable to watch.

Alfie couldn't bear the sight either, yet he couldn't seem to look away.

The Oni spun around and kicked out at Nova, she managed to dodge but the rush of air from the force knocked her backwards. The demon staggered, his grip loosened, and Tabby pushed herself down and dropped out.

"TABBY!" Hercules exclaimed as the girl tumbled through the air. Tabby landed on the beast's leg and slid down until she lay on the grass, everyone stared in alarm. She wasn't moving.

The Oni started walking towards Nova, it didn't seem to see Tabby lying within his path.

Nova sat up and cried out, she struggled to her feet and tried to direct the beast away from her teammate, but it was no use.

Alfie ran forward, he had to do something!

He couldn't let Tabby die!

He heard the others call his name, but he paid no attention.

He dashed to her side and fell to his knees next to his injured friend, he lifted her gently to rest her upper half against his thighs.

"Tabby?" Alfie whimpered fearfully as he looked over his friend. Her mousey hair was a mess, her pale skin was spilt and bruised across her head. Her lip and nostrils were bleeding and there was a deep weepy wound on the bridge of the nose.

"Tabby… Please…" Alfie begged jostling the girl.

Tabby opened one eye blearily, she looked up at Alfie with her bruised brow creased into a poignant expression.

"Run." She murmured breathily, "You'll get hurt."

Alfie shook his head as the others continued to call his name, it was then he realised a gigantic shadow was cast over them and quickly getting bigger.

It was in the shape of a foot.

"Alfie. Move!" Tabby pleaded, cringing in apprehension of what was to come.

Alfie looked up just in time to see the giant red mass coming down towards them, he threw his body over his friend and closed his eyes in anxious dread.

But something stirred inside him.

A warmth burst from his core and surrounded the two of them in a rush of air.

Alfie blinked open his eyes to see a golden veil of light shaped like a dome sheltered the two friends, a shield of sorts. He then realised there was a thread of light coming out of his chest and joining the dome.

So that was his ability.

He looked around with wide astonished eyes at his accidental creation, he barely noticed the Oni had fallen over from tripping on the forcefield.

"Makes sense…" Tabby hummed with a tired smile from where she lay, Alfie looked down at her. "Of course, your ability isn't violent… I couldn't see you being able to hurt anything."

"Stay awake." Alfie begged softly, "You're gonna be ok."

Tabby smiled up at her friend, her eyes then looked up to admire the golden light twinkling around them. They both felt warm and safe.

"I believe you." She nodded gingerly. "Thanks… Alfie."

Both friends glanced up to see the Oni tearing away back to the trees with a swarm of giant wasps chasing him, the purple cloud gliding behind them told the two that Nova was their creator.

Alfie finally looked around to see the four adults speeding over to them, he breathed a sigh of relief and allowed the shield to evaporate.

"Welcome! Finally!" Oculus cheered giddily, "Now you can rename yourself and drop your boring one!"

"What!? No! I like my name!" Alfie shook his head slightly offended.

"While I am happy for you... now is not the time to celebrate." Hercules stepped forward gravely. "Tabby needs healed."

Alfie looked back down at his friend to see she had passed out, he nodded sadly. He was about to move so Vera could get to her but stopped when Hercules picked Tabby up with gentle arms and carried her back to the door.

"She's in bad shape." Nova explained as they all hurried to follow. "We're better off getting her safe indoors to heal her than risk another encounter."

Alfie nodded wordlessly.

He was glad he had finally discovered his ability, but he hated the cost, he hoped Tabby would be ok.

She had to be.

Chapter 10

Alfie leaned back against the wall; his eyes closed. He was waiting for the door next to him to open and for Hercules and Vera to give him any news on Tabby's condition. Oculus sat cross legged in front of him while Nova was sat by his side, also resting against the wall. Alfie appreciated their company, but Nova's worry was causing a slight falling of snow around the three and it was starting to get really cold.

Hercules and Vera had disappeared into the sleeping quarters with Tabby the minute they arrived home, so the three had been sat just outside for about an hour and a half now.

"Vera will need to rest soon..." Nova mused quietly, "She must be exhausting herself..."

"I think we all need a good meal, especially you." Oculus informed Alfie seriously, looking at him pointedly. "If you don't fill your belly you're gonna crash pretty hard... first time using your ability and all..."

Alfie stayed silent, not even twitching.

"I'm sorry I wasn't more help." Oculus continued, bowing his head guiltily.

"You were more help than I was." Nova sighed softly, "You saw what was going to happen so Alfie could save Tabby."

Alfie finally opened his eyes.

"You didn't see me save her, did you? In your vision I mean?" Alfie inquired quietly, looking over at the tall man. "You thought she was going to die."

"Yes... I thought we'd made a mistake somewhere and the future had changed its course..." Oculus admitted with a downtrodden sigh, "This ability is just as frustrating for me as it is for all of you."

Alfie tried to relax as he listened.

"I wish I could control it… I wish I could do more." Oculus continued, his voice getting more frustrated. "I never see full visions, only ever flashes and somehow I'm supposed to just know what they mean!"

"That's why he has those notebooks." Nova explained quietly, "When he gets those flashes, he writes down what he saw so he doesn't forget."

"Forgetting one flash could be the difference between coming home in victory or losing one of our team." Oculus shook his head in weariness, Alfie watched him sympathetically. "And if we lose someone… it'd be all my fault…"

"What else have you seen?" Alfie probed, hoping to learn more and lift the heavy burden from those thin shoulders. He couldn't imagine how it must feel trying to remember flashes of images in fear of it being the difference between life or death.

"All sorts of useless nonsense… I've seen you two, packs of wolves, rats, a dragon, a flame, running water… nothing that makes sense out of context…" Oculus shrugged carelessly. Alfie opened his mouth to ask further questions but soon snapped it shut when the door next to him opened with a quiet creak.

The three on the floor instantly jumped to their feet and looked to the two, they were eager to hear any news about Tabby.

"I healed her the best I could." Vera nodded, looking mostly at Alfie – she looked like she needed a good sleep. "She has a scar on her nose but that's all that remains."

"Vera worked tirelessly. Tabby was asleep and unaware the whole time." Hercules nodded, placing a hand on Vera's shoulder. "Now, we must let her rest. We need to eat something to restore our energy."

With that Hercules and Vera shuffled off to the kitchen, Oculus not far behind them. Nova hesitated, her eyes on the door as she shifted her weight from one foot to another restlessly.

"I want to see her." Alfie sighed, "I don't want her to wake up all alone."

Nova smiled at him gently.

"Well… nobody said you couldn't rest up in there with her." Nova suggested in a light voice. "I'd rather someone stayed with her too, if you wanna go in there then go ahead."

Alfie smiled showing he was grateful before disappearing inside the dim room.

He shut the door softly behind him and turned around, his eyes fell on the figure on the bed.

Tabby was lying under her covers on her back, her arms lay upon the soft fabric. Her eyes were shut, her hair was still messy, but she looked unharmed bar the large pink scar running horizontally across the bridge of her nose.

Alfie shuffled forward, fearing if he breathed too loud he would disturb the peace.

Slowly and quietly, he lay down on the edge. He shuffled onto his side and took one of Tabby's hands in his own.

He swallowed at how cold and limp it was.

Suddenly, everything felt too much.

Neither of them had realised just how dangerous this new role was, they never even considered the risk to their lives.

Why would they?

They were only sixteen, their whole lives should still be ahead of them. They shouldn't have to think about getting so badly hurt or losing their lives in battle, they should be doing some boring old job and going home at the end of the day to their own homes.

Alfie let out a shaky breath as he watched Tabby's chest steadily rise and fall, he took comfort in the subtle movement.

He smiled as he continued to watch over the girl, he could remember when they were both young.

Neither had much to do with the other kids, they only really interacted with the others to remind them of the consequences of misbehaving. The other kids thought they were downers, but they just didn't want to watch their classmates being dragged out by The Masquerade.

The two had been born in the same birthing room along with many others, obviously they didn't remember this. Their parents had told them when they became older and closer.

Their first real meeting was on an awful day.

Alfie and Tabby were only six years old.

They were due to start their lessons in the coming week – they would have met eventually.

He could remember his mother sobbing and holding a striped card in her hand at the kitchen table, everyone knew what that meant.

Alfie had ran out of the house and into the street. He had just stood there staring off into the distance feeling lost, confused and broken hearted.

His father was taken in the night, and he didn't understand why. What had his hero done to warrant such a punishment?

He had met Tabby that morning as he stood in the middle of the street in nothing but his pyjamas and bare feet.

Honestly, he was lucky he hadn't been taken next. You weren't supposed to leave your house without your day clothes, pyjamas were not considered appropriate wear.

Luckily, Tabby had spied him from the window. She lived across the street and had been up, washed and dressed for a while. She had been watching the world go by in boredom.

The worried girl had dashed out into the street, grabbed Alfie's arm and dragged him back into the house.

They both ignored Alfie's mother's crying as Tabby dragged him upstairs and into his room, they both knew there was no way of comforting her at that moment.

Alfie had then broken down and told Tabby what happened, the girl had been kind and patient as she listened to the story. Once he had finished, Tabby hadn't said a word.

There were no false promises of a return they knew wasn't going to happen. No fake, pitying word of how he'll be ok.

Nothing.

She simply reached forward and pulled Alfie into a gentle hug, she had rubbed his back comfortingly as she let the boy try and calm down.

Alfie couldn't remember that day to the T but those few details he could remember always brought a small smile to his face.

Tabby had been the first truly kind person he had met outside of his family.

She was quiet, reserved and very observant.

The more time they spent together the more Tabby was able to talk to him, yet she still didn't say much. Alfie figured the girl was too guarded to try and make friends, after all she might be forced to move away for her assigned career.

It was only now that the other seemed to realise they were stuck together that she was finally lowering her walls, they were finally able to treat each other like the lifelong friends they had always been.

Alfie was thankful. He had always wanted to get close to the sweet girl, he often dreamed of spending every day with her.

He was startled out of his thoughts when he felt Tabby's hand twitch, he hurried to sit up and watch as his friend finally came to.

Tabby's body felt odd. That was the first thing she was aware of.

There was a deep, dull ache pulsing around her with her heartbeat. Her nose in particular felt like it was stinging, like when you have a paper cut and you use hand sanitiser.

She let out a breathy groan as she remembered her fight with the Oni, the whole battle had been disastrous. She was grateful Alfie was there, she wouldn't be waking up right now if he wasn't.

Tabby realised there was a warm hand clinging to her own. Her eyes fluttered open to see Alfie grinning down at her in relief, he looked exhausted.

"Tabby." Alfie breathed happily, "You're awake."

"Yeah... thanks to you I think?" Tabby smiled groggily, eyes crinkling with her smile.

"Well... probably more because of Vera." Alfie blushed shyly, "How do you feel?"

"A little achy." Tabby admitted with a groan, she slowly sat up and faced her friend. "My nose stings."

"Yeah... you've kinda got a scar there... but everything else was healed up!" Alfie informed her eagerly, "I'm sure once you start moving around the pain will go away."

"Yeah, you're probably right." Tabby nodded gingerly. There was a lapse of comforting silence, as the friends processed all that had happened.

Tabby slowly looked up and studied Alfie's face, she smiled knowingly.

"So... you can make forcefields..." She grinned, Alfie looked at her bashfully.

"I guess so?" He chuckled, his cheeks reddening. Tabby laughed but soon her face fell into a thoughtful expression, her brow creased, and she looked away.

"You're... are you?... You're not Alfie anymore, are you..." She sighed sadly, unable to look at the boy in front of her. "Alfie's gone..."

"No." Alfie shook his head, he grabbed the girl's chin and forced her to look him in the eye. "I am still Alfie. We're still a team... I just make shields apparently."

"What? Everyone else changed their name once they figured out their abilities?" Tabby pointed out in confusion.

"Because... I'm Alfie." Alfie nodded firmly. "Do you remember that first day we met? We were still going by Alfred and Tabitha; we shortened our names to make it easier for the other!"

"What a story." Tabby joked weakly. Her defeated tone made her friend frown, he tilted his head and scanned the downcast expression.

"You OK?" Alfie asked softly,

"... I'm not sure..." Tabby admitted, "You just... seem different now."

Alfie watched Tabby sadly, he didn't know what to say.

"I'm still the same." He tried,

"You're right." Tabby nodded, still not sounding sure. "I'm being stupid..."

In truth, Tabby wasn't OK. It wasn't that she didn't want her friend to discover his powers, it was just yet another change she couldn't control.

First, she lost her family and home, then she lost her clothes, she's supposed to lose her own name eventually and now, it feels like she's lost the one person she counted on to never change.

Alfie wasn't Alfie anymore.

He was now the boy who was part of the team and had his own special ability.

Tabby just felt alone.

What if she never discovered her ability?

What if the machine got it wrong?

Maybe she wasn't special.

After all, it was her life at stake and yet nothing happened. Nothing sprang forth to protect her or take out the enemy, not one thing. Instead, she was hurt. Injured like any other ordinary person would be in that situation.

She didn't want to be jealous of her friend, and really, she wasn't. She just didn't want to be the odd one out and she didn't want to be left behind.

What if her ability didn't exist and she was kicked out of the team, abandoned and all alone in a world she didn't belong in.

"Tabby?" Alfie's concerned voice interrupted her thoughts, Tabby sniffed and rubbed her nose. "Hey... it's ok."

"Why couldn't I save myself?" Tabby croaked as her emotions got the better of her, she tried to scrub her tears away but they just kept coming.

"What?" Alfie was lost, he had never seen Tabby so distressed.

"Why didn't my ability save me?" Tabby hiccupped, "What if I don't have any powers? What if I'm a nobody?"

"Don't be an idiot!" Alfie insisted as he pulled the girl into a strong hug. "Oculus saw what your ability was! I'm sure there's a reason it didn't do anything against the Oni! Tabby, you could *never* be a nobody!"

"If I'm useless I'll be kicked off the team!" Tabby wept pitifully, "Then you'll be with them, and I'll lose you just like I lost my parents and Matilda..."

"That will never happen." Alfie soothed, "You could never lose me. I should be the one crying! You nearly died!"

Tabby chuckled wetly against Alfie's shoulder, the boy smirked at the noise.

"You're exhausted and hurt... I am sure you will figure stuff out eventually, but you need to let yourself recover first." Alfie sighed calmly, "And I promise, you will never ever lose me."

Tabby nodded wordlessly, they stayed in their hug for a moment longer.

Tabby realised after a few minutes of quiet that she was now supporting most of Alfie's weight, she frowned and tried to move but the boy nearly fell off the bed.

"Alfie?" She questioned warily before mentally shaking herself, "Are you ok?"

"Hercules said if I didn't eat, I was gonna crash." Alfie yawned as he blinked sleepily, "I think that was an understatement."

Tabby snorted a fond chuckle.

"Maybe I should go get you a snack?" Tabby wondered aloud, "That might help."

"Nah... you're comfy..." The tired boy mumbled as his eyes closed.

Tabby slowly lowered them both until they were lying down, she blushed as Alfie cuddled into her side.

"Stay?" Alfie asked softly, barely even awake.

"Yeah, just relax and enjoy a nap... I'll be here." Tabby nodded with a whisper, wondering if she should be worried that they boy had dropped so fast.

"Ok..." Alfie breathed as he drifted off.

Tabby smiled softly as she heard the other's breaths even out, she too closed her eyes.

Chapter 11

Tabby lay on her back next to her snoozing best friend as she fretted over how quickly Alfie had crashed, she hoped her friend wasn't going to be under the weather for too long. She figured the ability looked pretty tiring, but what did she know? She had no power yet.

She flinched when the bedroom door was opened gradually and light filtered into the room, she breathed a sigh of relief as Nova's head appeared.

She squinted through the darkness before her face split into a wide grin, she slipped in and shut the door behind her before quickly tiptoeing over to the bed. She crept round and sat by Tabby's side. "You're awake!" She whispered with a happy smile, "I'm so glad! How do you feel? A little sore I imagine?"

"Yeah… a little…" Tabby nodded bashfully. "A little disappointed too…"

Nova frowned sympathetically at that.

"I'm sorry for messing everything up." Tabby apologised bowing her head in guilt, "And for scaring you all… and for making Vera heal me…"

"You have nothing to be sorry for, you did fabulously considering it was your first time in the field! You were amazingly fast and agile, I think we'll make a fighter of you yet." Nova shook her head with a coy smirk, "I mean it! You were a huge help, we should've protected you better."

"Why didn't my ability save me?" Tabby asked miserably, wishing someone could just give her a straight answer. "I was in mortal danger and… nothing…"

Nova bit her lip, she seemed to think for a moment before sighing in resignation. She settled down and lay next to Tabby – it was a tight squeeze having three bodies lying on one single bed - with a contemplative look on her face, the girl watched her curiously.

"I understand how you must be feeling… Vera was the same… I found my powers on only the second quest while Vera went months without anything." Nova nodded, her voice quiet with guilt and regret. "The problem was her ability had nothing to do with fighting. She wasn't going to unlock it by getting herself into trouble… which she did a lot to try and prove her worth. It was only when Hercules was knocked out by a unicorn that she finally learned what her purpose was."

"Hercules was knocked out by a unicorn?" Tabby snorted in amusement, Nova stifled her giggles with her hand.

"Yeah, he was so embarrassed!" She grinned widely, "We didn't wanna fight it, so he tried to spook it and make it run away… he did too good a job and got kicked in the head!"

The two snickered quietly.

"I spoke to Oculus because I knew you would be feeling the same way as Vera did all those years ago." Nova smiled softly as she lay her head against Tabby's. "He told me that your ability has nothing to do with the Oni… it's specific… We talked some more about how to help you out… We don't want you waiting months like Vera did, she got so depressed, and I know she felt terrible. We don't need you putting yourself at risk to try and get approval or whatever."

Tabby frowned in slight offence and intrigue as she listened.

"We both wondered… if it would be worth you sneaking out with us and seeing if we can figure this out together." Nova whispered secretively; Tabby gasped.

"But Hercules said-" She began but was hastily shushed.

"I know... he thinks The Masquerade are always watching... but, Oculus and I have snuck out before and... we're still here." She insisted with a serious expression, "I think they only care if we go into the city, I think outside is ok. They want us to protect the city after all, they're not gonna argue with a little overtime."

"Overtime?" Tabby repeated doubtfully. "What if that one time you were lucky?"

"We've snuck out way more than once." Nova gave her a smug smirk, "We go out there all the time."

"And Hercules doesn't know?" Tabby asked incredulously, she watched as Nova winced.

"He may be our leader, but he doesn't need to know everything, and we certainly don't need his permission." She insisted adamantly, "So no. And you're not gonna tell him either!"

"Of course not!" Tabby huffed with an eyeroll at the accusing tone. "When would we go?"

"It has to be at night." Nova informed her, her eyes on the shut door. "You wanna go tonight or do you need more rest?"

Tabby frowned in thought. On one hand her body was in desperate need of recovery but on the other, she just couldn't stand the wait. She needed to know so she could contribute, she wanted to know what her place was amongst all these remarkable people.

Then she looked over at Alfie, her friend was exhausted from discovering his own ability. What if he ended up needing her and she wasn't there? That was no way to treat the person who just saved her life.

"Not tonight." Tabby shook her head confidently. "How about tomorrow night?"

"Ok... Just you, me and Oculus, ok? Vera and Hercules can't know, you can't tell Alfie either. It'll just be a one off!" Nova pushed firmly, she was checking she could be trusted. "Yes?"

Tabby glanced hesitantly at her friend before heaving a sigh.

"Ok. Just us three…" She then had a sudden thought. "But, if we do figure out my ability and I decide to change my name or whatever, won't they find out?"

"You would have to hide your knowledge for now." Nova rolled her eyes in exasperation. "We're just trying to help you figure this out, you can then make a spectacle of yourself later if you must! Besides, you don't have to change your name immediately… I like your name as it is."

Tabby gave her a grateful look, Nova smiled back and gave her a quick side hug.

"I'm glad you're ok." She hummed softly, "I was so scared when I saw you lying on the ground like that… if I can do this so that never happens again then I will. Oculus will too… you really scared us."

Tabby said nothing.

Nova stood, gave her young friend one more smile before slipping back out of the room – no doubt to inform Oculus of their plans for tomorrow night.

Tabby smiled warmly; she was glad the others wanted to help. She wasn't sure how she felt about already having to keep a secret from half of their new team, especially when Alfie was in that half.

An hour later, Alfie woke up smacking his lips tiredly. His body felt heavy, and he was parched, his eyes felt dry and itchy despite being closed.

He just felt so drained.

"Alfie?" Tabby's voice whispered from beside him.

Alfie slowly blinked open his eyes and looking into Tabby's worried face, the girl was watching him wake in concern.

"You look more tired than you did when you fell asleep." The girl commented, studying the dark circles bruising the skin under her friend's eyes. "You ok?"

"Mm hm." Alfie nodded with a stretch, "Just feel a li'l drained."

Tabby smirked in fond amusement.

"Oh... makes sense I guess." She nodded reassuringly, "Do you want me to get you anything? Food, water?"

Alfie thought for a moment, his brain sluggishly processing his options.

"Yeah..." He said sleepily, Tabby snorted in response.

"Which one?" She asked clearly, trying to hide her amused grin.

"Which one?" Alfie repeated in confusion, his brow creasing. Tabby chuckled lightly before sitting herself up.

"I'm gonna go get you a glass of water and something to eat, ok?" She asked in a precise and slow voice in an attempt to get her groggy friend to understand, Alfie nodded his approval.

However, when Tabby stood up, she felt someone pull on the back of her jumpsuit. She glanced over her shoulder to see Alfie looking up at her pitifully.

"Don't go..." Alfie pouted,

"I have to if you want food and drink." Tabby smiled apologetically, "I'll be right back, I promise."

"No... use your ability to magic up stuff." Alfie yawned; Tabby laughed.

"Yeah, no. I don't think my ability has anything to do with miracles I'm afraid." She teased sarcastically, the hand finally released her and flopped back down onto the covers.

"Fine... but come back." Alfie demanded as he closed his eyes again.

"Duh," Tabby chuckled as she headed for the door. "Kinda hard to deliver the goods if I don't come back."

With that she left the room.

She stood outside the door for a moment and let herself breathe, her friend was a little out of it but otherwise seemed ok. She believed she made the right decision not abandoning Alfie tonight – she just hoped some food would help!

Tabby shook herself out of her thoughts, straightened up and marched off to the kitchen. She didn't want to be away too long, Alfie needed her.

Hercules, Oculus and Vera were nursing cups of green tea when Tabby walked into their kitchen area, Nova was lying on the tile floor.

"Why are you down there?" Tabby asked as she lightly kicked her leg, she needed it to move so she could get a glass.

"Why not?" Nova asked with a shrug, "It's clean, it's comfortable."

"I doubt it's comfortable." Tabby raised an eyebrow questioningly.

"Don't know 'til you try." The woman droned as she relaxed.

"How are you?" Hercules interrupted the conversation, staring intently at the girl.

"I'm ok... Alfie's kind out of it though." Tabby nodded as she filled the glass with cold water, she placed it down on the counter gently before hunting through the cupboards for a snack.

"Yeah, his ability looked like an exhausting one." Vera nodded, knowing too well what the boy was going through. "Making a shield of pure energy takes a lot out of you... like using pure energy to heal a wound."

"Huh, so were you the same way?" Tabby asked inquisitively as she studied a pack of crackers.

"Yes. Practice makes it easier." Vera smiled helpfully, "Even just the next time he won't be as exhausted."

"That's good." Tabby smiled back at her.

"How are *you* feeling though?" Hercules tried again, "You said 'ok' but... you were out for a while... you were badly hurt."

"Honestly, I'm fine." Tabby insisted a bit too firmly, Hercules breathed a heavy sigh.

"Don't be too frustrated." Vera piped up keeping her kind smile in place, "It took a while for my ability to show itself... just give yourself time, we'll figure it out eventually."

Tabby nodded, keeping her mouth shut tight to avoid giving Nova's plan away.

She grabbed the glass and nodded to her friends.

"Thanks for… y'know." She smiled in a way that she hoped came across convincing but definitely felt strained, "I'm gonna go make sure Alfie gets something in his stomach."

She hurried off before anyone could say another word, she didn't want to be rude, but she also knew she was a terrible liar.

She didn't want to hide anything from Hercules and Vera, the two sweetest people she'd ever met.

She finally reunited with her lethargic friend, she forced the boy to eat some crackers and drink the full glass of water. After the glass was drained of every drop and half the packet was consumed, Alfie began to become more like himself again.

The two rested together comfortably for the remainder of the day and night.

Chapter 12

Alfie was completely back to himself the next morning, all exhaustion completely gone. If anything, he seemed to be even more energised that day than he'd ever been! Tabby guessed there was something reassuring and exciting about discovering your role within the team.

She couldn't relate.

Alfie had slept like a log last night. Barely moving, not even twitching and he snored far louder than Tabby had ever heard him. She knew this due to herself not being able to keep her eyes closed or her mind quiet for longer than a couple of minutes, she swore she only managed to sleep for an hour or so in the early morning. She just couldn't stop worrying – this wasn't completely uncommon for her or others within Slately.

She could not shake the fear of this all being a huge mistake. The machine got it wrong, she wasn't special – she was just a normal girl like everyone else. She would forever stay on the side-lines as her friends saved the town over and over again, becoming closer and relying on one another.

She'd just be Tabby, the one that's just a liability.

How long would it be before the team gave up trying to help her? And how much longer after that would she start being left behind? She doubted they would bring some useless kid out with them every time the alarm rang.

What did this mean for her relationship with Alfie?

She didn't want to grow nasty and envious.

She didn't want to be forgotten and abandoned.

This train of thought then led her to her next one.

She spent half the night berating herself for being so self-centred. She should be happy for her friend, proud that he had such a kind and wonderful power. Especially seeing as he discovered it saving her useless ass.

She was a bad friend to be upset.

She was an awful person for only thinking of herself and ruining this big accomplishment.

She simply lay on her back and stared up at the ceiling.

She must have fallen asleep at some point because she was woken early when Hercules got out of bed – the man had walked into the door frame with a loud and heavy thump from being half asleep.

Apparently, Nova was already awake too because she dissolved into hysterical giggles at Hercules' blunder.

She continued to lie there as Nova, then Vera and last of all Oculus got ready for the day.

She stayed in her own bed by Alfie's side. Determined to be a good friend and cheerleader of her best friend – she hoped to keep Alfie close even if it turned out she was normal, she would be there the whole way.

Alfie was the last to wake but when he did, Tabby startled in surprise and was forced to catch her breath. Alfie had seemed to go from dead asleep to on his feet in seconds, he even grinned at Tabby immediately despite the dark bags under his eyes.

"Good morning!" He greeted pleasantly before getting ready, a jolly skip in his step.

Tabby sat there stunned, she had never met anyone who could just get out of bed the second they awoke – Alfie was always the kind of guy that would lie in for an hour as he swore, he was getting up now.

She shook her head as Alfie skipped out into the main room, leaving Tabby behind in the dark bedroom.

Tabby walked out to the smell of pancakes, herbal tea and coffee. The others were already happily gathered around the dining table digging into their breakfasts, a huge stack of pancakes sat in the middle.

"Morning!" Nova greeted enthusiastically through her mouthful.

"Help yourself!" Alfie gestured sheepishly to the stack in the centre, "I think I made too many."

"You think?" Oculus scoffed rudely as he sipped his green tea.

Tabby sat down smiling politely, she helped herself to a couple and poured herself a large cup of coffee – even opting out of sugar and milk, hoping black coffee would keep her awake.

Everyone else was happily chatting and eating their fill, nobody seemed to notice how quiet she was being or the dark bruises under her bloodshot eyes.

She didn't blame them; she wasn't one of them yet.

She stuck a fingernail into the flesh of her palm angrily, she told herself to stop moping and to stop being so dramatic. They hadn't been there long, Alfie got lucky – that was all.

Her heart broke as she thought about what Nova had told her about Vera. The poor girl had gone months without knowing her place, how awful she must have felt. She wondered if she took it as personally as she was, did she feel like a burden?

Did she worry that it was all a mistake?

These thoughts just wouldn't leave her throughout the day, she really hoped going out tonight would put an end to this self-torture.

After lunch, she found herself cornered by Vera.

She had sat herself on the kitchen floor, hidden by the island counter. The others were laughing and joking outside, theorising about what else Alfie might be able to do with his shields and forcefields.

She just needed some quiet, just for a moment.

Apparently, Vera had seen her leave and had subtly followed.

"Hey." She greeted gently as she gracefully sat beside her, "Not the most comfortable hiding place but... effective I guess."

Tabby responded with a soft chuckle.

"I just needed some peace and quiet for a moment." She shrugged, looking over at the girl. She nodded slowly; her shoulder then pressed against her.

"I know how you feel." Vera smile was sad and empathetic, "I was the same way... the day after Nova figured out she had magic I think I spent the whole day in bed... Claimed I wasn't feeling well."

Tabby said nothing, simply watched as she seemed to cast her mind back.

"It was months before I figured out my purpose... honestly, I probably could have worked it out sooner if I hadn't been so... low. I stopped going out with the others, I distanced myself... had I just kept getting involved I would have seen them get hurt and I would have learned about my healing ability." Vera confessed shyly, "The others tried to reassure me it was ok... they told me to be patient but... that's easy for them to say when they're useful and part of the team."

"I'm just scared this is all just some big mistake." Tabby admitted once Vera fell silent. "What if I don't have an ability?"

"Why do you think I distanced myself?" Vera chuckled with a soft smirk, "I thought the same thing... I didn't want to get close to the others in case The Masquerade came for me, in case there was a mix up and I wasn't supposed to be here."

"Yeah..." Tabby sighed, feeling almost relieved at having her biggest fear shared.

"Tabby, The Masquerade don't make mistakes." Vera assured her firmly, she finally looked over at her and met her eye. "You are one of us. It may take time to work out just what role you play but... have faith that it'll all work out eventually. We're here with you, every step of the way."

Tabby's smile wobbled emotionally at her kind words.

It was nice to have someone who truly understood.

They both leant against each other as they fell into a comforting silence. They didn't need to say anything further to one another, they already knew all the other was feeling.

Tabby wasn't worried about being left behind anymore, she knew Vera would always look out for her. She was on her side having experienced the same thing.

They jumped when the heard the shrill ringing of the alarm. Tabby glanced worriedly at Vera – She gave her a reassuring smile.

"C'mon." She nodded before standing up, she stepped forward and stretched her hand out to her.

Tabby smiled, took her hand and followed her out of the kitchen.

The six once again descended the slope from their home base, excitedly chatting and laughing as they stretched and hyped themselves up.

Tabby and Vera walked together in step; both quietly enjoying the other members' energy.

They all walked through the door, ready to take on the threat that waited for them out in the world.

Their grins soon fell off their faces when they looked around – there didn't seem to be anything there.

They then heard a wet gurgle. Their heads all snapped down to see something small, scaly and green sitting hunched over in the grass – it seemed to be searching for something.

"Aww!" Nova cooed happily, "It's so tiny!"

She stepped forward and the creature rose to its full height as it noticed her, it was tense and wary.

It was very odd looking. Its skin looked smooth with shining scales; it was a greenish aqua sort of colour depending on where the light hit it. It was about the size of a small child, had stubby legs and arms that seemed to disappear into its body in a disconcerting way – like if you pulled too hard they would come out. On its back sat a large turtle carapace, it seemed to be a part of its body rather than an armour choice.

Its head was far too large and there was a strange sort of divot that looked like a dish filled with water. It very much looked like a weird hybrid of human and terrapin. It had human eyes but a turtle's beak, it had hands and feet, but they were webbed.

Oculus grabbed a notebook and quickly scribbled in it; Hercules looked over at him.

"Do you know what it is yet?" He asked hopefully, keeping his voice low so as not to startle the mysterious little terrapin.

"Oh yeah, sorry." Oculus chuckled, not looking up from what he was doing. "It's a Kappa."

There was a beat of silence as they waited in vain for him to elaborate. He continued scribbling quietly while whispering to himself.

"Yes, thank you, Oculus." Nova rolled her eyes derisively, "That was very insightful!"

Oculus shoved his notebook back where it belonged and crossed his arms.

"There's no need to be snippy!" He looked down at the Kappa with a bored expression. "You asked what it was, and I told you."

"Well clearly we wanted more information than that!" Nova argued back, giving him a heated glower. "Which you know damn well!"

"I thought you said I didn't know *everything*," The man mocked with a sly grin, "Why don't you try learning about it for yourself for a change."

"Oculus!" Nova grit her teeth in frustration.

"Is it dangerous?" Hercules asked as his intelligent eyes observed the little creature, ignoring the argument.

"I mean… it depends if it's *feeling* dangerous." The skinny man gave a nonchalant shrug. "Be nice, even little Tabby here could be dangerous if you gave her reason to be."

Tabby glanced up at Oculus, wondering if that was supposed to be a cheap shot.

"What's the worst it can do?" Alfie asked in vain as he tried to get more useful information.

"Worst?" Oculus hummed thoughtfully, "I mean… they *could* eat your flesh, but they don't really tend to do that much."

Nova rolled her eyes irritably again before stepping closer to the little Kappa.

"Hello Kappa." She greeted with a nice smile, it looked up at her with beady black eyes. "What are you looking for li'l guy?"

The Kappa shied away, its movements were disturbingly human. Nova knelt down softly and reached a hand out to the nervous creature.

"Don't be afraid." She soothed hoping to reassure the Kappa she meant no harm.

The Kappa studied her.

Nova screamed as the Kappa leapt at her and clung to her waist, seemingly now trying to search through her pockets and belt.

Hercules hurried forward to help but was soon covered in other Kappa who had been hiding in the bushes and pond nearby, he stumbled to the side under their weight.

Alfie was next to try and help but very much ended up in the same position as the others.

"Umm… what now?" Tabby asked in concern, looking to Oculus and Vera for guidance.

"Well, that depends." Oculus smirked cheekily. "If you wanna get covered in greedy Kappa then you go ahead and join in, if you wanna stay away from the little creeps then stay here with the rest of us intelligent members of the team."

"That's not helpful." Vera scolded gently, "Won't they hurt the others?"

"Nah!" Oculus waved their worries off. "They like drowning people and there's no deep bodies of water for miles."

Hercules yelped as the group of Kappa lifted him off the ground and started shaking him.

"Huh…" Oculus hummed, completely fascinated, as he once again grabbed his notebook to write what he was seeing. "So, they're pretty strong… noted."

"They're clearly looking for something." Tabby pointed out as she observed the ambush in front. "What do you think they want?"

"Well… they're part animal so I imagine… food?" Vera calmly suggested, Oculus nodded wisely.

"Yes, but they're also part human." He reminded them, "So… I guess food still works but they might be pickier."

"Ok, so what food do they eat?" Tabby wondered to herself as she wracked her brain, the other two shrugged cluelessly.

The three yelped as more Kappa appeared, the little creatures ran at them and harshly dragged them into the fray.

They tumbled and tousled for a couple of minutes.

Then, the Kappa were tossed into the air as a golden, shimmering dome enveloped the six friends. Alfie's forcefield once again saved the day.

They all caught their breaths before scanning the crowd of now very upset Kappa, big crocodile tears were streaming down their green faces.

"Aww." Nova whined sadly, "You hurt them!"

"Sorry." Alfie shrugged, clearly not sorry at all.

"Ok. We need to think." Hercules announced in determination, "How are we getting these annoying turtles to leave? Any ideas?"

"Not turtles. Kappa." Oculus interrupted, "That's probably a very offensive thing to call them, never mind inaccurate."

"We think food." Vera nodded as she ignored the know-it-all, "What do you think they'd like to eat?"

"Oh!" Nova grinned in excitement; she waved her hand.

The Kappa screamed and jumped out of the way as lumps of slimy soggy kelp rained down on them. They all looked a bit sick as they cowered from the smelly water plants, they even hugged each other for protection.

Nova huffed as she waved her hand again and made the kelp disappear.

"That was a good guess." Hercules nodded with pride; Nova smiled up at him.

"How about some kind of vegetable?" Oculus suggested, "Maybe... lettuce?"

Once again, Nova magicked up what was requested, and it came raining down from the sky.

This time, the Kappa didn't look quite as disgusted. In fact, they seemed to have realised it was the humans causing it. The crowds looked over at the six and all shook their big dome heads, Nova stomped as she made the heads of lettuce vanish.

"They're so picky!" She griped moodily.

"Carrots?"

"Nope."

"Cabbage?"

"You made one barf."

"Turnip!"

"Gross... no."

"Potato."

The six flinched as the Kappa threw the spuds at them in frustration at all their wrong guesses.

"Well, what other vegetables are there?" Nova asked tiredly, getting fed up of trying to feed the picky eaters.

"Maybe vegetables are wrong, maybe they like fruit?" Vera suggested lightly, her head tilting to the side.

"Too sugary and acidic." Nova frowned, "Pretty sure that would have the same result as the cabbage."

"Well… cucumber isn't acidic, is it?" Vera pointed out; Nova looked at her blankly.

"Cucumbers are vegetables." She deadpanned; Vera cringed.

"Well… technically they're not because they have seeds that we eat in them… tomatoes aren't veggies either." She deflated as Oculus scoffed in boredom.

"We are not having this argument again!" He groaned, throwing his head back. "Just give the stupid things cucumbers and then we'll try tomatoes."

Nova sighed and waved her hand.

The Kappa all gazed up with wide, excited eyes. They're big beaks curving into smiles as they started jumping for joy as cucumbers rained down upon them.

Some of them even going as far as to leap up impatiently so they could finally eat.

The six watched in disgust as they swallowed some of them whole, chewing and gulping the vegetable-that-might-actually-be-a-fruit down.

In a matter of seconds all of the cumbers were chomped down, the crowds of Kappa were finally satisfied.

They all waved their thanks before scurrying off in the direction of the nearby river.

Alfie finally let his shield down with a relieved smile.

"Nice one team!" Hercules praised happily, "I'm proud of all of you except Oculus!"

"Hey!" The man in question gasped in offence.

"We would have been done much sooner if you had actually *tried* to help." Hercules pointed out sternly.

"Where's the fun in that?" Oculus chuckled mischievously. "I knew they weren't really dangerous so why not."

"That was quick thinking on your part, Alfie!" Hercules patted the boy on the back as they all headed towards the door. "Your ability is going to be very useful! I can tell!"

Tabby watched as Hercules, Oculus, Nova and Alfie all walked ahead. They were all praising the youngest and enthusing about his power.

Tabby smiled wanly as Vera joined her side, she placed a hand on her shoulder and leaned closer to her as they strolled along.

"You helped too." She reminded her. "I thought you did rather well... you kept out of trouble, and you helped us work out the solution."

"Yeah... maybe my place is in the background with you and Oculus... figuring everything out while the others do the heavy lifting..." She shrugged, trying to sound positive.

"It's the better place to be in my opinion." Vera smiled with a quiet chuckle.

Tabby appreciated her being so kind but, she wasn't so sure she could agree. Yet again, there was no sign of her ability – nothing that indicated she belonged with these wonderful, gifted people. It was hard not to overthink it.

She was glad she, Oculus and Nova were going out that night. She couldn't take one more day of wondering if she was a mistake.

Chapter 13

Night came much faster than Tabby wanted it to. She was excited yet scared to go out at night with just two other members of their team, but she kept wondering what her ability was. She had no real theories, she just hoped it wasn't useless or boring.

A large part of her didn't want to have the same as the others either.

It was hard not to confide this secret to Alfie.

Tabby had promised to keep quiet yet, she really wanted to tell him.

She wished he could come with her, but her friend was still exhausted from using his ability again, he needed the sleep.

Or at least, that's what Tabby told herself so she wouldn't feel so bad about hiding this from him.

Tabby lay in bed and listened to Alfie's deep breaths; she could also hear the others getting ready to sleep. She quickly shut her eyes as the door opened, she pretended to breathe deeply like she was asleep – all of her power went into not moving.

She could hear Hercules' bed groan with the weight as the large man settled in for the night.

She then heard Vera, Nova and Oculus come in, all chatting together quietly. Vera's voice was barely audible, the others' whispers were loud and pointless. They might as well just talk.

Tabby tried not to smirk.

They were not giving her any faith in their ability to sneak her out.

"Nova! Oculus!" Hercules hushed the two impatiently, "Quiet down! The kids are asleep!"

"Sorry!" Nova whispered back.

The three settled into their beds, there was a tense silence.

Tabby waited to hear the other two get up before she made any moves, if they sneaked out as often as they claimed then they were the pros. They knew when to move and how to keep from being caught.

Tabby nearly drifted off but was quickly woken when a gentle hand shook her, she blinked her eyes open to see Oculus grinning mischievously.

Tabby sat up quickly but froze when Oculus pointedly lifted his index finger to his lips, signalling she had to be silent. He then lifted his other hand to reveal he was carrying Tabby's belt with all his stuff.

Oculus helped Tabby slip out of bed and creep through the dark, both as silent as mice.

Once in the main area they met up with Nova who was bouncing on her toes energetically, she looked positively giddy when she saw them.

She waved excitedly, reminded them to stay silent and allowed Oculus to lead the way out.

No one said a word until they were hurrying down the stone passage to their exit.

"Awww!" Nova giggled quietly, "It's been so long since we did this!"

"It has!" Oculus agreed lightly, "It's nice to share our tradition with a newbie."

"Why did you guys used to sneak out?" Tabby asked curiously, "Did you really do it that often?"

"Yeah! We used to do it... was it twice a month?" Nova asked as she tried to remember.

"Originally it was once a week." Oculus reminded her with a laugh, "But we started to worry Hercules would figure us out, so we cut it down to twice a month and then we just... stopped..."

"Yeah..." Nova sighed as she reminisced, "We used to just go out to do stargazing."

"Nova was obsessed when she first saw them, I agreed to make sure she could see them regularly seeing as our missions tend to be in the day." Oculus explained casually, "It's also an open space for her to practice her magic harmlessly and honestly? It's just nice to relax in the fresh air once in a while."

"Yeah... I get that." Tabby nodded slowly, "Are the stars really that cool?"

"Yes!" Nova squealed excitedly, "They are the most beautiful things in the world!"

"The sky is pretty amazing out there when there aren't any clouds." Oculus admitted with a wry smile, "Do you know how many moons we have?"

"Moons?" Tabby asked in confusion, "One as far as I knew, you can barely see the night sky in Slately."

"We have three!" Nova gushed, "We have a large one which you see no matter what, I named her Luna! We also have Pandora and Aphrodite; Pandora is kind of a purple colour and she's half the size of Luna. Aphrodite is a pinkish colour and she's tiny! Only just bigger than a star!"

"Wow!" Tabby gasped in delight, now she was really excited.

They arrived at the door and rushed through it, their eyes immediately on the sky above.

"Woah..." Tabby breathed in amazement.

Twinkling stars littered the inky canvas above, there were swirls of colour which she guessed were galaxies. Sure enough, there were three moons lined up in a row. The biggest one was a pale silvery white, Tabby could finally see the details of craters on its surface. The second was a blue-ish purple, it blended with the sky well. The last really was tiny and was as pink as a fresh rose!

"Hi Luna! Hi Pandora! Hi Aphrodite!" Nova waved up to the sky ecstatically, "Sorry we've been away for so long!"

Oculus chuckled but secretly sent the three moons a wave.

"How come you know their names?" Tabby asked in wonder. "Do they talk?"

"She named them, they don't have names… as far as we know…" Oculus shrugged,

"Yup! I named them!" Nova nodded happily, "I believe they are three sisters. I think they get pretty lonely watching over the world at night, so I like to visit them and give them company."

"Yeah… Nova's insane." Oculus summed up cheekily, Nova ignored him.

Tabby finally looked away from the view, she glanced around the dark wilderness only to freeze.

There, standing only three feet away were giant wolves.

Tabby held her breath in fear, the others hadn't noticed the animals.

The two wolves were huge, nearly seven foot tall. Their coats were big, shiny and fluffy.

The first wolf was pure black with glowing red eyes, it also had a glowing red symbol of the sun in the centre of its breast.

The second was pure silvery white with bright blue eyes, it also had a glowing blue symbol of a crescent moon in the centre of its breast.

The two were sniffing the air in their direction and watching Tabby warily, she gulped in fear as the hair on her arms stood on end. She didn't want to get hurt again, maybe this *was* a bad idea.

It felt like her heart was going to pound itself right out of her chest – Alfie wasn't here to protect her this time.

Suddenly, there was a voice in her head.

"Are you dangerous?" The voice was deep and harsh.

"Umm… no?" Tabby flinched as the two stepped back in surprise.

"She can understand us." The white wolf looked at the black one as a lighter, much softer voice spoke. *"I have never encountered this before."*

"Neither have I..."

Tabby was seriously freaked out, were the voices in her head coming from the wolves or had she finally lost it?

It was then Nova and Oculus stepped up beside her, one on either side. They were glaring at the two wolves in front.

"These guys again." Nova growled protectively as she raised her hands, "Leave us alone fleabags!"

"These two are troublemakers Tabby," Oculus warned the girl, "We've dealt with them before, powerful and sneaky."

"Maybe she can help?" The softer voice spoke once more.

The white wolf stepped forward warily and sniffed in Tabby's direction, Nova's hands began to glow.

"Human... My name is Hati, this is my brother Skoll." The white wolf glanced over at the black one briefly, the soft voice continued. *"We are the leaders of the wolves around here. What is your name?"*

"My name is Tabby." Tabby nodded trying to sound confident. Oculus groaned as Nova watched in fascination.

"Aww! No! Don't tell me your ability was awoken by these mutts!" Nova gasped in amazement as she gazed between her friend and the animals.

"Wait... You're not going to change your name either, are you!?" Oculus groaned dramatically again, "I don't get you two! Why do I even bother?"

"Our names are already changed! They're the shortened version of the ones we were assigned!" Tabby huffed, "Now shhhh!"

"Greetings, Tabby." Skoll nodded his large head, *"How is it you can understand us?"*

"I have no idea, I guess it's just my... ability?" Tabby shrugged uneasily, "I wonder if it's only wolves I can understand..."

"You can really understand them!?" Nova squealed excitedly; the two animals flattened their ears at the noise. "That's so cool! What did they say?"

"Their names are Skoll and Hati, they are kind of the leaders of all the wolves in Emerelda." Tabby explained awkwardly.

"Which is which?" Oculus asked, watching the wolves suspiciously.

"Skoll is the one with the black fur and Hati is the white one." Tabby pointed to each wolf in turn.

"We do not like your friends." Skoll lifted his lip and growled, showing his sharp teeth. Oculus and Nova stepped back in alarm.

"They are fools." Hati agreed as he too snarled at the two.

"Oculus and Nova are not fools." Tabby scolded bluntly, crossing her arms.

Oculus and Nova looked offended and glared at the two brothers.

"We need help." Hati requested as the beasts ceased their aggression, *"We wonder if you may be able to provide it?"*

"What do you need help with?" Tabby asked in interest.

"We will show you." Hati nodded his head. The two then turned to lead the way but Skoll looked back at the girl.

"You must come alone." Skoll informed her warningly.

"I'm not sure my team are gonna like that..." Tabby worried as she rubbed her cheek.

"We do not trust them. We're sure HE does not like humans either, we can protect you but not them." Skoll insisted, he was a very bad-tempered animal it would appear. *"Come."*

Tabby sighed heavily then turned to the two adults with a sheepish grin.

"Oh no..." Oculus groaned in dread, "What did they say?"

"They've asked me to help them and someone else." Tabby admitted, shuffling on the spot under their gaze.

"Ok, let's go." Nova nodded looking serious, but Tabby raised her hand shyly.

"They said HE doesn't like humans... they want me to come alone." She cringed as the two looked furious, "They said they can protect me!"

"This is so clearly a trap!" Oculus insisted angrily, "They're trying to trick you! They'll get you alone then they'll eat you! You can't trust them!"

Tabby opened her mouth to speak but Nova stepped forward.

"No. Tabby, you are not going with them." She told her, leaving no room for argument.

"But I can speak to them and understand them! What's the point in being able to understand animals if I don't get to actually listen to what they have to say?" Tabby tried weakly but she could see she wasn't getting anywhere, she sighed sadly and faced the wolves. "Sorry, I can't come with you."

The two wolves growled and leapt forward, knocking Oculus and Nova to the ground.

"No! Hey!" Tabby snapped in betrayal as she rushed at the beasts, "Leave them alone!"

Hati jumped off Nova and ran towards Tabby, he lowered himself next to the girl.

"Climb on!" He ordered fiercely, *"We will leave them unharmed; I promise!"*

Nova was wobbling to her feet as Tabby glanced at her teammates in worry, she sighed before climbing onto Hati's back.

She barely got the chance to settle herself when the white wolf let out a long, loud howl and sprinted off quickly.

Tabby threw herself forward and clung to the soft pelt, the ride was bumpy as the fields flew under the thundering paws. Skoll appeared next to them, he was panting and kept glancing at the girl.

"Do not be afraid." Skoll assured her with a strong voice. *"If you help us, we will forever protect you and your team as a reward. We will be allies."*

Tabby nodded in silence, choosing to trust the two animals and praying she wouldn't regret it.

Oculus and Nova tried to run after the wolves, but they simply weren't fast enough, they watched as their friend disappeared into the distance.

They looked at one another feeling uneasy.

They heard the door open behind them, they winced and glanced round to find Hercules, Vera and Alfie running towards them looking furious.

"What are you doing out here!?" Hercules bellowed; Alfie had never seen him so heated.

"We can explain!" Oculus held up his hands in surrender.

Vera crossed her arms and silently glared at the two. Alfie looked around for any sign of his friend, his stomach dropped when there was none.

"Did Tabby come with you?" Alfie fussed nervously. "Where is she?"

He could immediately tell by the two's expressions that Tabby was with them, but she wasn't now.

Where was she?

"Where is she?" Hercules pushed impatiently, "Do you have any idea how stupid this was? You three could have been killed or hurt or who knows what else!"

It was then it dawned on the three that Oculus and Nova looked upset and guilty; they began to understand there was a reason Tabby wasn't with them anymore they weren't willing to share.

"Where. Is. Tabby?" Hercules' voice was dangerously quiet, it sent a shiver up Alfie's spine.

"Tabby… can communicate with wolves." Oculus grinned painfully, clearly trying to look more confident than he felt while standing stock still.

The other three waited for him to continue.

"And um… she kinda… made friends with them and now, she's gone." Nova gulped, wincing at how her statement sounded.

"Gone. Where?" Hercules demanded.

Oculus and Nova looked at one another.

"We don't know?" They both squeaked.

Hercules growled angrily while Vera and Alfie looked at the two in shock and fear.

"What do you mean you don't know!?" Vera stepped forward; her eyes impossibly wide.

"We'll explain everything." Oculus sighed in defeat, "It's just... kind of a weird story."

Oculus and Nova deflated as they began to tell the three everything that had happened, they spoke about Hati and Skoll, how Tabby discovered her ability, and the wolves that took her away to help someone.

It was going to be a long night.

Chapter 14

Tabby's fingers were cramping and freezing as she held on for dear life, the two wolves had now fallen silent as they continued their run through the pine forest. Tabby wondered what would happen to her if it turned out she couldn't help.

"Are we there yet?" She whimpered miserably, her teeth chattering.

"Not yet." Hati responded, sounding focused. *"But we are not far."*

"Maybe it would help to explain what it is we need you to do." Skoll hummed in thought.

"Well yeah?" Tabby huffed sarcastically, "It would be a start!"

"Perhaps you should have asked before you agreed." Skoll snapped back, sending her a no-nonsense glare.

Tabby blushed, the wolf wasn't wrong.

"We look after all of the wolves that live in our forest; we are one big wolfpack." Skoll began his voice much calmer now, *"The south, east and west have always been our territory. Over the last few days, we have been able to smell an intruder, we need to prevent this beast from entering our domain."*

"Ok?" Tabby frowned, still not entirely sure what she was meant to be doing. "And how am I supposed to help with that?"

"We're hoping your ability stretches beyond just us." Hati admitted sounding embarrassed, Tabby wondered if wolves blushed under all that fur. *"We're hoping you can simply explain to the intruder that he is on our territory, and he must leave. We'd rather have a discussion than start a fight."*

"Animals can't talk to each other?" Tabby asked in surprise, "Maybe they just want to pass through? There's no harm in that is there?"

"Animals and beasts all have their own languages." Skoll snorted nastily, *"How simple you are."*

"Y'know, I don't have to help you!" Tabby griped bitterly.

"And we don't have to let you live." Skoll snapped back, showing his teeth.

"There is much harm in them passing through." Hati explained patiently as he ignored his brother's behaviour. *"You see, our females have just had their litters. This beast is heavy enough to collapse our nursing dens! It is already heading towards them; our young will be killed!"*

"And that's a whole generation lost." Skoll agreed gravely.

Tabby thought for a moment, she didn't want to fail and end up letting a bunch of pups die.

"So, what is the beast?" She asked suspiciously, "And why can't you guys just... scare it away?"

"It is too big." Skoll answered coldly, *"It would take out many of our best fighters and hunters, we cannot afford to lose anymore else our pack will starve."*

"Huh... it doesn't sound easy being a wolf." Tabby hummed.

"To answer your question..." Hati sounded sheepish, *"The beast is a large male bear from what we can gather."*

"A bear?" Tabby fiddled as she wracked her brain, they weren't edible so she wasn't sure what they were. "Um... I don't think I've ever seen one before..."

The two wolves shared a look, she suddenly had a bad feeling in her stomach.

"Well..." Hati's voice echoed in her head unpleasantly, the creature sounded nervous.

"You realise you guys are way bigger than me?" Tabby checked, the wolves howled.

They ran down a slope to enter a wide, dirt pit. Many dens littered the earthy walls around them, and a rocky incline was on the other side, Tabby was disturbed by the animal bones lying around.

She clambered off Hati's back only to squeak in fear, a whole crowd of wolves were gathering around them questioningly sniffing the air.

"Umm... hi?" She greeted nervously, giving them a stiff wave.

"Why have you brought us a human?" One of the largest wolves inquired, it sounded old and experienced.

"I'm here to help!" Tabby nodded, flinching as all the wolves startled.

She listened as Hati and Skoll explained everything to their pack, however she saw something in the dens that she couldn't resist having a peek at. She gently headed over, none of the wolves noticing. She crouched down in front of the opening and grinned at the sight inside.

A silver mother wolf was watching her in interest with large brown eyes, beside her were four wolf pups stumbling and playing with one another.

"I hear you are going to negotiate with the intruder." Her silky voice was sultry and melodic. Her pups looked round at Tabby and came running over, they jumped up at her nipping and licking at her clothes and skin – the girl couldn't help but laugh at the cuteness.

"Yeah... well... I'm gonna try?" Tabby winced awkwardly.

"Thank you." The she-wolf nodded her slender head. *"My name is Tala; I appreciate you coming all this way and risking your life like this... Many humans are afraid of us."*

"I'm Tabby." Tabby nodded happily before tilting her head in puzzlement. "Why's that?"

"I imagine it has something to do with our sharp teeth and powerful jaws." The she-wolf nodded her head gracefully. *"But what do I know?"*

Tabby audibly gulped, wrapping a cold hand around her own neck absentmindedly. She scanned the other dens to see multiple families, she could also hear more mothers and pups deep in the earth. It seemed the hides were all connected.

She began to sweat as her head ached. It was so overwhelming hearing so many voices in her head. The cacophony of communication and gossip, she could barely make out any clear words. Her heart pounded painfully in her ears, she was so acutely aware she was both outnumbered and very edible to these creatures.

"*Tabby?*" Tala's voice cut through the deafening chaos but was soon drowned out again.

Tabby grabbed her head, trying in vain to stop listening to everything.

Her vision started swimming.

"*HEY!*" An incredibly booming voice bellowed down her ear, making all other noise fade into the background.

Tabby jumped as Hati and Skoll appeared at her side, they looked unhappy with her.

"*If you are quite done?*" Skoll snapped bitterly, raising his lip to show his teeth. "*The bear is close; we must stop it!*"

"Ok." Tabby stood up straight as the pups ran back to their mother. "Bye Tala! Wish me luck!"

"*Good luck, Tabby.*" Tala laughed, she panted as her pups snuggled into her side.

Tabby grinned and nodded before following the two head wolves away from their home.

They strolled through the long grass and trees for only a few minutes, all three were on alert for danger.

It was finally nice and quiet in the girl's head.

"*So, Tabby…*" Hati looked over at the human, "*How have we never seen you before?*"

"We run into your fool friends very often, there are only four of them." Skoll agreed, his voice quiet as his keen red eyes scanned the undergrowth. *"Always chasing us off like they own the place."*

"Oh, I'm new." Tabby shrugged absentmindedly, "My friend and I were brought over to join them really not that long ago."

The three were interrupted as an ear-splitting roar echoed through the trees, it sounded close!

They barely had a chance to gasp as a huge mass of tattered ash fur tore through the trees and bushes, it froze in front of the group. It looked over at them, dark beady eyes looked them up and down while a moist black nose sniffed the air. The beast turned to face them and rose itself onto its hind legs, it towered far above the group – it made Hercules look short!

Its ears were tattered and torn, it's paws and claws heavily scarred and still stained with blood. It had patches of fur missing and dried dirt and blood on its side and front.

"We may have made an error..." Skoll cowered beside Tabby, Hati was stock still and tense on her other side.

Tabby had never felt fear like realising the big bad wolf was scared. The bear looked down on them, growling and lifting its paws in preparation to fight.

"He doesn't look like he wants to talk!" Tabby whimpered, shaking terribly at the sight before her.

The bear cocked its head.

"Who?" It asked in a rumbling voice.

"Tabby." Tabby placed a hand on herself, "You?"

"I Tokka." The bear mirrored Tabby's movement.

"Hello Tokka, this is Hati and Skoll. They are the leaders of the wolfpacks around here!" Tabby smiled as the bear seemed to calm himself. "You're getting kinda close to their home, they have babies that could get hurt if you get too close..."

The bear lowered himself onto four paws.

"Nowhere to go." The bear sounded sad; his giant head bowed. *"Always in the way..."*

"What is he saying?" Skoll asked curiously, glancing between the human and the bear.

"He says he has nowhere to go." Tabby explained feeling bad for the wretched animal, she looked up at Tokka with sympathy. "What do you mean Tokka?"

"Tokka alone." Tokka explained dejectedly. *"He has no home. No family. Nowhere to go."*

"Oh... I'm sorry..." Tabby wasn't sure what else to say.

"Other bears attack Tokka. Hurt Tokka." Tokka continued as he finally slumped down onto his backside, he looked miserable. *"Tokka had cave, but bear took it from Tokka."*

"Aww, that's not fair!" Tabby nodded in understanding, "I'm sure we can find you a new place to live? Maybe get you some friends?"

"I am not being friends with this thing." Skoll protested in disgust.

"I might know somewhere he can stay..." Hati piped up as he gazed at Tokka. *"There's a huge cave in the east of the forest, it's by the river and it's in our territory so he'd be under our protection."*

"You hear that Tokka?" Tabby cheered after she translated for the bear, "You're gonna get a nice home and you'll have the wolves as your friends!"

"Tokka not sure." Tokka hesitated as he eyed the two wolves suspiciously, *"They might hurt Tokka."*

"No! They won't hurt you!" Tabby promised, "What can I do to prove it to you?"

Tokka seemed to think for a moment.

Tabby hugged the two wolves in hope of reassuring the bear, Tokka watched in fascination.

The big bear reached forward and pulled all three into a large hug.

"Tokka see new home!" Tabby grinned at how happy the bear sounded.

"Ok, Hati here will guide you to your new cave. Skoll's gonna take me back to my home." Tabby explained gently as she patted the bear's arm.

"Tabby not stay?" Tokka asked as he finally released the three, Skoll jumped away immediately.

"Sorry, I can't." Tabby smiled softly, "I have to go home… but we'll see each other again!"

Tokka nodded, he bumped his cold wet nose against Tabby's forehead.

Hati howled softly then led Tokka away to the cave, travelling the long way around so the pups stayed safe.

Skoll begrudgingly allowed the girl to climb onto his back, the wolf took off at top speed. Tabby held on, swearing she was done with riding wolves after today.

They finally made it back to the wall just as the sky was lightening, the sun would be up soon. Tabby cringed when she saw her team standing by the door, watching her arrival with angry yet relieved expressions.

Skoll trotted to a stop not far from them and lowered himself to let the girl down, the wolf eyed the other humans warily before tugging Tabby's sleeve so she'd face him.

"Looks like you are in trouble." Skoll observed untrusting of the other humans, *"Are you sure you are safe here? Remember, you are under our protection now that you are our ally"*

"Don't worry, I'm safe with these guys." Tabby waved the wolf off easily, "They're not mad because they want to hurt me, they're mad because they were worried."

The team stepped forward to join her side at that.

"I see… humans are strange…" Skoll shook his head, clearly still not entirely convinced. *"Thank you for your help, we will take care of the oaf Tokka."*

"Tokka isn't an oaf!" Tabby huffed in amusement, "Be nice to him!"

Skoll shook himself.

"We are creatures of our word. Ourselves, our pack and Tokka will be here when you need us – you need only call, and we will come running." Skoll yawned despite the meaningful statement,

"Thanks... I guess same to you? Just come find me I guess?" Tabby shrugged unsure, "I'm kinda locked in the wall most of the time..."

"Can you whistle?" Skoll asked curiously, Tabby tilted her head to the side in confusion.

The wolf huffed moodily before running off back to the forest.

"Not even a goodbye!" Tabby called teasingly, "Skoll!"

She turned to face her team; her head bowed in shame.

"Hercules-" She began apologetically but the large man held up his hand.

"I haven't decided if I am angry with you yet." Hercules warned her. "We are going back to bed and in the morning, you will tell us everything. Then I can decide if you're in trouble."

Tabby nodded silently.

"Tabby...?" Alfie smirked knowingly as his friend looked up at him. "You can speak to wolves?"

"I can speak to *animals*" Tabby corrected cockily; she was glad to see her friend wasn't upset with her. "And I'm keeping Tabby. I'll always be Tabby."

Both teens noticed Oculus' sour look, the man's attention was then taken by something in the distance.

"What does he want now!" Oculus groaned in dismay; Tabby looked round as Skoll padded over to her side.

The black wolf dropped a small shining piece of metal at his friend's feet before looking up at her sternly, Tabby leaned down and picked it up curiously.

"This is a whistle." Skoll explained sounding slightly annoyed. *"Blow in it to summon us."*

"Cool!" The girl grinned as she twirled the small thing in her fingers. "Where'd you get it?"

"Found it in a cave." The wolf answered easily, *"Among a pile of bones."*

Tabby cringed as she hurriedly placed the whistle in her belt, she was definitely going to be giving it a clean before it went anywhere near her mouth!

"Thank you Skoll." The girl nodded politely, the wolf shuffled restlessly.

"Goodbye Tabby. Until we meet again." Skoll bowed his head before turning and running off back home.

"Bye!" Tabby waved as she watched the wolf. "Be nice to Tokka!"

There was a loud howl that sounded an awful lot like mocking laughter, Tabby smirked and shook her head before following her team back to bed.

She suddenly felt lighter, happier and more confident. She was excited by her ability and the possibilities that came with it.

She finally felt like she was figuring this whole life thing out.

Chapter 15

A week passed without much trouble. Hercules and the group listened to Tabby's tale of what happened that night and, in a way, they understood. They couldn't be mad at her when she really did the right thing, Hercules even gave her a proud smile for her kindness towards the bear.

Oculus was giving the two teens the cold shoulder, neither were entirely sure why. Nova, Vera and Hercules didn't seem to understand it either.

Alfie and Tabby were getting closer and closer after their discovery, they were always by each other's side, and even had their own inside jokes – they would reminisce about their childhood and giggle like school girls.

Nova was thoroughly enjoying watching it all unfold, she and Vera often shared fond secretive smiles every time they noticed the teens whispering away to one another.

They were glad the two were already close, it took the pressure off – it was always better to meet new people and start a new life with a trusted friend by your side.

Meanwhile, Hercules was at his most relaxed. The bell had not rung once the whole week, not a single fight or patrol was needed. He was able to just chill out and read his beloved, dogeared book.

He very much ignored everything else that was going on.

It was laundry day. Their new clothes had been received and they had changed and sent away their old jumpsuits.

Nova was grumbling as she tried to upturn her pant cuffs, she had already fought her sleeves back into position.

"I hate these stupid things!" She complained moodily, "They always feel stiff and scratchy when they're new!"

Tabby agreed wholeheartedly. She was currently struggling to get comfortable where she sat on her bed, the seams kept digging into her.

"They fixed my sleeves!" Vera pouted as she examined her perfect length sleeves. "Now I can't keep my hands warm!"

"I'm kinda glad for the fresh clothes honestly" Alfie admitted from where he stood in front of Tabby's bed. "It's nice to actually feel clean!"

"Didn't help you dropped that tomato soup down yourself." Tabby snorted, "You stank!"

"I know!" Alfie laughed as he flopped down next to his friend, "Yet, you still let me sleep in the bed next to yours!"

"I'm not a monster!" Tabby smirked cheekily, "I wouldn't make you sleep across from poor Vera, she deserves better."

"Finally!" Nova huffed in exhaustion, finally her jumpsuit was the way she wanted it. "God! These clothes are the worst! We need someone with the ability to conjure up new clothes, I've always hated these things."

"At least yours fit the way you want them to." Vera sighed as she tried to pull her sleeves down over her palms, "I hate having my hands and wrists out on display."

Alfie and Tabby watched as Nova tried to help stretch Vera's sleeves.

Oculus and Hercules walked into the room; Hercules had a large smile while Oculus' face was still stony.

"Everyone happy?" Hercules asked as he scanned the room, "You all look great!"

"Ok *dad*" Nova huffed sarcastically, earning a snicker from the two youngest. "Why does it feel like you're trying too hard to keep things light?"

Hercules deflated with a sigh.

"Oculus wants a team meeting." Hercules admitted as he shuffled over to his bed, leaving Oculus still standing in front of the door with his arms crossed.

Tabby and Alfie sat up in attention, Vera perched herself on the edge of Nova's bed right next to the other girl. Nova slumped and gave Oculus a bored look.

"What?" She asked tiredly,

Oculus' eyes scanned the room, he cleared his throat and straightened his back. Making sure to puff out his chest so he looked tall and important, Nova rolled her eyes – Hercules was better at resisting this.

"We have a problem." Oculus nodded sternly, "I want it resolved." Everyone looked at one another in confusion.

"Um... What problem?" Vera asked timidly as she rang her hands, she hated conflict among teammates. "I thought we were all getting along very well?"

"We are." Oculus assured her. "But a couple of us are forgetting a few things."

Tabby and Alfie tensed; they had a feeling this was about them. This was confirmed when Oculus dramatically pointed at them with a long finger and frowned.

"You two have not changed your names!" He snapped accusingly.

"You cannot be Alfie and Tabby anymore! You must part with your old identities and embrace the new you!"

Nova and Vera groaned unhappily at the dramatics, Tabby and Alfie shared a look.

"Leave them alone." Nova sighed exasperate, "If they don't want to change their names they don't have to."

"That's where you're wrong." Oculus sniffed affronted. "They *must* change their names."

"Why?" Tabby asked curiously.

"Because young lady!" Oculus snapped, getting riled up. "Your current names are a sign of a life trapped in servitude! You are free, you are powerful, you are different and that's what those names represent! They make you part of the team!"

"I thought having abilities and being trapped in here made us part of the team." Alfie deadpanned; Oculus stomped his foot childishly making Nova snort.

"It's not enough!" Oculus nodded firmly, "You are not Tabby and Alfie anymore!"

"No, we're still Tabby and Alfie." Tabby stood up off the bed in defiance.

"Does it really matter?" Hercules asked in dread,

"Yes!" Oculus growled.

"Why?" Hercules raised an eyebrow.

"Because!" Oculus snapped back, "I saw my vision of them *being* their new selves! If they don't change their names, then that could change the future!"

"So?" Tabby asked with a puzzled frown.

"So!?" Oculus rounded on the girl,

Tabby flushed as she stepped back in slight wariness, Oculus tensed at the movement.

"If something's meant to be then it'll happen regardless." Hercules nodded calmly in an attempt to diffuse the situation.

"Oh, I'm sorry?" Oculus snarked, "Since when can you see the future? Oh wait, you can't! Only I can and yet nobody listens! Don't you people know I'm always right!?"

"So, in your little vision-" Alfie began carelessly, Oculus bristled.

"Did we have different names?"

There was a beat of stunned silence.

"Um… well… I mean…" Oculus flushed with a sheepish chuckle,

"Your names weren't really part of it, but my point still stands!"

Everyone groaned at the admission.

Tabby came closer to the irate man, Oculus glared at her as the others watched on tensely.

"What names are a symbol of servitude?" She asked quietly, her arms crossed and face passive.

"Yours!" Oculus growled in frustration, "Were you not listening!?"

"And what are our names?" Tabby's gaze was steady, once again staying calm and collected. This question seemed to shock Oculus out of his anger.

"Uh... Tabby and Alfie?" He said now unsure, he blinked when Alfie chuckled.

"Do those names really sound like something the council would approve of?" Alfie snickered with an amused smirk.

Oculus looked between the two, now completely thrown off.

"What are you talking about?" He wrinkled his nose.

"Our names are Alfred Knotts and Tabitha Murphy." Tabby explained slowly, "We already changed our names when we were six years old."

Oculus blinked as the new information sank in.

"We go by the shortened version of our names, which the council would never be ok with, because..." Alfie smiled nostalgically, "We wanted to make it easier for the other to say and remember our names. It's only the two of us and Tabby's sister that called us Tabby and Alfie."

"So..." Oculus coughed awkwardly, "You already broke free from servitude when you were... six?"

The two nodded.

"And you did it for each other...?" He tilted his head to the side. The teens nodded again.

Oculus seemed to think for a moment as the others awed at this new revelation.

He then grinned and pulled Tabby into a tight hug, he beckoned Alfie to join when the boy stared at him bewildered.

"My babies!" He cooed ecstatically, "You are greater than I ever thought!"

Alfie laughed and hurried over to join the hug.

"Alfie and Tabby it is! I never should have questioned you!" Oculus continued excitedly, almost getting emotional. "I'm just so proud!!"

"I'm sorry," Nova grinned wryly, "Did you just say they were 'your babies'?"

"They're my babies!" Oculus nodded affirmatively. "I officially adopt them as my children!"

Nova and Vera giggled as Tabby and Alfie tried to break free from the surprisingly tight hug.

"They are not!" Hercules stood up defiantly, "I'm the one who's actually been looking after them! I gave them the induction, I protected them!"

"What? You have not!" Oculus finally released the two as he rounded on Hercules, "I'm the one that's been guiding them!"

Hercules opened his mouth to continue arguing but was interrupted by the alarm, the six tensed and looked at one another.

They needed to go out once again.

They all gathered their things and marched off to head outside, all humour and arguing gone from their minds – they had enjoyed their time off and were sad to be back to work.

The Stone Guardians arrived outside to see empty open fields, they looked around in confusion. The sky was a bright orange as the sun was beginning to set.

"*Tabby!*" A loud and familiar voice made Tabby startle, which then spooked the others.

"What!? What!?" Oculus stressed as his head whipped around.

Tabby glanced round at where the voice came from and jumped when she saw Tokka sitting with his back against the wall, the others followed her gaze and gaped at the huge creature.

They fell into tense battle stances as the bear forced itself forward and onto its paws, it lumbered over happily towards Tabby.

"Watch out!" Alfie yelped as he, Oculus and Hercules stepped forward to protect their friend, but Tabby's friendly expression made them relax.

"What're you doing here Tokka?" She asked as the bear pressed his cold wet nose against her forehead in greeting, she lifted her hand and stroked the much cleaner fur.

"*This* is Tokka?" Oculus gaped in dismay at the towering beast, "You went up against *that* alone!?"

"No?" Tabby frowned in confusion, "Tokka's not a *that*! He's a sweetheart!"

She yelped and the others gasped as the bear's large thick arms circled the girl and lifted her off the ground.

They relaxed again as the bear cuddled Tabby into his belly and held her there happily, rocking back and forward.

"Tokka!" Tabby groaned as she struggled, "Let me go!"

"Tokka hug!" Tokka beamed cheerfully, Tabby sighed and smiled a little.

"Ok fine... Tokka hug." She huffed as she rested her head against the fur. "What are you doing here buddy?"

"Tokka lonely. Tokka needed to see friend Tabby." Tokka explained easily. *"Wolves don't visit Tokka every day."*

"Well... they're probably busy." Tabby soothed as she was finally released and placed back on her feet with her team.

Tokka whined sadly and bowed his head.

Nova couldn't take it, she rushed forward and hugged the bear tightly.

"Hello Tokka!" Nova greeted, "My name is Nova! This is Hercules, Oculus, Vera and Alfie!"

She motioned to each of them before cuddling the bear again.

Tabby had to relay this information back to the animal, the bear seemed overjoyed at the new company. He patted Nova gently on her head.

"Friends!" Tokka cheered giddily.

"Yup, we're your friends." Tabby nodded kindly before turning sad. "I'm sorry Tokka but... you can't just come over here every time you feel lonely."

"You shush!" Nova scolded as she buried her face further into the warm fur, "Of course he can!"

Tabby rolled her eyes as Tokka sighed in disappointment.

"No, Tabby is right." Hercules agreed. "It is far too dangerous, for all of us."

"How does a bear get lonely anyway?" Oculus crossed his arms bluntly as he looked Tokka up and down.

"Why wouldn't they?" Alfie looked over at the other, "If they're by themselves then they get lonely just like everyone else?"

"It's a *bear!*" Oculus shook his head as if it were obvious, "They're solitary creatures, they're supposed to live alone!"

"Tokka not like being alone." Tokka sighed as he continued to pat Nova's head.

"He says he doesn't like being alone." Tabby informed them all sadly, "Isn't there something we could do?"

Vera, who had been quietly circling the animal up until now finally gained the others' attention.

"He's hurt." She frowned worriedly, "His wounds are nearly healed but a few scabs have been scratched off and the cuts are open again."

"Yeah, the other bears attacked him which is why he lives in wolf territory now." Tabby explained solemnly.

"Tell him that I will heal him." Vera nodded confidently, "His wounds probably hurt and itch and that's making him antsy, maybe he'll settle down easier if he's all healed up?"

"Worth a shot." Tabby nodded before looking up at Tokka. "Tokka? My friend Vera here is able to heal others, she's going to get your wounds all healed up and you'll be as good as new!"

Nova stepped back as Tokka looked over at Vera.

"Hurt?" Tokka asked nervously.

"It won't hurt." Tabby chuckled, making Nova and Vera coo. "She'll be really careful! You can trust her!"

Tokka sniffed at Vera before settling.

Vera cautiously walked towards the large bear.

"Be careful!" Hercules winced, not liking tiny Vera being so close to such large claws and teeth.

"Tokka won't do anything!" Tabby scolded the man impatiently, she smiled when Alfie stepped forward to stand by her side.

"He's sweet." Alfie nodded fondly as he watched Vera heal the animal. "It sucks he's so lonely."

"Yeah..." Tabby nodded solemnly, "I wish there was more I could do..."

"There." Vera nodded as she stepped back, she smiled as Tokka pressed his nose against her forehead in thanks.

"Tokka better." Tokka sighed in relief, *"Tokka go home and sleep."*

"Sounds good." Tabby chuckled, "You go for a nap, you did great!"

Tokka stepped forward and pressed his nose to everyone's forehead in turn as a goodbye, he then wandered off in the direction of the forest.

The others watched him go as the sky darkened with the burning orange clouds, they felt a strange fondness towards the gentle animal.

They were satisfied that they managed to help him.

It was nice to come outside just to find a friendly face, they secretly hoped Tokka would come back to visit them again.

Chapter 16

The Stone Guardians had just sat down after meeting Tokka, they had barely even been back five minutes when the alarm went off once again. Instead of the usual tense reaction, all six let out tired groans. That incline is steep and no fun to keep running up and down.

"Again!?" Nova complained as she threw her head back.

"Is it just Tokka again?" Alfie wondered aloud as he forced himself to stand up.

"I hope not." Tabby huffed, still not getting up. "My brain's tired from talking to him... When does it get easier?"

"It takes time and practice, until then you must be careful." Hercules warned, "Your ability seems to be one that you cannot control, this means you're more at risk of collapsing and using too much energy."

"Join the club little Tabs!" Oculus smirked as he stood, he then waved his hand thoughtfully "Except, I have it harder than you of course... What with the terrible headaches and confusing visions... I'm a hero really for being able to handle it all..."

"It's not a competition." Hercules rolled his eyes.

"Not a close one." Oculus shrugged, Nova giggled as she stretched.

"Whatever!" Tabby huffed as Alfie took her hand and dragged her to her feet.

Tabby must have been tired because she forgot to follow him. Alfie walked off to the exit with the others, only pausing when they noticed Tabby wasn't following. They all looked back at her as she stood in the same spot, stretching and yawning.

"C'mon kiddo!" Oculus waltzed over to the girl's side, he threw an arm around her shoulders. "You don't wanna be left behind! How will you see me being awesome?"

Tabby just blinked at him, still not moving.

"Look, if it is Tokka it's gonna be real awkward when none of us can tell him to get lost." Oculus tried again, Tabby still just looked at him – this time with a smirk.

Oculus then proceeded to gently push Tabby towards the others, the girl shuffled along easily.

"There we go!" The tall man grinned as the two strolled passed the others, "Just needed a little push!"

"You talk too much." Tabby groaned, the others cackled in response.

The group stepped out onto the lush grass, the sky was now dark and speckled with twinkling stars. Nova said hello to the three moons she named while Hercules scanned the area, Vera and Alfie were on alert.

Oculus and Tabby were quite the opposite.

Tabby was exhausted, she simply stood there as the others watched out for threats. Every blink seemed to make her droop further towards the ground.

Oculus lay down and spread out his long limbs to mimic the stars above, he let out a dramatic sigh as he gazed up.

"I do not see anything..." Hercules frowned suspiciously.

"Me neither." Vera looked up at the other, "It's too dark... but... maybe it's a false alarm?"

"Oh!" Nova squealed happily as she jogged over towards a nearby bush, "I do! Look!"

She picked something up and turned to show it to the others, in her hands was a five-foot golden staff encrusted with emeralds and sapphires.

"It's beautiful!" Vera gasped as she hurried over to study it, "Looks so expensive…"

"Boring." Oculus huffed as he sat up, "It's just a glorified stick!"

"Do you know what this means?" Hercules frowned seriously, "We've found further proof of other beings in this world. Something like this… it's not from Slately."

Everyone looked at one another.

It was then an ear-piercing screech split the air making everyone jump, they could now hear the sound of large wings flapping above them.

"Nova!" Hercules yelled over as yet another screech rang out, this time much closer and louder. "Drop that!"

Nova didn't get the chance as a large creature landed between the team and the two women.

Tabby and Alfie gaped in amazement. The creature had the body, back legs and tail of a lion but the front legs, head and wings of a great eagle!

It was oddly beautiful and majestic.

"A Griffin…" Oculus breathed in awe.

"Griffin's are possessive!" Hercules warned Nova, "He's here for his Sceptre! Drop it!"

Nova pouted slightly, she had hoped to keep it.

"She." Tabby yawned, everyone looked at her. She suddenly looked very ill and drained. "She's a girl…"

"Uh oh…" Oculus winced, his eyes glued on his young teammate. "I guess she's speaking to her… How far do we need to drag her to cut the connection?"

"I don't know but we'd better find out." Hercules nodded in determination, "Get her to safety."

They all thought back to the night Tabby discovered her ability. She had been so exhausted from speaking with Skoll, Hati, Tala and Tokka that she didn't even make it up the incline before she passed out, one moment she was talking away about how cool the wolves were and the next there was a thump as she hit the ground. Of course, they freaked out at first thinking she had been hiding some sort of injury but soon figured out it was from overuse of such a new and powerful energy.

The poor girl had been out of it for two days straight, they had to hear her story as she lay in bed.

"She's cool." Tabby waved them off as she slowly lowered herself to kneel on the ground. "She just wants her treasure back... something about a mate or... babies or something..."

"Huh..." Oculus strolled closer to the girl and studied her in interest. "The more tired she gets, the less she can use her ability... interesting..."

Oculus wasn't too worried yet, the girl seemed to be doing a lot better this time around. The more she tried to push through the tiredness the quicker her body would adjust, he knew the signs of overuse and wouldn't let Tabby get that bad.

"I said move her!" Hercules commanded he then growled when he saw Nova was still holding the sceptre. "Nova! Put the damn thing down! Why is nobody listening to me!?"

Nova huffed moodily, she strolled closer to the beast.

"Nova..." Tabby warned sleepily, "Don't get too close, she doesn't like you."

Nova stopped, she slowly bent down and placed the ornate staff on the grass. She slowly backed up to allow the Griffin to inspect her treasure.

It circled the staff, scanning it with intelligent amber eyes.

Everyone watched in fascination, the two women were finally able to re-join the group.

Suddenly, Tabby's head snapped up in alarm. Everyone looked over at her in surprise as she seemed to listen to something worrying.
"There's a gem missing!" She looked at Hercules with wide eyes. "She's accusing us of stealing it!"
The Griffin screamed in rage as her large wings flapped furiously, raising her off the ground.
"Hey! Hey!" Tabby called desperately, waving her arms to get the beasts attention. "We didn't take it! Honest!"
The Griffin looked over at her, screeched and flew towards her. She divebombed the poor girl as she curled up on the ground to avoid her long talons.
"She's so mean!" Tabby yelped, "She just called me a liar!"
"Stop using your ability!" Hercules snapped as he sprinted over, "Why are you still here?"
"I can't stop!" Tabby snapped back, surprising the others with her sass. "Tell her to stop talking!"
Alfie jumped forwards and used his shield to bat the beast away, the Griffin flew up high so they couldn't see her anymore.
Oculus shuffled forward and dragged Tabby to her feet before pulling her away from the battle, the girl was mumbling about rude bird things. Oculus had to admit, he liked dozy Tabby.
Last time the girl had been hilarious. She had continuously called Hercules 'Daddo', she clung onto Alfie and whined incessantly whenever the boy left, asked Nova to magic her up ice lollies which she ate *way* too many of! Poor Vera was stuck being called 'Era' which would then make the loopy girl giggle for hours as if it were some sort of private joke that none of them understood!
Oculus had a lot of fun during that time, he was able to keep tricking the gullible girl over and over. He would make things 'disappear' by throwing them over his shoulder, Tabby would gasp dramatically and ask how he did it.
He was slightly disappointed that Tabby remembered none of it.

He sat the girl down once she stopped mumbling nonsense.

"Can you still hear the Griffin?" He asked curiously, watching the pale face for any sign of discomfort.

"Nope. Just you." Tabby smirked as she closed her eyes.

"Ok... so... we need to get around... eight feet away? I think..." Oculus frowned, Tabby let out a jaw cracking yawn.

"I don't like Griffins." She mumbled, not opening her eyes.

"Is that so?" Oculus smirked in amusement.

"Yeah..." Tabby scratched her chin lazily, "I like birds though... they're cool... so... tweet-y..."

Oculus snorted as he settled down beside the girl, Tabby immediately leaned against him, Oculus smirked as he looked over at the battle.

Vera was on the edge, watching and waiting for someone to need her assistance. Hercules and Nova were fighting well, though they were angering the Griffin greatly. Alfie also stayed close to them, ready to put up his shield when they needed him to.

The Griffin was incredibly tough, nothing seemed able to harm her. Oculus watched as something in the bush caught Vera's eye, she wandered off towards it.

He glanced back when he heard a yelp.

Alfie was working hard to be useful, he was getting better at knowing who needed a shield at what time. He had managed to protect his friends quite a few times against the angry feathered beast.

The Griffin seemed to be getting frustrated with him more than anyone else.

He supposed he was the reason no one was hurt yet, he wished he knew what had happened to that missing gem. If they could just return it to her she'd leave them be and the fight would be over.

Nova yelped as the Griffin soared up into the air once again. All three stood still, silent – listening for the beast coming back down.

It was quiet for a moment.

Hercules looked over to check on the two in the distance, he met Oculus' eye. The other man shrugged, communicating he wasn't sure where the Griffin had gone.

There was a rushing sound coming closer from above, before Alfie could even blink he felt talons stab into his shoulders before he was lifted up into the air.

The boy could hardly breathe as he watched the earth and his teammates grow further and further away, the air was getting colder the higher he went. His shoulders stung terribly but he didn't want her to let him go, in fact he began begging.

Alfie looked up at the Griffin, he was terrified at being at its mercy. "Please don't drop me!" He begged, choking on his lack of oxygen – he was still winded.

The Griffin didn't even spare him a glance.

She flew higher and higher, Alfie shut his eyes in fear.

Were Griffins really so heartless? Did they feel no guilt for such an unfair advantage?

His stomach flipped when he felt her claws rip back out of his skin – she let him go.

He opened his eyes as he plummeted back down to earth, the Griffin was above him and darting down after him. Poor Alfie couldn't even yell, he had no breath in his lungs. He reached an arm out towards the beast above, watching her with wide, panicked blues.

For once, he wanted the creature to grab him again.

Instead, the Griffin shot past him and out of sight. A few feathers drifted upwards, or maybe Alfie just dropped past them – his brain couldn't figure this out.

He felt sick as he closed his eyes, he didn't want to die like this.

He had only just begun living!

He wanted to get to know his team better, he wanted to get to know himself better. He wanted to just see his lifelong companion just one more time!

He wanted to see his quiet reserved friend grow into a powerful hero, something Alfie very much believed she was going to be. He wanted to see those wolves again, see Tokka again.

He wanted to live and explore this new world he had only just found out about, he wanted to see if there really were more people out there.

He didn't want all of this to end when it had only just begun!

In that moment he could trick himself.

He wasn't falling to his death. No, instead he was floating in the cool heavens.

A sensation no one else would understand.

He choked as he landed on a warm, feathery back. He managed to flip himself and cling onto the creature as she screeched, she shot back down towards the ground.

There, Alfie saw his team all standing together – Vera was holding up a loose sapphire.

She had found the missing gem.

The Griffin landed surprisingly smoothly, once she stopped Alfie shakily slipped off.

He knelt on the ground as the creature elegantly walked towards Vera to collect her missing gem, Tabby knelt in front of him hurriedly.

Alfie looked up at the girl. She was paler than usual, there were huge dark shadows under her red rimmed and bloodshot eyes. The scar on her nose stuck out against the white skin tone, her lips were ruby from worrying them.

"I thought you were gonna die." Tabby breathed as she studied her friend's face, she seemed more awake now. "Oh man... that looked so scary!"

Alfie nodded wordlessly.

"You're hurt." Tabby swallowed as her eyes scanned the bloodstains, "Vera will get you all healed up, I promise! You're gonna be ok!"

Alfie blinked, unable to look away from Tabby's face as his ears rang.

He had nearly died. They both had now.

They had been together for so long. They liked each other. They were stuck with one another until the day they died.

Alfie felt a sudden, warm surge of fondness.

He was glad he was still alive, he'd still get to stay by Tabby's side.

He just stared at the girl when his body decided to do its own thing.

He threw himself forward and wrapped his arms around Tabby's neck, he pressed himself into the familiar, warm body of his best friend.

Alfie closed his eyes.

He took deep breaths as he took comfort from the grounding weight, he barely noticed when Tabby wrapped her own arms around him. There was a soft whispering in his ear, he couldn't make out the words but the voice was reassuring and fond.

It was wonderful, warm and right.

Everything, all the fear, pain and noise, just stopped for a moment. There was silence.

Alfie blinked his eyes open as they finally parted, he gazed up at Tabby shyly. The girl was smiling gently at him, seemingly now relaxed and shoulders heavy with exhaustion.

"You ok now?" Tabby asked gently, tilting her head slightly.

Alfie imagined his cheeks were a similar rosy colour to Tabby's. He simply nodded, still too shaken to really speak. He wanted to hug again, he wanted to feel like he wasn't going to be whisked away again.

"That. Was. ADORABLE!" Nova cheered, snapping the two out of their haze. "Ahhhh!!!"

The two looked over to see the Griffin and her treasure were gone and their teammates were standing over them.

"Nice to know we were missed." Oculus huffed with a smirk, "You're not supposed to have favourites y'know, we were worried too!"

Alfie flushed in embarrassment, he stood and gave the rest of his team silent but strong hugs. They seemed to finally understand he was in shock and in need of reassurance that he wasn't in any danger anymore.

"You're ok." Hercules smiled gently, "Come you two... We'll get inside, Vera will heal you up and then it's time for bed. Especially for you Tabby."

Nova sang excitedly as she skipped off, everyone else still had happy smiles on their faces.

Both friends slowly stood as the others headed for the door, Tabby was slightly behind Alfie as they followed. The girl hesitantly stepped forward and bumped her shoulder against Alfie's the boy smirked and bumped her back.

Alfie smiled as they walked in step back home.

Chapter 17

The sleeping quarters were warm, dark and peaceful as the team snuggled into their beds. The only sounds were deep, relaxed breathing, the odd shuffle of bed covers and Hercules' soft snores. Most of the group had fallen asleep very quickly, it had been a busy day.

Once everyone had finally gotten back after the Griffin fight, they had all crashed. The team had barely spoken to each other, just muttered goodnights as they crawled into their beds and fell asleep. Vera and Alfie were the last to enter the bedroom, Alfie had thanked her for healing him and the two parted to sleep.

Despite being the two most exhausted members, neither of the youngest could seem to fall asleep.

Alfie was trying desperately. He lay on his stomach with his head buried into his soft pillow, he was doing everything he could to stop himself from feeling weightless. His mind was spinning, every time he closed his eyes he felt as if he were still falling. It made him feel terribly sick.

Meanwhile, Tabby lay on her back and stared up at the ceiling anxiously. She could hear her friend's laboured breaths as he jolted in his bed from time to time, as if he had just fallen. There would be a few moments of silence, the creak and sound of the poor boy jumping, a gasp then a sort of quiet growl.

They hadn't had the chance, or the energy, to speak about what happened or discuss anything. She knew what it was like to be vulnerable and in danger, she knew Alfie was not ok.

She kept thinking back to Alfie's desperate hug.

His slight tremble, his sickly skin.

His eyes wide and glassy as if he didn't understand how he was still even breathing.

Tabby just didn't know what to do, she didn't want to bring up the trauma when Alfie was trying to get some much needed rest.

However, she didn't see any other solution.

At this rate, neither of them would be getting any sleep tonight.

She let out a deep sigh as sleep continued to evade her.

Finally, Alfie let out a similar solemn sigh.

Everything fell silent at long last.

Tabby smiled in relief, her eyes slipped closed and she snuggled down into her pillow.

Then, the silence became too loud. The absence of Alfie's breathing and moving was eery, Tabby scrunched her face as her mind showed her a terrible world where Alfie had perished from the Griffin attack – they had gone home in mourning.

She couldn't stay in bed.

Tabby shakily rolled herself out from under her now too heavy covers, she glanced over to check there was a rise and fall to the neighbouring bed then, she shuffled out of the room as silently as she could. She missed the other boy's head lifting and listening to her leave.

She stumbled across the main area, trying to avoid tripping on anything in the dark. She rubbed her forehead in an attempt to make her pounding headache go away, she briefly wondered if Vera's healing abilities covered something as minor as that – headaches weren't injuries after all.

Tabby continued her way to the kitchen, she poured a small glass of water and sat down on one of the bar stools lined up by the island. She gently placed the glass down and watched as a droplet slid down the side of the glass and onto her finger.

She took a long sip of the cool liquid, somehow this was the best water she had ever had. She didn't realise just how thirsty she actually was.

She took a couple of deep breaths as she set the half empty glass back down, she just wanted to sleep.

She felt so tired, her eyes itched desperately so she tried rubbing them. The night air was cold against her skin, she chewed a nail in thought as she swung her bare feet to and fro – she was too short to reach the floor.

She closed her eyes and thought back to that terrible moment.

She had been dozing against Oculus' shoulder when she felt the other man gasp and straighten up. Her eyes had fluttered open groggily and she had scanned the view before her. It took her brain too long to realise Alfie was missing, she followed the groups' gazes to see her friend's shape drifting away until he was just a speck.

Then, they all watched as the Griffin dropped Alfie.

Tabby had woken up in that moment and sprinted forward until she was right under the shape of her friend, her eyes glued on the back that was getting closer and closer. She was going to catch him. She didn't care if it hurt or killed her, if there was a chance that landing on her might save Alfie's life then she would take it.

She had to wonder, if she hadn't been dozing would she have been able to prevent this?

Vera revealed the missing sapphire she found in the bush at that moment.

Hercules grabbed Tabby by the back of her jumpsuit and dragged her to safety, Tabby tried to fight but she was no match against someone with super strength.

By some miracle, the Griffin spotted the gem and made the decision to swap Alfie for it.

Thank goodness she did.

Tabby didn't know what she would do if Alfie had hit the ground.

"Tabby?" A worried voice called from behind, Tabby jolted in her seat and whipped her head around.

There stood Alfie, he looked tired, shaky but concerned.

Alfie walked over, his bare feet slapping against the cold floor before slipping into the stool next to his friend.

Tabby kept her head bowed slightly.

"You ok?" Alfie asked, his voice soft.

"Yeah... just... can't sleep." Tabby admitted weakly, "Did I wake you?"

"Nah... I can't sleep either..." Alfie admitted, his eyes locked on the side of Tabby's face. "Wanna talk about it?"

Tabby finally met his eyes.

"Talk about what?" She asked, scanning the others face as if searching for something.

"Why you can't sleep." Alfie answered with a slight frown at the strange question.

"Oh uh..." The mousey haired girl shook her head. "Just... thinking too much I guess."

The blonde nodded slowly.

"Why can't you sleep?" Tabby asked suddenly, she had a feeling she knew the answer.

"Oh uh..." Alfie cringed slightly, "It's silly but... every time I close my eyes, I feel like I'm falling?"

Tabby's face fell in worried sympathy, Alfie gave her a weak smile.

"I'll be ok." He insisted, waving the other off. "You didn't freak out after being nearly stomped on by the Oni."

"That's because you saved me." Tabby cocked her head, she didn't like that Alfie was dismissing his fears. "I was never in any real danger because you were there... you were... you were completely alone up there, nobody could do anything for you. It's ok to be freaked out by it."

Alfie smiled but stayed silent. He didn't seem to agree.

"Could I get a sip of your water?" The boy asked, Tabby answered by sliding the glass over.

Alfie took a quick sip.

Tabby bit her lip, she wanted to talk about the incident more but felt it wasn't the time – it was just all too fresh. Her friend was dealing with the trauma of falling helplessly through the air, he probably didn't need reminding that Tabby could have just begged the Griffin to catch him.

"So, I told you why I couldn't sleep..." Alfie looked at his friend. Tabby cringed.

"Yeah? So?" She asked trying to sound casual, her heart pounding nervously.

"Seriously, you can talk to me." Alfie continued awkwardly, Tabby felt her heart drop.

She sighed guiltily, she was worrying her friend needlessly.

"I can talk to animals..." She frowned cautiously, refusing to look Alfie in the eye. "Don't you remember?"

"Ok...?" Alfie pushed, still not understanding.

Tabby grit her teeth, biting the inside of her cheek in the process. "In that moment, you were about to be killed by an animal." Tabby snarled, furious at herself. "A magic animal, yeah... but still an animal I could talk to! Why didn't I? I literally did not say a word to the Griffin, I didn't ask her to save your life or to punish me instead! I just stood there! I could have helped, I should have helped! If you had died..."

Her jaw snapped shut with an audible click, her throat closed and stopped her from continuing.

"You were tired... I didn't even think about it..." Alfie cringed as he tried to find the right words. "I mean... it's not really your job to save me?"

Tabby wondered if she was supposed to be offended by that statement.

"What?" She asked, accidentally raising her voice. "Of course, it is!" Alfie shushed her desperately, glancing towards the bedroom door. Tabby took a deep breath before looking straight at the boy with as much seriousness as she could.

"Alfie." She began, her tone made the other's eyes widen. "You are one of the most important people in my life. You save me, I save you – nothing more, nothing less. That's what we've always done, and we'll continue doing. If you had died today – it would have been my fault for not acting quick enough."

Alfie seemed to think about this for a moment, his face was creased with sadness and resentment.

"Oh..." The other began to bite his thumb nail, still deep in thought. Tabby sighed tiredly.

"Do you really think that?" Alfie asked, his hand leaving his mouth to tap the surface of the counter. "That if I had... You would really be at fault?"

"Well... I mean..." Tabby shrugged, she couldn't deny her trepidation. "Yeah? If anyone could have done something in that moment it was me... all I did was stare up at you like an idiot." Alfie nodded thoughtfully.

"Ok... You realise how dumb that sounds right?" The boy asked, almost sarcastically. "I mean, you were literally exhausted and barely even able to keep your eyes open. I'm amazed you were awake enough to even notice the Griffin had taken me at all, you can't blame yourself for that! Besides, Nova has magic – she could've done something too."

Tabby smirked half-heartedly.

"That's true." She chuckled still not convinced. "I just don't know why I froze... You didn't."

There was a beat of silence, Alfie turned to face his friend.

He thought back to the Oni, how he hadn't even hesitated. He had ran to Tabby's side without a care about what would happen to him, he had just felt a desperate need to save his companion.

"Ok, but… I wasn't exhausted from using my power too much. I didn't even have a power at that point, we had never even fought anything before!" He insisted with a wry chuckle. "You're being way too hard on yourself! It was a completely different situation!"

Though she knew Alfie was right, Tabby couldn't deny her disappointment in herself.

She didn't want it to happen again, she couldn't bear the thought of freezing and not being able to help when she was needed.

"Ok." She nodded feebly; Alfie seemed to notice she wasn't entirely reassured yet.

"I mean… I don't know what to say…" The boy coughed, "I'm sure you're braver than you give yourself credit for, it was just bad timing…"

"Maybe." Tabby nodded slowly.

"If you really wanna blame someone…" Alfie hummed with a small smile. "We could always ask Nova what her excuse was? She wasn't exhausted, you'd think she would have at least tried *something!*"

Tabby couldn't help but laugh, both friends looked at one another with amused grins.

"Oh yeah!" She nodded enthusiastically, feeling lighter now knowing Alfie wasn't angry with her. "We're totally grilling her for that tomorrow!"

"Absolutely!" Alfie chortled.

"Sweet." Tabby slipped off her stool with a yawn. "We'd better get some rest."

She turned to head back but hesitated. She watched as Alfie emptied the glass of water down the sink and placed it nearby to be washed in the morning. The boy didn't seem to want to go to bed despite the way his feet were dragging sluggishly.

"Alfie? C'mon." Tabby beckoned, "We gotta sleep."

Alfie nodded wearily before shuffling towards the other. Tabby opened her arms and hugged him.

"I don't wanna feel like I'm falling again." Alfie whispered emptily, "If I go to bed I'll be back to that awful feeling."

Tabby frowned sadly, her grip tightened.

"I know... I think I can help though." Tabby nodded confidently, Alfie sent her a curious look.

Tabby took her friend's hand and pulled him towards the bedroom, shuffling along as quietly as possible to avoid waking the others. They pushed their beds together again and slipped under their comforters, Tabby pushed and pulled at the covers, so they didn't separate them anymore and most of the weight was atop of Alfie. She then shuffled closer to the other, cuddling into him by resting her head on the other's chest. She smiled when she heard the quick heartbeat.

"Is this, ok? I just thought if you can feel my weight..." Tabby whispered sleepily. "...then you'll know you're not falling."

Alfie smiled at the kind gesture; he was about to thank her but quickly shut his mouth when he heard his friend's steady breathing. Tabby had already drifted off to sleep, she must have been more exhausted than she appeared.

Alfie slowly wrapped his arms around the other, pulling her in close. He closed his eyes and focused on the warm weight on top of his chest, he wouldn't let his mind wander this time.

Before he knew it, he too had slipped away to sleep.

Instead of falling through the clouds, that night he dreamt he was lying outside with Tabby and the rest of the team beside him. They were watching the clouds above, completely at peace.

Chapter 18

It had been a month since the Griffin attack and everything was going wonderfully! The team had been able to relax again, only going out to patrol around the city now and then – no real threats or battles. They had eaten good food, played fun games and learned a lot about each other.

It was a bright and sunny afternoon. The sky was clear bar the flocks of birds flying high overhead, it was cold despite the lack of breeze. The six Stone Guardians were on patrol, just simply wandering aimlessly around their area of The Wall. They weren't allowed around the other sides, they had deep rivers and lakes there so no threats as a result.

They had now wandered over to the edge of the pine forest – Hercules planned for them to reach the trees, turn around and head home.

He, of course, was up front and leading the way in relaxed silence. Oculus, Nova, Tabby and Alfie were in the middle and Vera was trailing behind, she would stop here and there to gather herbs.

"We'll be heading back soon." Hercules informed them over his shoulder, "There isn't any sign of anything."

"I'm hungry." Nova whined, one hand on her stomach. "Vera, you got any food?"

"Yup!" Vera skipped over to her friend as she searched through her belt pouches. "I have… blueberries… raspberries and… elderberries!"

Nova wrinkled her nose in disgusted disappointment.

"You haven't got anything good?" She asked bluntly.

"Berries are sweet, tasty and healthy!" Vera defended with a shrug. "More for me."

"I'll take some raspberries?" Alfie asked hopefully, Vera beamed at him and was quick to hand him the pouch containing the sweet snack.

Alfie only managed to eat a couple before a huge rat ran up his leg, snatched the bag out of his hands and jumped back down into the long grass to escape.

This all happened with Vera, Nova, Oculus and Alfie screaming in horror and disgust at the sudden theft. Tabby watched in shock before frowning at the long grass.

"Aww!" Vera and Alfie pouted in disappointment.

"Hey!" Tabby called out sternly as she stomped forward. She reached down and grabbed something, there was a startled squeak as she straightened back up with the thief in tow.

The huge rat squirmed in her hand, teeth still clenched around the pouch of sweet treasure. The others watched as Tabby seemed to listen to the rat, a frown on her face that was slowly becoming sympathetic much to their dread.

"It's ok..." Vera piped up awkwardly, "I can probably get more?"

It was then Tabby plucked the pouch out of the rat's mouth, the little thing shrieked in dismay.

"No." She scolded, "They don't belong to you, you didn't even ask nicely! If you're hungry you can ask Vera for some food and she'll offer you what she can, you are not taking a whole pouch."

The rat deflated in disappointment.

"Um... He can have the elderberries?" Vera cringed when the rat began to squirm again.

"Ok fine." Tabby rolled her eyes, "Just don't snatch!"

She placed the rat gently on the ground as Vera emptied some fruit onto her palm, she then knelt down and wrapped it in a large leaf to make it easier for the rodent to carry.

"He says thanks." Tabby chuckled as the rodent bounced off through the grass.

"Rats are cuter than I thought they'd be…" Vera hummed in delight, she skipped off in a daydream to continue her foraging. The team trundled on.

They finally reached the shade of the trees, they stopped for a moment to scan the murky undergrowth for movement.

After a moment of nothing, Hercules shrugged and began leading everyone back home.

Tabby stopped in her tracks when she heard a rustle, the others didn't notice. She turned and gazed suspiciously into the dark.

"I think it's her…" A nasally voice whispered, *"The wolf kid… pretty sure anyway…"*

"Is someone there?" Tabby asked cautiously, edging closer to the forest.

"Do you know the wolves?" A different voice asked, it seemed unsure.

"Skoll and Hati?" Tabby asked, relaxing – any friend of the wolves were friends of her.

"I knew it!" The nasally voice cheered, *"It is her!"*

"Do you need help?" Tabby crouched down, still trying to see whatever was speaking to her.

"Come a little closer." A hushed voice beckoned innocently, *"We can't come out into the open, too dangerous!"*

Tabby understood, there were a lot of scary animals out there.

She shuffled so she could steady herself on a tree, she leaned forward – still unable to see anything through the vegetation.

She glanced round to call over to her retreating team but never got the chance.

Sharp teeth dug into her arm and pulled her into the undergrowth, she hissed in pain but was winded as her front hit the ground – her temple bounced off a branch. Her vision spun as leaves, stems, plants and trees whipped past – she yelped as multiple creatures bit her to help move her over the root patterned ground.

She tried to struggle but she was too disorientated, everything was getting darker and mistier as she was dragged further into the vast forest.

Eventually, she was dropped.

She simply blinked stupidly up at the green leaves towering above her, she felt so small – just like when she and her sister stood against The Wall.

"Uh... did we kill her?" A timid voice whimpered. *"The wolves won't be happy about this... they have a bear now, remember!?"*

"Relax, they won't know about any of this until it's too late." A dark voice chuckled. *"We'll deliver her to them and teach them some manners."*

A lot of chatter started up among the creatures sending flashes of agony through Tabby's already pounding head – she groaned as she gripped her skull.

She couldn't bear it.

The creatures all fell silent when they heard her groan.

Tabby already felt sick and drained, she looked down at herself and cringed at her deep wounds. She shuffled trying to get onto her feet, she finally looked up and got a good look at the creatures who kidnapped her.

They were all huge hares of various colours and patterns with long, sharp antlers protruding from their heads.

There were thousands of them all surrounding her in the clearing – there was no way out.

"What's going on?" She demanded, keeping her voice angry to hide how scared and exhausted she was. "What are you?"

"We are Jackalopes." The biggest, darkest creature hopped forward. *"and you are here so we can teach those bloodthirsty wolves a lesson!"*

Tabby recoiled in pain as all the creatures piped up again.

They stopped once more when they noticed.

"Interesting... understanding us animals comes at a cost for you..."
The head Jackalope sounded thrilled.

"What did they do?" Tabby ground out, the world blurring around her.

"Your little wolf friends keep eating our kin, we're down to half our population!" A female stomped her hind legs in fury.

"We will not take it any longer!" The leader nodded. *"We're going to give them a taste of their own medicine!"*

"Y-You're gonna eat me?" Tabby gaped, looking around guardedly at her captors.

"What?" The leader chuckled in disbelief, *"No! We don't eat meat! We were just gonna kill you and leave you near their dens to find!"*
Tabby didn't think that was much better.

"It looks like our chatter weakens her." A greying grizzled old Jackalope observed. *"I say we knock her out first, then kill her. Less messy and far more quiet. The last thing we want is for those savages to show up."*

The Jackalopes all seemed to agree.

A cacophony of noise, yelling and screaming filled poor Tabby's eardrums. She covered her ears and whined as she fell to the ground in pain, of course covering her ears did nothing to subdue the volume.

This was a hot, pulsing agony she had never felt before. She became vaguely aware of her nose beginning to bleed, she faintly wondered if this was how Oculus felt when he had those bad visions.

The Jackalopes hopped closer, increasing their volume.

It felt like hot daggers were being thrust into every spot in her head and face.

Tabby couldn't even hear her own screams as they ripped out of her throat, everything was fading and her body was feeling colder and heavier.

"Hey! Hey!" A familiar voice barked, Tabby keened at the added voice. *"Stop this!"*

The Jackalopes all screamed before falling into a stunned silence.

Tabby panted, flinching when she felt a cold wet nose bump against her skin. She opened one eye to see a white wolf sniffing her, giving her a soft nudge.

"Tabby?" Hati tried, keeping his voice very quiet. *"Are you ok? What have they done to you?"*

Tabby simply moaned and shook her head.

"Skoll and Tokka are on their way but... now I'm not so sure that's a good idea..." Hati sniffed her again.

"TABBY!" A fearful voice called as thundering and desperate footsteps came closer.

Tabby jolted, a voice that wasn't in her head didn't hurt as bad. Plus, she recognised it as Hercules which instantly put her at ease.

"Ewww, what are they?" Nova stomped at the Jackalopes threateningly.

Her team gathered around her, gentle hands grabbed at her and shook her – equally as soft voices called her name and whispered reassurances to her.

She was finally able to open her eyes again as she became aware of Vera's healing touch, she looked up into the worried faces of her friends. Her heart lurched when they all breathed a collective sigh of relief when they met her eye.

"You're ok." Alfie smiled joyfully, "We were so scared! We looked around and you were gone! Then we heard you screaming, we found a trail of blood and then when we got here you looked... well..."

Oculus helped Tabby sit up gingerly, he then used his thumb to tentatively wipe away the blood from under her nose.

"Been there kid," He hushed, massaging Tabby's shoulder. "You got pushed way too close to the edge there..."

The girl nodded, still too tired to speak.

She then noticed Hati guarding them all, glaring at the Jackalopes. They were all glancing at one another, Tabby had a bad feeling.

That moment, four of the Jackalopes leapt onto Hati's back and started biting him. He howled in pain as he tried to shake them off.

"Take out the human!" The leader commanded.

The screaming started up again, her team looked round at the strange squeaky breaths coming from the weird little animals.

"What're they doing?" Nova shuffled away, she spotted poor Hati.

"Hey! They're attacking Hati!"

The others were about to try and help only to be stopped when Tabby cried out, she was writhing and howling in pain and scratching at her face and head.

It was awful to watch.

Hercules grabbed the distressed girl's wrists to prevent her from hurting herself, Vera was quick to start healing her again.

"This is getting out of hand." Oculus grit his teeth, starting to get panicked as Tabby's nose gushed much heavier this time. "If they keep going they're gonna end up killing her!"

"What do we do?" Nova whimpered, tearing up as she listened to her friend's agony.

Vera was tense and panting, her face twisted into a grimace.

"I can feel it..." She whined, the others stared at her in shock. "As I'm trying to heal her... it's too powerful... I'm feeling it all..."

She yelped and let go, panting as she swayed in a daze.

"We need to get her out of here!" Hercules nodded, he then eyed up the creatures and their very dangerous antlers. "But... how..."

Alfie panicked, he didn't know what to do.

So, he created a forcefield.

The dome of warmth covered all six of the team and Hati, which in turn freed him from his attackers.

"Good job." Hercules smiled proudly, clapping Alfie on the back.

Vera began healing the hurt wolf as Tabby blinked her eyes open – they all watched as she sat up groggily yet again.

She suddenly looked panicked.

"Did I go deaf?" She asked shakily.

"Doubt it." Oculus soothed, pulling a tissue out of his pocket so he could mop up the nosebleed.

Tabby relaxed slightly, knowing she could hear.

"Are you alright?" Hati panted tiredly, Tabby looked at him and gasped.

"Oh Hati!" She pushed Oculus out of the way and scrambled over to the wolf, hugging him tightly. "I'm so sorry I got you hurt!"

Hati rested his chin on Tabby's shoulder.

"It is not your fault... Jackalopes are nasty, vengeful creatures..." Hati soothed, still keeping his voice quiet. *"We have been eating more of them recently because they are becoming a liability... they are slowly killing off the forest. I will ask Tokka to start helping himself."*

Tabby smiled as she snuggled into the soft fur of her friend, she closed her eyes.

"Still..." She murmured with a half-hearted shrug, she enjoyed the sound of the wolf chuckling.

"Please give Vera my thanks... she has completely healed me." Hati mused as he began licking the sweat and grime from Tabby's neck, grooming her paternally.

"Vera, Hati says thank you." Tabby mumbled, enjoying the wolf's care.

"Stop using your ability!" Hercules scolded, though there was no anger in his voice. "You've pushed it far enough today."

"So, how are we getting out of here?" Alfie interrupted hurriedly, "I don't know if my shield can move with me."

They all thought for a moment, it was then they saw Skoll and Tokka leading hundreds of wolves in an attack on the Jackalope.

The hybrid rabbit creatures dashed in different directions as they escaped into the undergrowth.

The wolves chased after them.

Alfie let his forcefield dissolve once only Skoll and Tokka were left. The bear and wolf hurried over, both sniffing and fussing over Tabby and Hati. The team watched in concern as their exhausted teammate was surrounded by huge animals, they just wanted to grab her and get her home.

"Stop!" Tabby whined as she tried to push the animals away, "I just wanna go home… No! I am not sleeping in a den! I can make it home!"

The others chuckled at that.

Finally, Hercules strolled over. He marched straight past the animals and scooped Tabby up in his arms, the girl squeaked in surprise, but the animals didn't attack.

"Home time." Hercules nodded firmly, Tabby smiled up at him feeling incredibly grateful.

"Bye guys…" Tabby waved lazily at her four-legged friends as she and her team headed off back home.

She wasn't even embarrassed when she fell asleep in Hercules' arms.

Chapter 19

Tabby heaved a heavy sigh, her feet were starting to ache and her stomach was grumbling terribly. She was also freezing cold and drenched through from the never-ending rain, the sky was pitch black with heavy clouds. She wondered if the others would be up for a break, Oculus and Nova were lagging behind so they would probably be on her side. Hercules would very kindly say no, Skoll would absolutely call her pathetic and tell her to stop whining.

The team were strolling through the emerald fields, it was now mid-afternoon, and they had been out since six in the morning.

The alarm had blared sending the six outside only to discover a pair of horses, the poor things were dripping wet and seemed distressed. They let out pitiful cries before galloping off through the grass.

The team had begun their journey with the intention of helping the poor animals out.

Then they met Skoll and Tokka, the two were also searching for the horses but for different reasons.

Tokka had seen the horses in the lake outside his cave, Skoll and Hati had come to visit him and tried to help the animals only for one of them to grab Hati with its teeth and drag him under.

The poor wolf had nearly drowned – Tokka had been the one to rescue him.

Now they were on a revenge hunt and had asked the team to join them.

So now they were marching through the grass, bushes and woods together.

Skoll and Tokka were up front closely followed by Hercules, Vera strolled just behind him humming a jolly yet gentle tune, Tabby and Alfie walked together and Oculus and Nova were bringing up the rear. They were lagging further and further behind the longer they walked.

Tabby was worried about poor Hati, he was apparently recovering back at the wolf den. On the other hand, she was delighted by Skoll and Tokka. The two seemed to be getting along great considering the language barrier, they were learning how to communicate with one another.

Tabby startled when she felt Alfie's shoulder bump her own, the boy sent her a relaxed smile.

"I still can't believe those horses tried to drown a wolf." Alfie shook his head in disbelief. "Horses aren't carnivorous."

"What is the human saying?" Skoll asked curiously, glancing behind at Tabby who was quick to translate. *"What a fool your friend is."* Tabby frowned a little.

"What do you mean?" She asked, stifling a yawn. She hadn't had to talk to animals for this long since the Jackalope incident, her head was beginning to pound, and she was feeling drained.

"Those were not real horses." Skoll growled as he faced the front once again. *"Even Tokka knows that!"*

"Tokka does!" The bear agreed happily, *"Tokka knows horses. Those were not horses. Tokka thinks they are bad things instead."*

"They are Water Spirits known as 'Kelpies'." Skoll sighed, he liked Tokka but the bear could be exhausting sometimes.

"Kelpies?" Tabby repeated curiously, her team looked at her.

"Wait? Kelpies?" Oculus asked once Tabby explained everything to her team. "But I thought they showed as women?"

"They can shapeshift into anything they need to." Tabby shrugged, "Apparently horses tug the heart strings more."

"So, they just like drowning people? For fun?" Alfie asked in disgust, Tabby shrugged in response.

"It doesn't matter why they drown people." Hercules pointed out as he scanned his surroundings, "They just do! Our job is to stop them."

"I can't heal dead people." Vera reminded them all.

"Why do we need to stop them?" Nova asked tiredly, the group looked round at her.

"What kind of question is that?" Oculus raised an eyebrow as he lightly pushed Nova, "They're killers!"

"They're just creatures doing their thing." Nova frowned at them all. "The wolves kill and eat deer and rabbits, I don't see any of you trying to kill them. Before Tabby these two would've happily killed us too so don't say it's because they don't kill people!"

They all looked at one another.

"They tried to drown Hati!" Tabby rolled her eyes as she scowled at the group, "Hati is our friend, we're helping these guys avenge him!"

The others shrugged, it was as good a reason as any.

"Poor Hati is a sweetheart." Tabby continued pointedly, "I wouldn't wanna stop 'em usually… they're just doing what they do like Nova says, but they attacked my friend."

Alfie smirked at her proudly.

"I guess… so we're really just helping you out." Nova summed up as she stretched her arms above her head.

"Mostly just making sure she doesn't drown." Oculus nodded sending Tabby a teasing smirk.

"Tabby." Skoll called over, his voice far too sweet for Tabby's liking.

"What's up Skoll?" She asked suspiciously, the others quietened down as they waited to hear what the wolf wanted to say.

"Could you do me a favour?" Skoll continued, his voice getting more aggressive. *"Kindly tell your friends to SHUT UP!"*

Tabby flinched at the volume as the wolf barked back at her, the others looked at her questioningly.

"Uh… Skoll said 'Shut up'." She chuckled sheepishly, the others laughed but did as the wolf asked.

"Nice of friends to do that for you," Tokka nodded, clearly pleased. *"Friend Tabby is good friend for passing on the message."*

"Tokka. Stop talking." Skoll growled, his ears twitching as he tried to listen.

"You're such a grump." Tabby huffed moodily, "I wish Hati were here."

Skoll snarled at that. Alfie's hand wrapped around Tabby's forearm in warning, he leaned his head over so only his friend could hear him.

"I'm not sure it's a good idea to make a wolf angry." He whispered pointedly, "Especially big wolves."

Tabby shrugged, she couldn't argue with that.

"Can't we take a break?" Oculus finally groaned, unable to take the silence for more than a minute.

"No way!" Nova snapped sulkily, "Normally I'd be with you, but I am so sick of this rain! I feel like I'm never gonna be dry again as it is! I'm not about to sit out here in it!"

"Awww C'mon!" Oculus pouted childishly, "We're all tired! A break would lift our spirits!"

"I don't mind." Vera shrugged easily, her hands brushing over the tall grass.

"We're not taking a break." Hercules nodded firmly, "We'll give up at nightfall."

"Stop." Skoll snapped as he halted his stride, everyone stopped at the tense behaviour. Tokka flopped down to sit and lazily scratched his ear.

"Tokka doesn't hear anything" The bear then sniffed the air, *"Oh! Tokka smells something!"*

Tokka raised himself onto his hindlegs, he stretched up and sniffed the air. Tabby smirked as her team stepped back at the height of the bear, they still found him intimidating apparently.

Tabby strolled forward to stand between the animals, Alfie stayed just behind her.

"What is it?" Tabby looked between the two.

"I hear splashing." Skoll's body stayed low as his ear flicked this way and that.

"I smell... salty water!" Tokka looked down at Tabby.

"I guess we found them then?" Tabby smiled softly up at Tokka.

"The splashing could've been anything but... We're nowhere near the sea these guys keep telling me about so, the salty smell's gotta be the Kelpies, right?"

"Finally!" Oculus rubbed his hands together, "Let's deal with the evil water horses and then we can go home and get dry and warm!"

"Such an old man." Nova smirked humorously, "But I agree, let's do this!"

"Tabby," Hercules nodded at the girl, "Please ask Skoll and Tokka to lead the way."

Tabby nodded and did as she was told but the two animals hesitated.

"Maybe you humans should stay behind." Skoll suggested awkwardly, *"These creatures... they're very strong."*

"Just lead the way." Tabby huffed, she pushed the wolf softly. Skoll took great offense to this, he turned round with a snarl and snapped at the girl's hand. Tabby just managed to save her fingers by jumping back in alarm, her friends stepped forward.

"Don't touch me!" Skoll growled showing his sharp teeth, *"If I say they are dangerous then they ARE DANGEROUS! How dare you argue with me and push me around!"*

Tabby blinked in stunned silence.

Tokka let out a low groan. Skoll's threatening stance was then ruined when the bear's large paw came down and gently pushed the wolf over, poor Skoll fell onto his side and Tokka was quick to lay his paw down and hold him there.

"Bad Skoll." Tokka shook his large head, *"We don't threaten friends. Friend Tabby didn't mean to upset you."*

"TOKKA!" Skoll growled furiously as he struggled beneath the weight. *"GET OFF!"*

"Not until you apologise and calm down." Tokka soothed, *"Anger is not good."*

"TOKKA!" Skoll snapped impatiently, his paws making divots in the dirt from all his struggling.

"You ok?" Alfie asked worriedly as he stepped forward and looked his friend over, "What was all that about?"

"Apparently I offended him." Tabby shrugged as she watched the two animals' quarrel.

"I hate that fleabag." Oculus crossed his arms furiously, "I never trusted him."

Hercules stayed silent but Tabby could see the rage on the other man's face, he may actually end up hurting the wolf.

Tabby sighed tiredly.

"Look, let's all just calm down." She insisted stepping forward towards the two animals, her friends watched – tensing in preparation. It was comforting to know they were ready to step in and help if she needed them.

She placed a light hand on Tokka's side, the bear looked down at her.

"Let him go." Tabby nodded to the big bear.

"But-" Tokka began but Tabby's smile stopped him.

"I really appreciate you looking out for me but... I'm the one that needs to apologise to him." Tabby explained gently, "I'm the one that overstepped the boundaries."

Tokka looked down at Skoll, the wolf was looking at Tabby but had now stopped struggling.

The bear seemed to think about it for a moment longer before finally lifting his paw.

Skoll slowly raised himself back onto all four paws, he then shook the water and dirt off his dark coat.

His red eyes looked up into Tabby's.

"I should not have snapped at you." He bowed his head and tucked his tail between his legs.

"It's ok… You're a wolf, I shouldn't have pushed you or ignored what you said." Tabby nodded, she crouched down so she was eye level with the wolf. "You've been out here longer than I have… Which means you know better than me if something is too dangerous."

Skoll gazed at Tabby, he understood what the girl was doing. She had placed herself at eye level and in a vulnerable position to show she trusted Skoll despite their earlier dispute, the wolf knew he couldn't take that lightly.

"Let us avenge my brother." Skoll nodded before turning away and walking forward, only stopping to indicate that everyone should follow.

Tabby smiled and was quick to follow the leader of their makeshift pack.

They arrived through the trees to a small lake surrounded with weeds, steep rolling hills were the backdrop. It looked like it would usually be a serene, peaceful area. Instead, the water spirits were splashing around and howling in their horse forms, Tabby hated how awful it sounded. They really knew how to tug the heartstrings of animal lovers.

"Tabby, can you understand what they are saying?" Hercules asked curiously.

Tabby suddenly realised that she really couldn't, she could only hear what everyone else was.

"No." She admitted worriedly, "I'm hearing the same as you."

"That's weird." Oculus frowned in puzzlement, "I thought you could talk to all animals? You talked to the Griffin and the Jackalope."

"Yeah, I know that!" Tabby snapped impatiently, "I don't know why I can't speak to them, maybe my power doesn't like horses!"

"You don't like horses?" Nova asked in shock, looking down at the girl. "Why not?"

"Who has a strong opinion on horses?" Oculus asked in confusion, looking between the two.

Meanwhile, Skoll and Tokka were taking on the Kelpies alone.

"I never said I didn't like horses!" Tabby insisted.

"I love horses!" Nova pushed a finger into Oculus' ribs. "How can you not? They're so graceful and pretty!"

"I don't like horses." Hercules huffed, remembering the unicorn incident.

"Wh-?" Nova gasped, rounding on Hercules. "What do you mean!? I didn't know I was surrounded by horse haters!"

"Umm... guys?" Alfie tried but the four were still squabbling, he looked round to Vera who was watching the Kelpie battle worriedly. "Should we try and fight without them?"

"No... I'm not sure how useful we'd be..." She sighed, giving the boy a longsuffering smile. "We're not offensive team members, you're defensive and I'm a healer. We need Hercules and Nova, they're the only ones with actual attacks."

"Man." Alfie sighed tiredly, "This sucks."

Vera hummed in agreement.

"TABBY!" Skoll yelled from the pool, *"WHY AREN'T YOUR TEAM HELPING!?"*

"Whoops!" Tabby cringed, "Um... we might wanna go help the others?"

Hercules and Nova ran over to the pool, Hercules had no choice but to enter the water, he warned everyone else to keep their distance.

"And what are any of us supposed to do from over here exactly?" Oculus asked with an eyeroll, "We have blades, we have to get close to attack!"

Nova dropped a boulder on one of the Kelpies, she then looked over at the others.

"You have a pistol!" She reminded him in exasperation.

"Yeah, but I don't like using it." Oculus huffed moodily, "I like blades better."

"Then why did you swap your knife for it?" Nova asked angrily as she used a hurricane to lift the same Kelpie into the air and away from Hercules who was currently trying to make a hit on the other spirit.

"Because I wanted to be different." Oculus shrugged nonchalantly. "I'm nothing if not original."

"Just shoot!" Hercules commanded, "But watch the friendly fire!" Oculus huffed moodily before pulling his pistol out of his belt, he shot at one Kelpie but his bullets just went straight through with a splash.

"Wow, how useful." Oculus grinned sarcastically, "So glad I decided to listen to you."

The sound of the shot had gained the water spirit's attention, while the others were busy with its companion it headed towards the group of four purposefully.

"I'll swap you for your dagger?" Oculus waved the pistol towards Tabby, the two friends ducked out of the way. "Aww c'mon! Like I'd shoot you."

"Accidents happen." Vera reminded him as she eyed the gun warily.

"Yeah? Still, even if an accident happened you could still heal them? It's no big deal." He huffed.

"Still hurts!" Alfie frowned as he dragged Tabby and Vera out of harm's way.

Tabby pulled her daggers out and handed them over, she snatched the pistol and eyed it warily.

"Relax, the safety's on." Oculus chuckled in amusement, "Just put it on your belt and look after it for me while you sit on the side-lines."

"But-" Tabby tried but the man turned to Alfie.

"You have a blade don't you?" He asked, the boy nodded warily.

"C'mon then, you can help."

With that the two ran off to help the others. They didn't see the other Kelpie as it disappeared under water.

"Why is it always us watching them?" Tabby griped, crossing her arms with a slight pout.

"Because we're the best ones." Vera giggled jokingly, her eyes didn't leave the battle.

Tabby huffed a laugh and sat down at the edge of the pool, Vera was walking around with her eyes on the fight. She was ready to jump in and heal as soon as she was needed.

It was then, the water horse rose from the liquid before her. It towered over her and looked down into her eyes.

"Hi?" Tabby tried, there was no response. "Why can't we communicate? Don't you count as an animal?"

The water spirit transformed into a curvy woman and then back into a horse, Tabby realised what it was saying.

"Oh!" She grinned excitedly, "You're not an animal! You're a spirit and shapeshifter! You don't count!"

This happiness was quickly ruined when she noticed the spirit was scanning over her with its hauntingly empty eyes.

She opened her mouth to speak but it all just happened too fast.

The horse snapped forward and grabbed her leg before dragging her roughly into the murky water, Tabby didn't have time to close her mouth and choked as it filled with water.

She was being dragged further and further down into the depths; she had no way to call for help.

She hadn't realised the pool was so deep.

It was then she realised – the pool wasn't deep but there was a single tunnel that led down into the earth, this was where the Kelpie was dragging her.

Tabby could only think to do one thing.

She dragged the pistol from her belt, she fumbled for a moment before clicking the safety off and shooting upwards. The bullet never reached the surface.

As she was beginning to lose consciousness and just before she was dragged into the dark tunnel she pushed the pistol so it landed beside the hole – hopefully if someone started looking for her they would see the gun pointing the way.

The last thing she saw were the bubbles of precious oxygen as her lungs finally gave in.

Chapter 20

The first thing Tabby became aware of was a hand on her shoulder violently shaking her, the second was a familiar panicked voice calling her name from above. She could feel a cold stone floor beneath her, her skin was wet and there was a cold breeze chilling her further – but she was no longer feeling or hearing the patter of raindrops.

Either it had stopped, or she was now under shelter and far away. It was then her name was called once more. She felt, what she assumed was, spit hit her face.

She grimaced in disgust and opened her eyes to see a red-faced Alfie crouched over her.

The boy looked thrilled that she was looking up at him.

"Tabby!" Alfie breathed in relief, "I thought you'd drowned! I'm so glad you're awake, are you ok?"

Tabby blinked at the hurried speech, she was still feeling a little dazed.

"You spat on me." She looked up into Alfie's stunned face.

"Wh-What?" The boy asked with a slight shake of the head, as if clearing his ears to ensure he was hearing right.

"When you said my name... you spat on me." Tabby explained blankly – still trying to clear her vision, Alfie made a mystified face.

"Oh uh... Sorry?" He scanned Tabby's face perplexed by his friend's behaviour.

"You should be... it's gross." The girl nodded, scrunching her eyes and blinking.

"Ok?" Alfie sat back on his heels, watching his friend with a bemused smile. "You literally just almost drowned from a Kelpie, is this really the conversation you want to have?"

Tabby blinked before chuckling.

"No, you're right." She shook her head, she still felt a little woozy. "Thanks for saving me!"

"I didn't." Alfie cringed, Tabby cocked her head questioningly. "Vera noticed you had disappeared and called over to the rest of us, I immediately assumed a Kelpie got you so I dove into the water, saw the pistol you left behind and just swam down the tunnel… I honestly thought I was gonna find you drowned in there but it sorta curved back up? I just followed it and I found you here."

"Wait… so the Kelpie just… dragged me here and left?" Tabby frowned, puzzled by the strange situation. "Why? What did that accomplish?"

"I don't know." Alfie shrugged, glancing around worriedly. "Maybe something scared it off?"

Tabby took a moment to actually look around her.

They seemed to be in some sort of cave, there were a few cracks and crevices in the walls that allowed small slivers of sunlight in. Nearby was a circular pool of water with drips and splashes around it – their way in and out. The cavern itself was dusty grey-brown stone, it was vast and seemed to carry on further into the darkness. Tabby gasped as she struggled to her feet, the walls and ceiling were covered in carvings and paintings of animals and mythological creatures alike. Alfie stood and strolled over so he was next to her.

"Yeah, it's pretty amazing." He nodded as he looked around. "There are so many creatures we've not even seen yet!"

Tabby couldn't find the words to express how breath-taking it all was.

"Griffin." She squeaked, pointing out the carving. Alfie grinned as he spotted it.

"Yeah! There's wolves over here!" Alfie showed Tabby the wolf illustrations on the left wall, Tabby beamed as she ran a light hand over the carvings.

Both friends jumped when they heard a vicious hiss from the shadows, they looked over in fright.

Another hiss echoed.

Slowly, a portly, fluffy grey creature waddled towards them. They had never seen such a strange animal before.

It had fuzzy grey fur all over its body, it had a white pointed face finished with a pink nose and long whiskers, large black eyes and black round ears atop its head. It's four short legs were followed by pink clawed hands and feet, they didn't really look like paws. Finally, it had a long, pink tail.

"What is that!?" Alfie gawked, stepping back from the curious creature who was sniffing in their direction.

"It's adorable!" Tabby cooed eagerly as she knelt to greet it. "My name's Tabby and this is Alfie."

The creature toddled closer and surveyed Tabby with its huge eyes.

"Aww, she says her name is Pokey." Tabby explained in delight to her friend, "She says she's an Opossum or Possum."

"Just looks like a big rat to me." Alfie frowned unimpressed; he knew exactly where this was going.

"You say that like it's a bad thing." Tabby chortled as she reached forward, she grabbed Pokey the Possum and lifted her up as she stood. She simply hung contentedly in her hands, her long body swinging slightly from lack of support.

"Hercules isn't going to let you keep her after last time." Alfie deadpanned knowingly.

Last week during a patrol, Tabby made friends with a couple of rats. She snuck them home in her pockets and before the team knew it, the whole HQ was infested. Apparently, Tabby hadn't realised how quickly rats reproduced. There was an added problem of the rats constantly chatting to each other so poor Tabby was relentlessly drained from her power being used to hear rats talk about food, sleep and filth, they needed to deal with it as soon as possible.

Nova had to use a spell to make all the rodents fall asleep. It had taken two trips with everyone filling their arms to get rid of them all, even now they still found evidence of the odd one still living in hiding.

"This is different! She's on her own!" Tabby huffed as she allowed Pokey to wander along her arm and settle on her shoulder, she seemed perfectly at ease.

"We're not taking another rodent home." Alfie frowned sternly.

"She says she's not a rodent." Tabby pointed out as the possum sniffed her ear.

Suddenly, Pokey jumped off her shoulder. She looked up at the two expectantly, she wandered down the cavern before stopping and doing the same again.

It didn't take a genius to work out she wanted them to follow. Of course, Tabby was more than happy to - while Alfie huffed a sigh before following begrudgingly.

The three wandered through the cavern, they spotted carvings of normal animals like birds, fish and deer but also spotted Oni, Minotaur, Kelpies and Manticores.

It was very helpful that all the creatures were labelled by whomever had carved them.

It was then Tabby noticed something intriguing on the right wall - a carving of a beautiful woman with long flowing hair and an elegant robe surrounded by what looked like light. Her mind flashed back to the Kelpie when it transformed into a woman.

"Gaia?" She read aloud as Alfie joined her side.

"She looks like some sort of goddess." The boy hummed in interest, "We were told such things didn't exist."

"Which means they must." Tabby agreed firmly.

Her attention then fell on the possum as she sat on one of her feet.

"Pokey says Gaia is 'The Creator'." She translated for her friend, "What does that mean?"

"Oh… Tabby, look!" Alfie gasped as he shuffled along the wall, Tabby followed – struggling to walk with a possum perched on her foot.

There, carved deeply into the stone wall next to 'Gaia' was a map of the world.

At the top 'Portus Naturae' was written in delicate calligraphy.

They could see the four island regions for the first time, they were captivated by how big it all was compared to them.

Emerelda was coloured green and was in the middle towards the right – it had illustrations of trees, streams, hills and some figures that looked like people. There was also a grey smudge, they wondered if it represented Slately.

Blossoming was coloured pink and could be seen just above Emerelda – it had illustrations of flowers, mountains, ponds, animals and, again, people. It seemed to be one of the smaller regions.

Bronze Forest was coloured yellow, it was the opposite end of the map from the previous two and seemed to be the biggest – there were drawing of colourful trees, mushrooms, toadstools, frogs and fruit. There were people but they looked like they were sitting atop something strange.

The White Rocks were very small and at the bottom middle, it was just a white outline with its name. Nothing else.

"This is our world…" Tabby breathed in awe, "It's so big… and to think… all this time we thought Slately was all there was."

"I thought Hercules said there were only four regions?" Alfie questioned quizzically, Tabby looked over at him.

"There are?" She frowned, Alfie shook his head and raised his hand. He placed a finger on what looked like a small hill rising out of the ocean in the dead centre of the map.

"There's a fifth region." He pointed out quietly.

"There's no name." Tabby studied it closely, "There are no drawings on it... nothing..."

The two friends stared in shock, what was this strange piece of land and why did no one seem to know about it?

Their thoughts were interrupted by a forlorn roar from further down the cave, they both startled and snapped their heads in the direction of the sound.

"What is that?" Alfie gulped nervously, he was backing away slowly and holding Tabby's sleeve.

It was then Tabby felt her heart break, the sound had been so sad and broken. She swore she could hear faint crying.

"C'mon..." Tabby began to walk forward but Alfie stopped her.

"Tabby." He looked his friend in the eye, "We're both tired, inexperienced and alone. What if it's dangerous? We're in no condition to defend ourselves or each other."

Tabby hesitated, she knew Alfie was right.

There was another roar from the gloom, this one crackled and ended in a sort of whine.

"I don't think it is dangerous..." Tabby cringed, knowing she sounded insane.

"Can you understand it?" Alfie asked in amazement, Tabby shook her head.

"No but..." She squirmed in place, "It just sounds so sad."

Alfie still looked unsure.

"We won't engage with it if it seems unsafe, we're just gonna go check that it's ok?" She pushed a little, Alfie deflated.

"Fine..." he groaned, Tabby smiled and gave him a quick hug.

Pokey trotted toward the sound, she then looked back at the two friends pointedly.

"See! Pokey says it's nothing to be scared of!" Tabby insisted as the two strode forward to follow the marsupial.

"You're really putting too much faith into that big rat." Alfie grumped with an eye roll.

"Pokey is not a rat!" Tabby huffed moodily, "It's not my fault she's so wise."

It was then the possum attacked the wall, the friends looked at her to see she was fluffing up and hissing at her own shadow.

"Oh yeah…" Alfie nodded sarcastically, "So very wise."

After only a few minutes of walking they arrived in a huge, cavernous room. It was bigger than any home in Slately, bigger than their base in The Wall! It was spacious, light and airy – they could hear the wind whistling through various cracks. They could also hear dripping water and smell wet rocks, salt and dirt.

In the back of the room was a huge, white, scaly dragon. It was lying on its stomach, eyes closed, wings spread out across the ground. Both friends trembled with awe at the intimidatingly ginormous creature before them.

"That's a… d-dragon." Alfie gasped, eyes so wide they may just pop out of his head.

"Ok… ok… I vote dangerous?" Tabby squeaked anxiously, she turned to hurry out as Pokey climbed up onto her shoulder, but Alfie didn't follow.

Tabby looked round and nearly fainted, Alfie was now stood inches away from the huge beast.

"What are you doing!?" She hissed panicked, "That thing could eat you without even chewing! Get away from it before you wake it!"

"Her." Alfie corrected absentmindedly, still observing the rare sight before him. Tabby let out a longsuffering sigh.

"Excuse me?" She glared at her friend's back.

"There are eggshells scattered around… I think it's a nest which makes her a she." Alfie explained easily as he tiptoed around the beast to inspect it.

"Alfie." Tabby growled urgently. "I really don't care about the dragon's pronouns; please can we just leave before we get eaten!" Alfie ignored her, he seemed to spot something on the other side of the room.

"Uh oh..." The boy stepped back, he looked over at Tabby before pointing across the room. "There's two of them!"

Tabby looked over in alarm to see another, dark green dragon lying in a hole at the other side of the room. This one didn't look well, all Tabby could see was a torn wing, two back legs and a tail sticking up in the air.

"I think it's... dead..." Alfie winced with pity, inspecting the poor creature.

"Yeah? Well, we'll be joining it if-" Tabby gasped in horror as Alfie stepped back, his foot landed on the white dragon's wing. "ALFIE!" Alfie jolted with shock at the panicked scream, he looked over to see Tabby reaching out towards him. Those golden eyes darted between Alfie and the dragon, slowly getting confused.

"Wait... how stupid are these things?" Tabby asked as she jogged forward, "You're standing on her wing and she's not even noticed, are these things heavy sleepers or something?"

Alfie hurriedly stepped off the torn wing, he then looked over and studied the creature's side. He deflated with realisation, a deep sadness crept through him.

"She's dead too." He shook his head despondently. "What happened here?"

Tabby joined her friend's side only to pause, she could hear something moving under the dragon's wing. She gently nudged Alfie's side, she motioned to the wing with her head.

Alfie seemed to understand.

Both friends shuffled over and crouched down, they heard a hiss. They bent further down to look under the limp wing to see a pair of fluorescent yellow cat eyes staring back, both flinched in surprise.

They then heard frightened whimpering and growling.

They shared an uneasy look.

"Try talking to it?" Alfie suggested in a whisper. "Sounds like an animal."

Tabby nodded, she took a deep breath.

"Hey... we aren't going to hurt you." She soothed gently, "It's ok..."

Pokey leapt off her shoulder and disappeared under the wing. They heard a lot of sniffing and scurrying before the possum returned, she sat next to the wing seemingly waiting for something.

They heard clawed steps coming forward from under the wing, slowly and cautiously a little dragon's head appeared.

It had two white curled horns coming from its head, it's scales were a light, fresh green. Clearly a baby.

"A baby dragon..." Alfie breathed in wonder, he looked at the mother then the father and, finally, the baby. His face fell as he put two and two together. "You poor thing..."

"It's lost its entire family." Tabby looked to Alfie in distress.

"Know how that feels." Alfie sighed bitterly.

"Mama?" The small, scared voice asked. The dragon looked up at the white dragon, it nudged its snout against the cold scales.

"She's a female." Tabby nodded, watching the heart-breaking scene.

The little dragon finally looked up at the two friends, her yellow eyes wide with fear.

"My name's Tabby, this is Alfie. Do you have a name?" She asked gently, wanting the baby to feel safe.

"Kaida." The baby answered meekly, *"My mother named me Kaida."*

"Hi Kaida." Tabby greeted kindly, "Do you know what happened to your parents?"

The dragon shook her head.

"I was... Asleep." She answered hesitantly, glancing at her mother.

"You were asleep?" Tabby clarified; she nodded her head.

"Poor thing." Alfie looked over at Tabby, "What do we do now?"

Tabby had no idea. A few minutes ago, she didn't even know dragons existed, much less what to do if you found an orphaned baby one.

Both friends stared at the infant, she simply stared back. Neither party seemed to know what to do next or what to say.

Tabby opened her mouth.

"Hercules will not let you keep her as a pet either." Alfie deadpanned bluntly.

Tabby closed her mouth again and deflated.

It was then Pokey stepped forward to stand beside Kaida, she looked up at Tabby pointedly.

"What!?" Tabby gasped in disgust before looking at Alfie, "Pokey saw what happened! She says they were killed by shadows in white masks!"

"The Masquerade..." Alfie looked down at the little possum gravely.

"But... why would they go around killing dragons? I didn't think they were even allowed outside the city?"

"I-... I don't know..." Tabby shook her head in shock, "I think there's way more going on here than we thought."

"Dragons are worshipped and thought of as sacred." Kaida informed Tabby shyly, *"Only a monster would kill them."*

"Huh... So... those carvings of people?" Tabby thought carefully, "They worship dragons? Is that what you mean?"

Kaida nodded, as did Pokey.

"So, if we can get Kaida to those people-" Alfie began excitedly.

"They'd keep her safe and take care of her!" Tabby finished, equally excited.

"But... How do we do that?" Alfie scrunched his nose in thought, "I don't see any way out of here, do you?"

"Well, her mother and father must have left and entered here somehow…" Tabby shrugged as she looked up at the ceiling, scanning it for any sign of an exit. "Maybe through the tunnel we came from?"

Alfie stared at Tabby causing the girl to look at him uncertainly.

"What?" She asked feeling like she said something stupid.

"Are you serious?" Alfie asked, in slight amazement. "Dragons breathe fire. Somehow I don't think submerging them in water is such a good idea."

"Why not?" Tabby frowned, slightly affronted.

"Because water puts out fire?" Alfie tilted his head, "Duh?"

"We're not asking her to drink it!" Tabby huffed as she crossed her arms, "We can swim in it! Granted we don't breathe fire, but we still die if we breathe it in!"

"I don't think it's the same thing." Alfie still wasn't sure, "You really expect a baby to hold her breath that long while swimming? Can dragons even swim?"

"All animals can swim!" Tabby rolled her eyes before facing the two females, they were watching the argument in interest. "Hey, can you swim, can you fly and will you die if we put you in water?"

The dragon and possum shared a look, Tabby chuckled.

"Kaida says most animals can swim, she can fly and the underwater tunnel is the only way in and out – her parents used it all the time to go find and bring back food." Tabby then stuck her tongue out at Alfie, "So there!"

Alfie smirked in amusement as he raised his hands in surrender.

"Fair enough." He chuckled, "Guess we have a plan. Guide Kaida out and send her off to the people."

"Yes!" Tabby agreed confidently.

"We're still not bringing Pokey home with us." Alfie reminded her as he turned and walked away.

Tabby looked down at Pokey who just looked back up at her, the girl smirked before hurrying to follow her friend.

Alfie led Tabby, Pokey and Kaida down back through the cave. The two friends were worried about the baby dragon flying off on her own to find people they knew nothing about, they hoped she would be ok. There was nothing else they could do for her, if she was right about them worshipping dragons then she'd be very welcomed.

They stopped briefly in front of the map, Kaida scanned it with her catlike eyes. She seemed to be trying to remember the shape of the region. Pokey yawned as she clambered up Tabby's back and settled down on her shoulder, she curled up and snuggled in for a nap making the girl smile fondly.

Alfie pretended not to see.

Once Kaida seemed satisfied, they continued on down and back to the tunnel, they found it easily. They all stood around it peering into the dark water below, nobody really wanted to go swimming again.

"Have you swam before?" Tabby asked Kaida, not bothering to look over at her.

"No…" Kaida sounded on edge, her clawed feet tensed to keep her hold on dry ground. *"My parents could… so I should be able to…"*

Tabby cringed, she hoped she was right. She quickly informed Alfie of her answer, the boy rubbed his arm thoughtfully.

"Ok… so… we have the two of us, only one of us has actually been conscious swimming through the tunnel which, by the way, is pitch black in the day… meaning it's definitely impossible to see through this late." Alfie looked up at Tabby pointedly. "We have a baby dragon, who may actually be the last of her species, who apparently has never swam before… and a big rat."

"How many times do I have to tell you?" Tabby shot a glare at her friend, "She's not a rat!"

Alfie smirked as he looked back down into the water.

"So, what's the plan?" He asked quietly, Tabby shrugged uneasily.

"That's more Hercules' forte…" Tabby admitted nervously, "Is it too dangerous for us all to just… go?"

"I would say yes. We'll be essentially blind, disorientated, cold, unable to breathe and there's a possibility that Kaida can't swim." Alfie scratched his head, "Which means there's a real chance of her drowning and us not noticing until we're out the other end."

"I'm not hearing any solutions." Tabby huffed impatiently, looking down at poor Kaida. She didn't look very confident, she looked pretty scared in fact.

"Ok… ok…" Alfie hummed as he thought, he looked at the three waiting for him. "So… chances are – Pokey's just gonna hang out on your shoulder so… I doubt we need to worry about her… I've swam through before so it's best I take the lead to make sure we don't get turned around…"

"Isn't it just a straight line?" Tabby deadpanned, raising an eyebrow.

"No! I told you it's curved!" Alfie insisted pointedly, "Plus the rocks are sharp!"

Tabby shrugged but allowed her friend to go on.

"So that leaves Kaida." Alfie continued slowly, "Tabby? How confident are you that you can follow me and keep track of her at the same time?"

"In freezing dark, pitch black water?" Tabby asked sceptically, "I would say about…50 percent."

Alfie gave her an exasperated look.

Pokey yawned and looked down at the water, she then clambered down onto the ground and jumped onto Kaida's back. There, she settled herself and held on.

Kaida flapped her wings and lifted herself into the air, she then landed so her front feet gripped Tabby's shoulders while her back feet pushed against the small of her back.

Tabby nearly toppled over from the heavy weight, it was only thanks to Alfie grabbing her that she didn't.

"This isn't gonna work!" Tabby choked out, still being steadied by Alfie's arm. "We're gonna sink like a stone!"

Neither creature gave a response, instead Kaida pushed her weight to force Tabby forward. Again, Alfie saved her from falling headfirst into the tunnel.

"It's the best we've got." The boy shrugged, though his face betrayed how worried he actually was. "Maybe she'll float really well in water?"

Tabby glared at the boy once again, Alfie sighed tiredly.

"I'll jump in first, then you. Once we dive down, you can grab onto my shoulders if you can't carry the weight alone." The boy compromised, slowly releasing Tabby to ensure she stayed balanced.

"Fine. Let's just go." Tabby wheezed breathlessly.

Alfie nodded, took a deep breath and jumped into the frigid water. He came up panting and gasping desperately, his whole body shivering and becoming numb.

"Ok... Ok... It's r-really c-cold." He whined as he swam out of the way. "Get in."

"Are dragons cold blooded?" Tabby asked nervously, she screeched as a wave of cold water splashed her.

"GET. IN." Alfie commanded impatiently.

Tabby sighed and did as she was told.

Both friends took a deep breath before diving down into the dark. Alfie led the way, immediately noticing that Tabby was struggling to swim with the weight. The girl sank like a stone and moved as fast as one despite the desperate kicking and paddling. Alfie followed the noise and movement until he found her, the poor girl was already wearing herself out.

He grabbed Tabby's wrist and guided it to his shoulder, the girl held on tightly – giving a grateful squeeze.

They worked together to swim through the blackness. Tabby kicked her feet, Alfie kicked and used his hands to feel his way around.

They didn't need anyone getting hurt on top of all this.

It wasn't long until they could see the moon and sky up ahead.

This wonderful sight gave them all the boost they needed, together they pushed themselves toward freedom – their lungs begging for air.

Kaida flew to the grass as soon as they broke the surface of the pool, she forgot to let go. Poor Tabby squeaked as she was lifted into the air, she grabbed onto Alfie's arms and dragged him upwards. Alfie grabbed her back with a strangled gasp.

Both friends were dropped unceremoniously on the ground, Kaida landed beside them as she panted. Pokey was still happily perched on her back, she was licking the water from her fur.

It took a moment for Tabby and Alfie to get their bearings but when they did, they realised their team, Tokka and Skoll were long gone.

They slowly sat up and looked around, there was no sign of life anywhere.

They couldn't deny the sad and betrayed feeling that gripped them at being abandoned.

Kaida used her fire breath to scorch an area of grass, she then dragged over a log and set fire to it. She curled up on the scorched ground while the other three gathered around the fire.

"Thanks Kaida." Tabby nodded gratefully.

"Rest. I'll leave in the morning once you wake... for now, I'll guard our camp." Kaida responded gently, *"My payment for your help."*

Tabby nodded, too tired to say much more.

She glanced over as Alfie leaned into her side.

Both were trembling violently, their lips were blue and their hair and clothes were dripping wet. It didn't help that the ground was still soaked from the heavy rain throughout the day. It was not going to be a pleasant night's sleep for them.

But in that moment, the warm crackling fire, the deep soothing breaths of the baby dragon, the squeaky snores from the possum in her lap and her friend's warm and wonderful weight against her side – Tabby found she wanted to stay in this moment for as long as she could.

This moment was bliss.

Chapter 21

The day looked like it was going to be much nicer than the last. The sun rose from behind the pine trees and illuminated the dewy grass making it twinkle like glass beads, it's warm rays would make quick work of drying up yesterday's downpour. The sky was clear, not a cloud to blemish it. The mysterious pool glittered with the morning rays as black smoke lazily floated from the ashes of last night's campfire.

A flock of birds flew overhead, calling out in fear when they spotted the dragon below them. A large armoured black beetle scuttled through the grass, avoiding the sleeping humans and dragon. It crawled around the fire, seemingly heading for the shelter of the raspberry bushes ahead.

Or it was until a large, fat possum landed on top of it. The little creature picked up the struggling bug with her hands, gave it a sniff before shoving it in her mouth and crunching noisily.

She then wandered past the friends towards her dragon friend, her tail whipped a lock of wet brown hair onto the slumbering girl's forehead.

Tabby awoke feeling cold and damp. Her nose was runny, her eyes dry and tired but her skin warming from the morning sun. She smiled softly as a breath tickled her cheek, Alfie was huddled against her from behind.

He didn't seem to be awake yet.

Tabby opened her eyes, blinking as the light pierced them.

She could see Kaida cleaning her claws gracefully from where she sat on the charred grass, Pokey was sat next to her simply staring straight at the sleeping humans.

Tabby thought it was a little creepy but she was glad she was still here.

She was especially glad Kaida had kept her word and hadn't left without a goodbye.

Tabby hummed sleepily as she enjoyed this peaceful moment, she was almost tempted to try and fall back asleep.

However, her body was begging her to get off the cold, hard ground.

The girl tried to shuffle out of her companion's grip to sit up without waking him but, unsurprisingly, this did not work. The minute Tabby slipped in Alfie's grip the other was wide awake and sitting up, he looked around as if expecting a foe as a dome of light surrounded them. Alfie had made a protective forcefield around them without even noticing.

It was warm and welcome, Alfie blushed in embarrassment when he noticed.

Tabby sat up too and smirked at him.

"Good morning." She chuckled lightly as Alfie rubbed his eyes.

"Morning." The other yawned, he too had a red and runny nose from camping.

"I didn't mean to wake you up." Tabby admitted awkwardly as she prized herself to her feet, Alfie followed her sluggishly as the forcefield fell away. It had warmed the two up and even dried their hair and clothes.

"It's ok." He groaned as he stretched out his arms and spine, "It's better you woke me up, sleeping on the ground hurts."

Tabby chuckled but fully agreed, she had all kinds of aches and pains – especially after all the action of yesterday.

"Oh. I see ratty is still here." Alfie joked as he strolled over to the two creatures, Tabby rolled her eyes.

Alfie patted Pokey gently on the head, then moved to Kaida to stroke her smooth scales.

"I'm glad you're both awake." Kaida nodded her head and stretched her wings, "I felt uneasy resting out in the open, I'm eager to find myself a new home."

"Thanks for waiting on us first." Tabby smiled softly, "I was scared you'd had left during the night."

"I owe you two my life." Kaida stood up and looked at the two friends, "I never would have left the cavern or even the safety of my mama's wing had you two not found me, I never would have made it through the tunnel on my own either."

"That's ok." Alfie waved the dragon off once Tabby translated. "We were happy to help!"

"Do you think there are any more dragons out there?" Tabby asked sadly, Kaida bowed her head.

"I am unsure... I've never seen any but I haven't been alive for very long." She admitted honestly, "Once I have found the people, I may look for others of my kind, it will be chaos if all the dragons die out."

Tabby didn't get the chance to ask what she meant before the dragon was flapping her wings.

She lifted up into the air and hovered for a moment, gazing down at the two humans.

"Thank you for your help. I am beginning a new journey now but I'm sure our paths will cross again." She giggled as the two friends gave her a small wave. "Goodbye Tabby! Goodbye Alfie!"

Pokey clambered up onto Tabby's shoulder, she stood on her hind legs and sniffed the air in the dragon's direction.

"Bye Pokey!" Kaida added in amusement.

"Bye!" The teens called as they watched her fly up into the sky and away over the hills.

They just stood there, watching the sky long after she disappeared. She was only a baby, they hoped she'd be ok on her own. It hurt to know they'd likely never find out, it was unlikely they would see her again but they couldn't keep her with them.

They just had to hope she was ready and capable.

Both teens shuffled awkwardly in the grass, their hearts heavy from the bittersweet goodbye. They weren't sure what to do next, where were their teammates? Had they really just left them behind without knowing if they were alive or dead?

Did they think they were dead?

Tabby petted Pokey gently as she thought about what to do, the little creature leaned into her touch affectionately.

"Should we leave?" Alfie's quiet voice asked, it was almost a whisper – as if he was afraid of Tabby hearing him. Tabby looked over at Alfie curiously, unsure if she had heard him correctly.

"What do you mean?" She asked, also keeping her voice quiet in case her friend knew something she didn't.

"I mean... do we follow Kaida and look for others?" Alfie kept his eyes on the sky above, his face was twisted with conflict. "Do we go into the world and figure everything out or... or do we go back?"

Tabby couldn't believe what she was hearing.

Alfie didn't want to go back? He didn't want to reunite with their team?

"What are you talking about? How is that even a question?" She gaped, wishing the boy would just look at her. "We go back to base of course! We have a team now, we have a home! They must be worried about us, we can't just run off and leave them behind – not after all they've done for us!"

Alfie pressed his mouth into a thin line as his brow creased.

"You mean like *they* did to *us*?" He asked bitterly, finally looking down and into his friend's eyes.

"Alfie, we don't know what happened." Tabby pressed as Pokey jumped back down onto the ground, "We have to go back."

"Back to what? Being imprisoned in The Wall? Protecting a city of slaves for a Council that doesn't care? Living in the same building with dragon murderers?" Alfie asked, his voice getting louder and sharper with each word. His face was twisted with ugly anger and betrayal. "I don't want to be a prisoner or a slave anymore, I don't want others pushing me around and having no control over anything!"

Tabby stared in surprise as Alfie stepped towards her and grabbed her shoulders tightly, the other now looked distraught as tears welled up in his blue eyes. Poor Pokey had to leap out the way to avoid being stepped on, she watched the two with her big, blank eyes.

"We keep losing and being left by people. Don't you see? They don't care about us, nobody cares about us." Alfie pleaded miserably, "How long is it until there's another change? How long is it until..."

Tabby frowned as Alfie shook his head.

"...Until I lose you?" he finished weakly, Tabby felt her heart break.

"Alfie-"

"No!" The other backed away hurriedly as if he'd been stung, "Don't say it! Don't say it won't happen when neither of us knows! All my life, you are the only one that's been there by my side. My dad was taken away, my mother barely looked at me because she knew I was next to go, the kids in class ignored me, when I was dragged away from home and off to a whole new life you were there! When I woke up to my dad missing... you were there. When kids were mean, when people were being killed, during the scariest and most stressful moments of my life – you have been there every time."

Tabby blinked, hoping to keep her own tears at bay as her friend broke.

"I can't lose you, you're my one constant in this hell!" Alfie yelled, his face bright red. "If we go back there, you could be taken away! They left us behind, they don't care about us! If we left to go out into the big wide world together, just the two of us... we'd never have to lose anyone again."

Alfie looked straight at Tabby, seemingly begging her to understand how desperate he felt. Tabby did understand, how could she not? She too was sick of being pushed around, she was sick of losing those who mattered most to her. She wanted control over her own life but, there was one thing her friend was forgetting.

"Alfie... I feel the same way, I do! But-" Tabby began, Alfie deflated in defeat. "But we don't know for sure there's a better life out there. What if the people beyond those trees are cruel? What if they hurt us or do something to us? What if everywhere is just the same as Slately or worse?"

"But what if it's not? What if it's open and wonderful and free?" Alfie pushed desperately.

"You say you don't want to lose anyone anymore... If we abandon our friends, we lose them." Tabby tried, stepping towards her friend softly. "We need to at least see them one more time... then... then maybe we can all leave together."

Tabby couldn't help but think about the rest of the team, she wouldn't believe they had just left them willingly. She could see in her mind how they all must feel. She could see Hercules angry and conflicted pacing the length of their home, no doubt the one who had to convince the others to follow him home and end the search. She could see Oculus, pushing himself to use his ability to ensure they were alright. Maybe he already knew and was telling everyone to chill out and enjoy the quiet while they can.

She could see Nova also pacing and muttering away to herself, berating herself for letting them down. She would fiddle with her rings, pull her hair and bite her nails anxiously. Lastly, she could see Vera. She'd simply be sitting silently, watching the others with that look on her face. The hopeless look that begged the others to think of something or to make a plan because she knew there was nothing she could do.

It broke her heart thinking of their new family this way. It hurt to think Alfie was so willing to just abandon them and leave at the first chance, didn't he care about them the way Tabby did?

Alfie blinked a couple of times as he thought about what Tabby had said, clearly he hadn't considered the others may feel the same as them. He couldn't seem to see anything in his mind's eye other than the four leaving and heading home, not knowing what happened to their two youngest members.

If he hadn't followed Tabby, would they have forced him to leave too? Would they be trying to convince him that his best friend was no longer alive or able to be rescued? Would he have believed them without evidence? It was just all so painful to think about.

"I'm just so tired, Tabby." Alfie admitted as he looked at his friend. The poor boy looked as if he had the weight of the world upon his shoulders, like the fight was done and over and he had lost.

"I know." Tabby nodded sympathetically. She hurried forward and pulled her companion into a tight hug, she just couldn't bear to see her strong friend look so beaten. "But... But this is bigger than us." Alfie buried his face into Tabby's neck as he hugged her back.

"We have to go back. We have to see the others and get them to leave with us." Tabby nodded in determination. "We need to figure out why The Masquerade are killing dragons, why Slately exists and who The Council are. The people on the other side of that stupid wall have no idea what's out here, how much bigger the world is than Slately. Maybe... Maybe we can break all of them free too?"

Alfie stayed quiet for a moment, he slowly pushed Tabby away so she was at arm's length. He had a tired smile and a twinkle of rejuvenation in his eye.

"You're right." He nodded proudly, "We can't just run away. We have to save the others, we need to stop The Council, The Masquerade and put an end to the slavery our friends and family are going through."

Tabby smiled back, relishing in the pride on Alfie's face.

"We can do this." Alfie smirked in determination, he straightened up to his full height. He was back to looking like his strong self again, the fight had finally returned to him.

"Together?" Tabby bumped Alfie's shoulder cheekily, giving her friend a smile.

Alfie grinned and nodded.

"Together."

They both laughed as Pokey clambered onto Tabby's shoulder. They felt stronger now that they had a plan, they knew how to change their world and, hopefully, make it a better place.

There was only one problem.

They couldn't remember the way home.

Chapter 22

The two sixteen-year-olds stood for a moment still in their campsite, they each spun around as they scanned their environment. Their eyes were trying to find any indication of which direction they needed to go, anything familiar. Pokey clung onto Tabby's shoulder as she spun, she hissed angrily as she nearly fell off.

"Well…" Alfie cringed as he turned back to face his friend, "This is kind of a problem."

Tabby frowned as she looked at the hill, then to the trees.

"I think… I feel like the hill was behind the pond when we arrived…" She contemplated with a hum, Alfie glanced at the hill.

"I mean… I didn't notice… we definitely came through the trees though…" Alfie nodded as he headed towards the woodland. "So, I guess we just head into the trees and hope for the best?"

"I guess so, I hope we don't run into anything." Tabby looked around uneasily before following the boy into the dark forest.

Pokey was having a lovely time, she jumped and ran and rolled around in the long grass as the three made their way through the woodland. She even found a few bugs to snack on, she thought it was the best day ever. She was completely unaware of her human companions' discomfort.

They both walked with tense shoulders, their heads turning this way and that, every sound made them jump. There was something spooky about being lost in a forest of towering pine trees – it didn't help that their little possum kept snapping branches under her weight making the two jolt.

"We didn't walk in a straight line." Tabby pointed out shakily, she flinched as Pokey snapped another stick. "We were following Skoll in the rain! There's no way we can find our way back!"

"The trees have to end eventually." Alfie shrugged, keeping his alert gaze forward "And I imagine we'd be able to see The Wall right? So, we can just follow that when we see it."

Tabby smiled as she relaxed slightly, she was glad one of them was feeling calm enough to figure out a plan. She strolled closer to Alfie's side, she jumped again as yet another crack split the air – she grabbed onto Alfie's arm for protection.

Alfie smirked in amusement as he pretended not to notice, he didn't miss the way the girl seemed to relax at the contact. He was glad his friend felt safe with him, she truly believed she could rely on him wholeheartedly – it made Alfie feel stronger and braver.

"Isn't this crazy?" Tabby chuckled as she shook her head. "Never in a million years would I have thought we'd end up here."

"I know, it's amazing how quickly everything can change." Alfie agreed softly, "I'm glad it went this way though... even with all the danger and panic and stuff... I wouldn't change it, would you?"

"Only slightly." Tabby admitted shyly, "If I could, I would go back and make sure to grab my sister and bring her with us. Then she'd be free too."

"Somehow I don't think The Masquerade would be too pleased with that." Alfie smirked in amusement.

"Probably not... I bet Nova would adore her though!" Tabby grinned cheekily, Alfie groaned and threw his head back.

"Oh man! The two of them together?" He laughed, "That would be a nightmare!"

During the two's early friendship Alfie had gotten to know Matilda relatively well, the girl immediately seemed to warm to him and would often tease the two for being 'lonely losers'. He liked her well enough but he didn't tend to pay much attention to her, back then he still figured he was going to be whisked away on his own so he didn't bother getting close to anyone.

Tabby laughed, she had to agree. Nova and Matilda would get up to all sorts, nobody would be able to relax.

"I wonder if Matilda has hidden abilities," Tabby thought aloud, watching the grass under her feet. "I mean, if we're related maybe we're similar in that way?"

Alfie glanced at her with a soft expression.

"I don't know how it works, but… maybe?" He suggested gently, "Would you want her to?"

"I don't know…" Tabby hummed with a frown, "In a way… yeah? If we don't manage to save anyone then she'd join us and we'd be together again but… man, it's so dangerous out here! All these freaky creatures just ready to attack whenever?"

"Yeah, it makes it even weirder that nobody in the city knows about all this." Alfie nodded slowly.

"Well, Slately's huge and that wall is thick." Tabby shrugged easily. "And those guys deal with it."

"It's so crazy to think that while we were growing up, those guys were out there fighting beasts and protecting us!" Alfie shook his head in amazement, "I wonder how many kids right now have this future ahead of them?"

Tabby smiled, she raised her head and closed her eyes as she enjoyed the warmth of the sun radiating through the swaying trees. She opened her eyes to gaze up at the blue sky bordered by dark green pines.

She still couldn't quite get over how beautiful nature was, she didn't know how she survived growing up in such a grey, concrete city.

It saddened her that the citizens of Slately had no idea about the beauty that lay just outside of their home.

Tabby continued her musings as she watched the sky above, trusting Alfie not to let her trip and fall.

It was then, her eye caught something unusual.

A bright orange light was high up in the sky above, it was gliding slowly above the trees.

The girl frowned as she tried to work out what it was, it looked like it was getting bigger. Her eyes widened as she realised – it wasn't getting bigger, it was getting closer!

"Um… Alfie?" Tabby gulped as she looked over at her friend, Alfie looked back in concern.

"What?" He frowned, wondering why Tabby was suddenly so worried.

"I think we need to run." Tabby looked up into the sky again, she was alarmed to see the orange light was getting closer. "Like, now!" Alfie looked up and gasped, Tabby pulled him along as she broke into a run.

"Pokey! C'mon girl!" Tabby called hurriedly, patting her thigh. Pokey was quick to run up her back and sit on her shoulder again.

"What is that thing?" Alfie stressed as he finally picked up his feet to run, Tabby accidently let go of his arm.

"I don't know, and I don't wanna find out!" Tabby insisted through pants, "We don't have Oculus and his stupid notebook!"

Alfie looked back before slowing to a jog, he stopped as he studied the trees behind them. Tabby skidded and nearly fell over when she realised she was alone, she looked back to see Alfie's back to her.

"What are you doing!?" She yelled in bewilderment, "Why are you waiting for it!?"

"I'm not!" Alfie snapped back as he looked back towards his friend, "I don't think it was aiming for us… or following us?"

Tabby huffed a sigh and began walking towards Alfie only to be knocked over by a lump of glowing orange feathers, poor Pokey screeched as the bird grabbed her. Tabby tried to protect her but yelped as talons clawed her cheek as she hit the grassy terrain.

"Alfie!" She yelped as she punched the bird away, "It's a chicken!"

Alfie dashed over and grabbed his friend before pulling them both into a run again.

"That is not a chicken you idiot!" He looked back to check on Tabby, "It's a giant glowing bird!"

Pokey shrieked again as she fluffed up, watching the bird fearfully.

"She says it's a firebird." Tabby panted, lifting a hand and placing it on her possum's back to keep her steady and safe.

"Ok? What else does she know?" Alfie asked worriedly, he glanced over at the two.

"Oh! Not such a stupid giant rat now!" Tabby smirked triumphantly, Alfie rolled his eyes as Tabby translated his question to Pokey. "She says she doesn't know much, always hid from them because they eat possums but this one doesn't seem right – she doesn't know why."

Alfie cringed, he couldn't blame the marsupial really.

"I'm so tired!" Tabby complained suddenly as her head pounded, "It's shrieking!"

Alfie frowned, he couldn't hear a thing.

"Wait… so it's communicating to you just… noise?" He asked in confusion, "That doesn't sound right."

Tabby didn't respond as she used her other hand to grip her head, Alfie was worried now.

The bird was gaining on them and neither teen knew what would happen when it caught them, it was massive, it would absolutely try and eat Pokey and its beak and talons were clearly sharp.

Alfie's frown deepened as music reached his ears, it was high pitched and breathy, but the melody was beautiful. It sounded like a slow lullaby.

He smiled dozily as he slowed down, the music was so pretty.

Tabby groaned through the pain in her head, she only looked up when she realised that Alfie had stopped running despite the thumping wings behind them.

"Alfie?" Tabby ground out through the headache, she circled her friend so she could see his face. She was alarmed to see a drowsy smile and slow blinks.

"Can you hear that?" Alfie hummed happily, "So pretty..."

Tabby stared in shock, she didn't understand what was happening. All she could hear was shrieking in her head, she looked past her friend to see the bird's mouth was open. She grabbed Alfie's shoulders and shook him roughly, it made no difference.

"What can you hear?" She pressed seriously, Alfie simply yawned. "Alfie! What are you hearing!?"

It was then she realised Pokey had fallen asleep on her shoulder, she had a bad feeling in the pit of her stomach.

"Music..." Alfie mumbled sleepily, "Pretty lullaby..."

Tabby blinked as her friend fell forward, she just managed to catch him. She lowered him onto the ground gently and knelt beside him, she shook Alfie's shoulders desperately.

She felt sick when she realised he wasn't responding.

"Alfie! Alfie!" She pleaded but the teen was fast asleep. "C'mon! We gotta move!"

Tabby looked over at the bird as the shrieking in her head got louder, her vision was becoming blurry. She knew she too was going to pass out soon, she looked down at Alfie as she tried to figure out what to do.

She tried shaking Alfie one more time. It still did nothing, so the girl placed Pokey atop her friend as she tried to figure out what to do.

"What do I do!?" She cried out in panic, not expecting an answer.
It was then she remembered, the wolves had given her a whistle for
when she needed them!
She pulled the whistle out and blew into it as hard as she could, a
shrill, high-pitched shriek came out of it.
Tabby groaned as her headache became worse.
The world spun and before she knew it, she was lying on her side,
the bird landed on Alfie the shrieking was now unbearable! Tabby
just manged to pull Pokey away from the predator and tuck her
safely against her chest.
The last thing Tabby saw was something blurry and white coming
towards them then, everything went dark.

Alfie groaned groggily as he came to, he felt slightly sick and cold.
He could feel grass under his hands, he was propped up against
something rough – stone? A cold breeze swept his hair, making
strands fall and tickle his cheek. He frowned as he tried to will his
eyes open, he couldn't remember what happened to get him in this
situation.
He wracked his brain as he shifted slightly, his back felt stiff from
the position he was in. He remembered walking through the forest
with Tabby, they were just chatting.
Tabby…
She had seen…
Alfie gasped as his eyes flew open, he cringed as his back twinged.
He fell asleep while Tabby was suffering from a headache, he
needed to find out what happened and if his friend was ok.
He rubbed his eyes to clear his blurry vision. He realised he was
back at The Wall. His back was against it, before him lay that
familiar view of rolling green hills, dark forest beyond. What was
not so familiar were the three animals sitting in front of him
watching, not moving.

He blinked at Skoll, Hati and Tokka, neither party seemed to know what to do.

Hati stood and sniffed in his direction, he then tilted his head to the side with a twitch of his ear. Alfie smiled softly at the attempt, he always liked Hati more than Skoll.

"Hi Hati." He waved, the wolf wagged and straightened up. Tokka strolled forward and pressed his wet nose against the boy's forehead in greeting, Alfie stroked his soft fur in return.

He allowed the bear to back away before turning his head to the side, he gasped when he saw Tabby also propped up against the stone wall – Pokey lay curled up in her lap. The girl's eyes were closed and she appeared to still be unconscious while the Possum was staring over at Alfie.

Alfie grunted as he shifted himself to kneel by his best friend's side, he then rested his hand against the cold, pale cheek. The girl groaned at the touch, Alfie smiled and let out a breath of relief. He released Tabby and then reached down to pet Pokey, the little creature crawled onto his lap making him smile. He settled down and gently shuffled to sit closer by his friend's side, he noticed the animals were watching Tabby closely.

"She seems to be ok." Alfie nodded with a relaxed smile, Hati and Skoll's ears flicked his way but there was no other response.

He huffed, it was no fun hanging out with these guys when there was no translator.

He tried to relax as he waited for Tabby to come to, but he couldn't seem to quiet his brain down. He kept wondering what happened once he fell asleep; what was that bird thing? Why did it attack them? How did they get to The Wall and where did those three come from?

He looked down at Pokey, she seemed to be watching the other animals closely – it looked like she didn't trust them. When Skoll glanced at them she fluffed up and hissed, it almost looked protective. Alfie chuckled and focused on keeping Tabby's new friend calm.

He jumped when he saw movement out the corner of his eye, the animals stood to attention. He looked round and grinned.

He'd never been so happy to see those eyes.

Tabby groaned and rubbed her eyes, she looked around dozily.

Their eyes met and Tabby gave him a lazy smile.

"It worked." The girl murmured, her smile was tired but relieved. "I got us out."

"You sure did." Alfie nodded happily as he pulled his companion into a warm hug, "How'd you do it? What happened?"

"When you fell asleep I kinda started to panic... I was about to pass out from that stupid bird's screaming but then I remembered!" Tabby grinned as her energy returned, "The wolf whistle!"

"Wait? So, you passed out after blowing the whistle and these guys rescued us?" Alfie frowned as he gestured to the three waiting animals.

Tabby startled as she looked at her three furry friends, she beamed and greeted them. She thanked Hati profusely as Tokka placed his nose against her forehead, Tabby nodded as she listened to whatever the creatures were saying to her. Pokey crawled onto her lap and looked between her new friend and the other animals, Tabby introduced them all to each other. Pokey let out another hiss before stomping over and settling herself on Alfie's shoulders, apparently, she was the jealous type.

It was strange to watch when Tabby used her ability.

Alfie could see the animals' subtle movements but mostly, he could see Tabby looking between the creatures, pulling faces and talking to thin air. She just looked like she was insane more than anything.

It was oddly amusing and disconcerting at the same time.

"Yeah, Hati says he heard the call and came running. The other two came shortly after to help him move us." Tabby explained easily, looking over at Alfie. "Apparently, the others were searching for us for hours! The Masquerade came and took them back, Skoll and Tokka saw the whole thing!"

Alfie frowned in concern.

"They were taken back? I've never seen The Masks have anything to do with us, why were they looking for them in the first place?" He asked as he began chewing his thumbnail nervously.

"They don't know, couldn't understand what was going on." Tabby sighed sadly, she glanced between the animals and her friend, "They said it looked threatening though... they think they're in danger."

Alfie's eyes widened at that.

Both teens prized themselves to their feet and looked over towards the door, now they weren't sure what to do.

"What now?" Tabby asked quietly, clenching her fists. "Do we go home?"

Alfie shook his head.

"I don't know... what if... I mean..." He swallowed thickly, "The Masquerade taking you away usually means..."

Tabby shuddered.

"But... maybe they were just out way longer than they should've been? Maybe they're perfectly fine and are worrying about us?" The girl suggested hopefully, "I don't understand why those creeps would want our team! They protect the city!"

Alfie shook his head once again, he too was lost.

"I don't see why they were killing dragons either." He pointed out seriously, "Something's going on, I just don't know what..."

The two stared at the door for a moment longer, Skoll stepped forward with his head tilted to the side – Pokey hissed angrily at him.

"Pokey! Language!" Tabby scolded gently, the possum looked at her. "Yeah well, Alfie can be your new favourite all you like but without me you can't talk to him! If you don't behave, we'll have to leave you behind!"

The possum sniffed Alfie's ear, the boy smirked weakly as it tickled.

"She's such a suck up." Tabby huffed moodily, Skoll barked loudly to regain their attention.

"You two are not really thinking of going in there, are you?" He demanded angrily, *"We didn't save your lives just for you to go get yourselves killed."*

"What choice do we have?" Tabby asked hopelessly, "What if they need us?"

"What if they're dead?" Skoll growled, stepping forward again.

"Skoll. Stop." Hati warned as he stepped between the human and his brother, *"They are a pack, you of all wolves should understand her actions."*

Skoll growled and looked away, Hati turned and faced Tabby purposefully.

"We will not stop you." He promised softly, *"But you must understand, if you go in there and get into trouble – we can't help you. You two will be on your own."*

Tabby nodded in solemn understanding.

"Ok… good luck." Hati nodded wistfully, *"I hope we see each other again."*

Tabby smiled softly, waving goodbye as the three animals wandered off back to the forest. Tabby turned and faced Alfie, the boy was watching the creatures leave with a forlorn expression.

"We're heading in then?" he guessed, finally meeting his friend's eye.

"Yeah." Tabby sighed, "They'd do it for us."

"Ok, but we gotta be careful." Alfie pointed out as they strolled towards the door, "We keep quiet and as hidden as we can until we know if it's safe."

Tabby nodded in agreement, the two humans and their possum faced the door. It was time to reunite with their team, they only hoped they were ok.

Chapter 23

The stone sloped corridor felt colder than ever before. There were no cheerful or exciting sounds coming from outside, just the haunting howl of the wind. The incline had never felt so steep nor so long before, maybe it was the jarring loneliness.

Alfie crept up the stone walkway, Tabby with Pokey on her shoulder not far behind. They could hear their soft footsteps and short breaths echo along the walls.

It was odd for this area to be so quiet. Normally it would be full of the team's chatter and laughter. Either talking about what was waiting for them as they descended or celebrating a win as they headed home.

The last time it had been silent was, Alfie winced at the memory, when Tabby had been hurt by the Oni.

Tabby felt particularly jumpy as they tried to stay quiet.

There were no hiding places or doors or anything in this area, realistically they were fine until they reached their base. For some reason though, the image of The Masquerade pouring down from the top while more of them stormed from the bottom wouldn't leave Tabby alone – she felt trapped already.

What was also concerning was that they were getting close to the top now, but they still couldn't hear any voices or movement. The door wasn't soundproof and, normally, their group was pretty loud. Especially Oculus and Nova.

Neither dared to utter a word. Though, Alfie could tell Pokey was talking away to Tabby. The girl seemed to keep glancing at her, giving subtle nods and shakes of her head.

The little possum yawned, clearly bored of Tabby's silence.

She steadied herself as her eyes fell on Alfie's back, she tensed as she readied to jump.

If only Tabby had noticed, maybe then she could have warned her friend or stopped Pokey.

But she didn't.

Alfie let out a startled yell when he felt something heavy collide with his back, in a lame attempt to get away he leant forward but his foot caught on the uneven stones. He immediately tripped and fell into a heap on the hard floor. All of this had startled Tabby too, she let out a loud gasp and clapped her two hands to her mouth as her wide eyes watched the commotion in front.

Alfie groaned as he pushed himself off his stomach, he glanced at Pokey who was clinging to his jumpsuit in fright. She made eye contact with him and slowly relaxed despite the heated glare she was receiving.

"Y-You ok?" Tabby squeaked as she placed a hand on her chest in an attempt to calm her thumping heart.

"Yeah, no thanks to you or your stupid rat." Alfie grumbled bitterly as he finally got to his feet, he sent Tabby an annoyed glance over the shoulder as they started their journey again.

"Not a rat." Tabby huffed under her breath, her eyes firmly on the back of her friend's head.

Both teens only managed a few seconds more of silence before they dissolved into quiet yet hysterical giggles. Both covered their mouths in an attempt to silence their snickers but failed miserably – Pokey's wide-eyed glancing between the two didn't help any.

"We're such cowards." Tabby whispered with a laugh, Alfie nodded his head in agreement.

They finally arrived at the door, both friends glanced down the incline as they took a deep breath – they wondered if they would be heading back down there soon.

Tabby watched as Alfie knelt and pressed his ear against the door, she watched her friend's face as his brow creased into a frown.

"Can you hear anything?" She whispered nervously, Pokey looked at her and then back at Alfie.

"I can hear…" Alfie looked at Tabby quizzically, "I can hear hushed voices?"

"Maybe we should peek?" Tabby suggested as she lay a hand on the door to push it open.

"I guess so, just open it a tiny crack." Alfie agreed, Tabby pushed the door enough for Alfie to look through.

Both held their breath as Alfie scoped out their home.

"I can see the team… they look unharmed." Alfie smiled in relief, "They're sitting at the table and whispering away to each other… I don't see any sign of the guards, but I don't see why they would be whispering if no one's around…"

"I feel like just waltzing in would be pretty stupid." Tabby hummed thoughtfully, "Is there any way to signal to them that we're here without being seen?"

Both thought for a moment, they then turned to look at Pokey who had just landed on the floor. She looked up at them both cluelessly, the two humans shared a smirk.

"Ok, one more time." Tabby explained slowly to her possum friend, both friends were knelt next to her waiting for her to understand the plan. They'd been over it a couple times now and, apparently, Pokey kept adding her own ideas to it. "All you're gonna do is go in there, jump on the table to get their attention and run back to us. That's it."

Pokey scratched her ear.

"There is no need to go anywhere near the kitchen, no need to steal food, trash or anything else… there is also no biting anyone. Do you understand?" Tabby gave her possum a firm look.

Pokey sniffed in her direction, Tabby deflated.

"Why would there be food on the floor?" She asked with a sigh, she pinched the bridge of her nose with stress.

"We might need to think of something else." Alfie frowned sympathetically as he stroked Pokey's head, "She seems to kinda have a one-track mind..."

"Ok, if there's food on the floor you can pick it up on your way back to us as long as you make sure the others are watching you the whole way." Tabby reasoned with the animal pleadingly.

Pokey stood up and scurried over to the door, she looked at them as she waited for it to be opened so she could start her mission. Tabby opened the door wide enough for the possum to slip through, she ran out excitedly as the friends watched.

"There's something we didn't consider." Alfie frowned suddenly, he looked concerned.

"And what's that?" Tabby asked in surprise as she looked at her friend.

Three screams erupted from the room along with a series of explosions.

"We just sent a wild creature into a room full of dramatic people with abilities." Alfie cringed as Tabby stared into the room.

Poor Pokey was hissing violently as she ran back across the floor, fireballs hitting the ground behind her as she just managed to stay out of the way. Hercules was frowning from where he still sat at the table, Oculus and Vera were stood and clinging to each other while Nova was chasing Pokey – her hands alight with the fire spell she was casting.

"Pokey! Hurry!" Tabby whispered worriedly,

Pokey arrived at the door, Alfie's hand grabbed her by the scruff of her neck and dragged her to safety. The teens slammed the door shut and flinched when they heard the spell slam into the other side, all fell silent.

Poor Pokey was trembling as her two humans held her between them, all three staring at the door with wide eyes.

"I am so sorry." Tabby winced as she finally let out her breath, "I didn't think they'd do that! I thought they'd just... y'know... be confused."

Alfie crawled forward and listened closely, he frowned at the silence.

Tabby and Pokey watched him as he turned towards them, still against the door.

"I don't hear-" The boy began only to be cut off as a hand grabbed him by the back of his collar and pulled him through the door, slamming it behind him.

Tabby gasped in horror, she and Pokey immediately crawled over. Tabby shook slightly at the sudden disappearance of her companion, she panted in panic as she cracked the door open a little and peeked in.

She saw Alfie knelt on the floor trying to catch his breath as the team surrounded him, Hercules looked particularly guilty – Tabby guessed it was him that grabbed her friend.

The girl frowned as she finally stood and stormed through the door, Pokey was quick to follow her in but stay behind her where she was safe.

She opened her mouth to yell at the others, but they shushed her hurriedly.

Tabby took the hint, instead choosing to kneel beside Alfie – she placed a gentle hand on the other's back. Alfie looked over at her and gave a weak smile, Tabby matched it with her own relieved one.

The others knelt in front of them and gave them both apologetic yet pleased smiles.

"I am so glad you two are ok!" Nova whispered happily, "We were so scared when you disappeared."

The two blushed.

"Listen." Hercules whispered hurriedly, he kept glancing at the front door. "You two can't be here!"

"Why?" Tabby asked as she tilted her head.

"The Masquerade came to get us when we were looking for you, we're under arrest." Hercules explained, his voice low and guarded.

"They know you two are missing and they're thinking of sending search parties, we're worried they need the whole team together for whatever it is they're planning. They were furious when they brought us here, kept asking where you two were hiding. There are two guards at the front door."

The two youngest shared a troubled look.

"I even made a bird just to keep you guys away!" Nova whispered sulkily, "Did you even see it?"

"*You* sent the firebird!?" Alfie gaped in shock, struggling to keep his voice low.

"Wh-? Yeah!" Nova frowned in confusion, "You saw it? Didn't you get my note? I literally had to use my magic IN FRONT of The Masquerade to send it!"

"There was no note!" Alfie growled, "Just a vicious bird!"

"It wasn't vicious!" Nova argued back, "Firebirds are gentle creatures! They sing and put you to sleep! I chose one because I hoped it would make you guys take a nap and leave you the note!"

"Yeah, well it tried to kill Pokey, it attacked me, put Alfie to sleep and made me pass out!" Tabby pointed out irritably, the others appeared taken aback at this.

"I have so many questions." Oculus shook his head tiredly, rubbing his eyes as he processed all the information.

"I assume this is Pokey?" Vera cooed at the possum, Pokey stepped forward shyly and sniffed the air.

"What did I say about bringing wild creatures home?" Hercules scolded sternly, Oculus gave the bigger man an exasperated look.

"She followed us!" Tabby defended weakly, "Besides, she's more Alfie's pet than mine!"

Alfie rolled his eyes.

"All of that information and it's the possum you're focusing on!?" Oculus gaped at Hercules, completely astonished. "Were you not listening when they said Nova's bad idea nearly killed them?"

"What do you mean you passed out?" Nova pushed, pointedly ignoring Oculus and Hercules as she fixed the girl with a forceful frown.

"I couldn't hear the singing! My head was just filled with screaming!" Tabby explained angrily,

Nova cringed with embarrassment.

"Must be something to do with it being a temporary (and technically not real) animal." Oculus hummed thoughtfully as he wrote in his notebook, "Interesting... we'll need to test that."

"No thank you." Tabby groaned disapprovingly, watching Oculus write.

"None of this is important right now." Hercules pulled their attentions back. "You two need to get out of here before The Masquerade find you, you need to get out and run."

"But we came to rescue you!" Tabby insisted, Alfie hurriedly nodded. "We found some stuff out and we need to go investigate! We figured we'd come get you guys first then the six of us could save Slately!"

The four adults looked worried and confused, but no one got to say another word.

The front door was slammed open as a group of Masks charged in, they immediately targeted the group kneeling in the middle of the floor.

The team leapt to their feet, the four adults standing in front of the teens. Alfie grabbed Tabby's hand and dragged her as he ran to the double doors in hopes of making it back outside, but the doors opened revealing more Masks.

The teens yelped as they changed course. Alfie pulled them both into the safety of the sleeping quarters and shut the door, he leaned against it in hopes of being able to keep them both safe.

The two panted in panic as they heard yelling and fighting outside. They heard Pokey hiss and realised she was still out there, they shared a scared look.

"What do we do!?" Tabby panicked, looking to Alfie for help.

"We're trapped." Alfie swallowed as he rested his head back against the door, his eyes darted side to side as he tried to think up a plan. "We don't know what they want."

Tabby shook her head, she was petrified.

They were even more scared when the fighting noises stopped, both tensed – were their friends ok?

Alfie and Tabby jolted as something banged against the door, they pushed themselves against it to keep it closed. Whoever was on the other side continued banging into it, clearly trying to force it open. Tabby squeezed her eyes shut and grit her teeth, the next hit was harder.

Alfie seemed to make a decision, he grabbed Tabby and pulled her further into the room.

"We're gonna get hit." He whispered hurriedly as he forced the smaller girl to crouch and get under her bed. "We gotta hide!"

Tabby whimpered but did as she was told, she listened as Alfie ran to the other side of the room intending on hiding but the door was broken open first. Tabby watched tearfully as The Masquerade stormed in and dragged a yelling and kicking Alfie out into the main room.

She heard Hercules call Alfie's name in desperation.

Tabby covered her mouth and nose with her hands in an attempt to keep her breathing quiet, she watched the shadowy feet as the guards searched the room and bathroom for her.

She closed her eyes, she hoped Alfie was ok along with the rest of her team.

Then, she felt a hand on her leg.

Her eyes shot open as she was dragged out, she yelped as two guards took one of her arms each and dragged her forcefully out into the main room.

Tabby looked around, everything seemed to slow down as she was pushed through.

Hercules had a whole group of guards sitting and standing on top of him, the man was yelling and struggling – his face red with rage. Oculus was held by four guards, one of which had him by the neck. His purple irises stared deep into Tabby's soul, he appeared scared and sorry. Nova was pinned to the floor by six guards, she was screaming and writhing. It was then Tabby noticed she had a deep wound in her side, one of the guards had a blade and it was now being used to threaten her – she guessed it was to prevent her from using her magic. Vera was held by only 1 guard, she wasn't fighting or screaming or making any kind of fuss. She was stood stock still, her eyes firmly on Nova's wound.

Tabby's stomach turned as a pang of fear hit her. Alfie was missing. It was then she realised she was being guided towards the front door, she was being taken away instead of pinned down like the others.

What could this mean?

She held her breath and tried to put on a brave face, but her mind kept racing. Her friends were being kept at base but Nova was seriously hurt, would Vera be able to heal her in time? Where was Alfie? Where were they taking her?

There were no answers, just a terrible feeling deep in her gut.

She realised Alfie was right and how she wished she had listened to him.

They should have just ran away when they had the chance.

Chapter 24

They seemed to walk forever, Tabby swore they must be on the other side of the city by now. Inside The Wall was so dark, cold and depressing. How she missed the wide-open space outside where she and Alfie had such a lovely time together, if you don't count all the fighting, injuries, attacks, drowning and terror that is. She even wished Pokey was here with her, she didn't see her as she was taken away – she could be anywhere!

She wished they had just run, the wolves had warned them they couldn't help. They had known it was too risky and stupid, but the two friends just had to play hero, they were so sick of being told what to do and who they were going to lose that they walked straight into hell without even knowing it.

Tabby flinched as they arrived at a huge mahogany door, it even had a knocker on it in the shape of a skull.

Tabby figured this wasn't a good sign of what was to come.

Two guards were stood outside, they opened the door wordlessly. Tabby was pushed through, she didn't get a chance to see anything before she fell flat on her face with a squeak. She winced when the door slammed shut behind her.

She slowly lifted herself up onto her knees and scanned the room. It was pitch black bar five spotlights shining down on five wooden thrones, the room was cold and seemed vast despite the lack of vision. Tabby smiled as Alfie appeared by her side, she was glad to see he was unharmed.

"You ok?" Alfie fussed anxiously, his voice no louder than a whisper.

"Yeah, I'm ok." Tabby nodded as Alfie helped her to her feet.

"Well... this is extra dramatic huh?"

Alfie elbowed her warningly.

The two friends crept closer to the row of thrones in interest. All five were made of dark rosewood, they were all the same style and height – the only difference being the colourful symbols in white circles painted on the backrests.

The first was of a white gust of air, the second an orange flame. The third seemed to be a black swirl, the fourth a blue tidal wave and the last was a green leaf.

"Where are we?" Alfie breathed fearfully, not daring to get any closer. He watched warily as Tabby slowly edged closer to the centre seat. "Maybe we shouldn't get too close to those?"

"What does the swirl symbolise?" The girl ignored her friend with a puzzled frown. "I mean... the other chairs have the four elements... There isn't a fifth one... is there?"

Tabby looked back at Alfie.

"I don't think so." The taller boy thought carefully. "There are only four; fire, wind, earth and water."

Both friends looked forward at the chairs again, staring at the fifth and centre symbol in confused fascination. Their minds whirled as they thought about what it could mean or what it represented.

Both jumped as the figures simply appeared in the seats in a flash of light. Tabby tried to back away to join Alfie's side, but the centre figure lifted a hand, Tabby yelled as she was thrown back and sent skidding across the ground.

Alfie hurried over and helped her up carefully, they then turned to face the towering figures in fear – these were the strangest people they had met yet and that was saying something.

The first appeared to be part male and part bird. He had pale white skin dotted with silky white feathers, his torso was of a man but his thighs down to his feet looked as if they belonged to an eagle! Instead of arms he had large, feathered wings with pale hands on the ends. His head was bald, his eyes appeared pure white, and he wore a grand toga.

The second figure looked like a female but inhuman. She was slightly shorter than the others but by far one of the most frightening! She seemed to be constantly aflame, they couldn't see anything beyond the inferno. Thick black smoke poured down from her skull to look like her hair.

The fourth also appeared to be female though she didn't seem to be entirely human either. Her body was covered in shining blue scales like a fish, she was curvy and just as tall as the first figure. She had pure black lips and eyes but no nose. Her hair was long and looked like a tidal wave falling over one shoulder, she wore a cloak that was a literal waterfall.

The fifth figure was a large male made of earth and stone. He had long brown hair, and a crown of twigs but, strangely, he had a small tree sapling sticking out the top of his head. He wore a long flowing cloak made of colourful flower heads and fresh green leaves, instead of feet he had hooves like a deer.

But it was the final and centre figure that was the most frightening. This being had no real form, instead it was ever shifting. It seemed able to morph into anything it needed to with fluidity and speed. It was made of flowing shadow and pure darkness, but there were two piercing violet eyes where the head seemed to be.

"Tabitha Murphy. Alfred Knotts." The shadow being spoke with a voice that sounded both high and low pitched, it sent shivers through the two kids. "Do you know who we are?"

The teenagers shook their heads stiffly, not daring to speak.

"My name is Zephyr and I am Air." The first figured bowed his head with a smirk.

"I'm Hestia. I am Fire!" The woman made of flames announced loudly as she gestured with her arms – the two could see charcoal flesh when the flames were moved too quickly.

"Azura. I am Water." The fourth nodded, she seemed pretty bored.

"I am Earth and I go by Bryn." The large male smiled at the two, his voice was deep and gravelly.

"And I am Onyx." The shadow figure announced, "I am Void. We are The Council of Slately."

There was a beat of silence.

"I don't think they know who you are." Azura smirked in amusement, "Wanna show 'em?"

"Is this true?" Onyx snarled in offense, "You only know of four elements?"

Alfie and Tabby just stared at them, wide eyed and terrified – this only seemed to make the five that much happier.

"I did say void was too confusing for people to remember." Bryn shrugged as he plucked a weed from his chin.

"Void is everything." Onyx growled, the room shook. "Void is both creation and destruction. That which is corporeal and that which is beyond human comprehension."

"Just show 'em!" Hestia cackled excitedly, "We all know you want to!"

"Very well." Onyx chortled mysteriously.

Their body grew twice the size and from their shadowy flesh more bodies formed – white masks adorned their faces. Tabby and Alfie gasped as they recognised The Masquerade. Onyx then stretched out a hand and the figures evaporated with animalistic screams. Onyx then formed a second hand, they lifted everyone into the air and the room changed so it was made of wood instead of stone, they changed it back then stomped two feet against the floor. It darkened and the two kids fell into the inky blackness, they tried to swim in the thick cold liquid but it was exhausting.

Alfie reached for Tabby but Onyx wasn't finished.

The two teens were tied up with the liquid tendrils and it carried them upwards as the floor became stone once more, both were dropped as the tendrils turned to dust.

Alfie grunted as he hit the floor, he looked over to see Tabby had been caught. She was floating just above the floor surrounded by purple mist, she couldn't seem to move. She looked terrified.

"I can create life and destroy it as I please." Onyx explained darkly, "I can twist your minds, turn your blood to water, make you see things that aren't there, make your entire personality change... I can do everything..."

Tabby gulped fearfully.

"But my favourite thing to do." Onyx continued, their purple eyes glowing brighter and brighter. The other elementals shuffled in their seats excitedly, leaning forward to watch. "Is this..."

Tabby yelled out.

Alfie watched in horror as his friend's limbs separated from her body, there was no blood or wounds or anything but clearly his friend felt it as if they had been pulled off.

"Leave her alone!" Alfie begged as he ran forward, the five looked at him.

Onyx put Tabby back together before dropping her to the ground, the poor girl was shaking like a leaf but seemed to be ok.

"Very well..." Onyx sounded amused. "Let me show you another trick I enjoy."

Alfie glared at Onyx as he waited for something to happen, Tabby was watching in terror from her place on the floor.

Alfie choked as his mouth and throat filled with water, he bent over and tried to spit it all out, but it was only replaced with more. He couldn't breathe, his lungs burned and his vision blurred as he fell onto his hands and knees.

The silent room was filled with splashing, spluttering and choking coughs.

Tabby scrambled over to Alfie, she thumped him on the back in an attempt to help him. She gripped her friend and shook him fearfully, not knowing what to do to stop him drowning.

"That's enough." Azura sighed in boredom, "I've already told you I don't like it when you use my element without my permission."

"My apologies." Onyx nodded.

As quickly as it started it stopped.

Alfie sucked in a huge breath as his lungs, throat and mouth finally cleared. Tabby breathed a sigh of relief as she patted her friend's shoulder gently, hoping to give some kind of relief.

The boy sent her a grateful look.

"Ok. On your feet." Onyx commanded dully.

Both teenagers felt their legs move against their will, painfully pushing them to stand on their two feet.

"Alfred, Tabitha... We allowed you to live when we discovered you were... broken." Onyx began darkly, the teens flinched. "We sent you to be with the other failures, to be with your own kind... We allowed you the honour to defend your birthplace, your home. But you wandered too far."

The five elementals straightened up to their full heights, they looked down upon the shaking kids.

"Now," Onyx continued gravely. "I know you have seen far more than you needed to, we will forgive you on one condition."

Alfie and Tabby looked at one another before facing Onyx, they knew they would have to give them whatever they wanted.

"I know you saw the dead dragons." Onyx nodded bluntly. "I *was* originally just going to erase your memories, but I have just heard about something very interesting, something that caused us to be late to this meeting."

The other four looked at the fifth, they clearly hadn't heard this news.

"A dragon infant has been spotted flying into the clouds." Onyx revealed with a nasty sneer, the other elements gasped loudly. "I have a suspicion that you two have some involvement, am I correct?"

Tabby opened her mouth to speak but Alfie beat her to it.

"We saw the dead dragons... it's true!" The taller boy began, his voice strong but polite. "But we don't know what you're talking about. We didn't see an infant dragon, only dead adults. There was nothing else in the cavern."

Tabby kept her face steady, even nodding along.

Zephyr, Hestia, Azura and Bryn all looked over to their leader, their faces serious and grave. Onyx didn't even flinch.

"Which one are you?" They asked conversationally.

"Alfred." Alfie answered confidently, "And I'm telling the truth."

"Knotts..." Onyx hummed in thought, the other four smirked.

"Yeah... his dad is the idiot from years ago!" Hestia cackled, Alfie flinched. "You remember? Begged you to spare him!"

Suddenly, Alfie's father's voice echoed around the room.

"Please! Please! I have a young son! He needs me! I'll never disobey you again! Spare me for my boy!"

Tabby glanced at Alfie to see tears in his eyes, his lips trembling. Yet, he stood tall and strong – not breaking eye contact.

"Ah... Yes..." Onyx chuckled darkly.

"And the mother." Zephyr piped up, watching as Alfie's head snapped in his direction. "She begged us to at least tell her what was going to happen to him before she died."

Alfie was stunned.

His mother was dead?

"Oh Zephyr!" Azura scolded with a playful smirk, "He didn't know she was executed yet! So naughty!"

Alfie shook his head tearfully; his chest was tight as he tried not to cry in front of these heartless monsters.

"She was executed because of you." Onyx's voice sounded grave, "Once we find... mistakes among our people, we have to wipe out the relations... Just in case. I'm sure you understand."

Alfie let out a strangled cry as he bowed his head and panted shakily, his mind was reeling. His shoulders and hands shook, his face felt hot and his chest painfully hollow.

Tabby gasped and stared at the five in fearful shock and dread, she felt Alfie look over at her as he seemed to reach the same conclusion.

They execute the relatives?

Wouldn't that mean...

"The little girl was the bravest." Bryn hummed pleasantly, closing his eyes. "Whatever her name was... she didn't beg or cry or... really do anything... silent."

Tabby choked as her own tears stung her eyes, she shook her head refusing to believe the cruel words.

"Your parents were whiny." Hestia grumped, "Kept insulting us and arguing with us! So rude."

The two stepped back as the news sank in, their families were dead, and it was all their fault.

Tabby could only think of her little sister. How kind and intelligent she was, how she had always believed she would go far in life.

She grit her teeth as tears poured down her cheeks, she saw Alfie sit on the floor next to her as he tried to stay brave. Tabby wasn't about to breakdown, instead she let her grief turn to anger.

She yelled as she ran forward, she wanted to hurt these awful beings. She wanted to avenge all those people they had hurt or killed, she wanted to make them pay for executing her baby sister. She didn't get very far.

"Tabby!" Alfie yelled as a gust of wind lifted the smaller girl into the air.

Poor Tabby was spun around before being dropped heavily back on the floor, she moved to try again but a stone vine materialised from the floor and wrapped around her. She groaned and snarled as she struggled against it, but it was no use, she was pinned down by her restraint.

"Calm down." Hestia huffed moodily, her flames climbing with her annoyance. "So over the top, you weren't gonna see them again anyway! What difference does it make?"

"You know… I am able to bring them all back." Onyx suggested knowingly, "Just tell me the truth and I will do so."

Alfie shook his head defiantly; he scrubbed his face of all wetness as he rose to his feet.

"We were telling the truth! We know nothing of the baby dragon!" He insisted angrily. "You can't blackmail us!"

The five council members howled with laughter, Tabby glared at them after she was finally released. She too scrubbed her tears away pointedly.

"We need to know where it's gone. Just tell us where it is and we'll fix everything." Bryn chuckled softly, he was the first to calm his laughter.

"We already told you." Tabby growled, "We don't know anything!"

"Isn't that obvious?" Onyx joked, "You two don't seem to understand the position you are in. I can tear you apart, make you feel unimaginable pain, see soul destroying things… I only need one of you alive to tell me what I need to know."

Onyx had expected this to frighten the sixteen-year-olds. They were surprised to see this only seemed to anger them more.

"No matter what you do, you'll still get the same answer." Tabby snapped, face reddening. "We don't know anything about it."

"We can't give you information we don't have." Alfie then seemed to come up with an idea. "But… if you're right, we might be able to help. Surely a dragon would leave a trail, our team could head out and hunt for it?"

The five elementals gaped at him for a moment, Tabby nearly did too.

How suicidal was her friend?

The room was once again filled with loud, mocking laughter.

Alfie grit his teeth, he was really getting sick of this.

"I like this one!" Hestia cheered excitedly, "He's so sassy!"

Both teens were stuck watching The Council laughing at them. How were they going to get out of there? Were they going to be able to keep hiding the truth? They couldn't help but think back to their team, they hoped to reunite with them once more.

They hoped the six of them would get a chance to escape this hell.

They just had to get through this questioning alive first.

Chapter 25

Alfie lay on his back on the cold hard ground, he was too exhausted to move. He could hear yelling and laughter echoing around the room from The Council while they continued to torment poor Tabby, his friend was staying strong though and sticking to their original answers.

There was no good reason to tell The Council what they knew. These monsters were not going to spare the two teens or bring back their families as a reward. More likely, the two would be killed (Maybe even their team as well) and then Kaida would be destroyed too.

They didn't know what would happen if all of the dragons disappeared, Kaida had said it would be chaos but that could really mean anything.

Plus, if there really were others out there and Kaida had joined them, these elementals were not above hurting and killing people to get to her. Maybe they would even create yet another Slately. They couldn't allow that.

They would both rather die here today than cause whatever pain would come of them telling the truth.

Alfie glanced over as Tabby landed on her face beside him, the girl gave an exhausted groan as she turned her head to look at him. They made eye contact, neither dared to say a word.

"This is getting kinda boring now." Hestia yawned tiredly, "They're not playing!"

"Maybe it's time we kicked it up a notch?" Bryn suggested as he slumped further in his throne. "I'd like to go back home at some point y'know, this place is a dump."

Both friends frowned in interest at one another at this new information. The five elementals did not stay in the city they ruled, so where did they come from?

"I mean, you said we only needed one of them." Zephyr pointed out dully, "Maybe it's time to act on that?"

"Which one though?" Azura cocked her head, "They're both as useless as each other."

"I feel it would be a waste of my power to destroy such a meaningless life." Onyx sighed heavily, clearly disappointed. "It would not change anything."

This was very true.

"What a waste of time!" Hestia groaned loudly as she stretched. "I mean it was fun and all but, we're no further forward."

Tabby and Alfie both gasped as they felt themselves being pulled over towards the thrones, the floor covered their legs and forced them back up into standing positions. Both spread their arms in an attempt to balance themselves, they looked up at the five.

"Ugh, don't look at us like that!" Azura scolded them heatedly, "We're the ones that should be angry, you two have nothing to complain about!"

Both wanted to point out that they had literally been tormented endlessly while the five just sat there but they knew that would be a mistake, they wisely kept their mouths shut.

"Look, would this be easier if the other wasn't here?" Onyx asked, their voice dull and fed up.

"Worth a shot." Bryn huffed as he stood up, he strolled over towards the two and studied them.

This was odd. None of the five had left their seats the whole time.

"Let's see." Bryn hummed thoughtfully, he placed a hand on Alfie's shoulder.

Tabby watched in horror as from his touch her friend's body turned to stone, she couldn't look away as Bryn stepped back and seemed to wait.

"It's just you and us now." Zephyr pointed out, gaining Tabby's attention. "Just tell us where the dragon went and your little friend will never know! You two can go back and just continue as you were."

Tabby swallowed as she glared at the birdman.

"How many times!?" She growled furiously, "This changes nothing! I don't know anything!"

Zephyr deflated in his seat with a frustrated sigh.

"Bryn." He waved a wing vaguely.

Bryn nodded and strolled over to Tabby's side, he placed a hand on her. Tabby felt freezing cold and sleepy as her body became numb, she let out a shuddering breath and everything went dark.

Alfie gasped as his eyes shot open. His flesh was bright red with cold, his chest ached as if he'd held his breath for far too long. He shook his head in confusion, a statue caught his eye.

He did a double take as he slowly realised it looked very familiar. Then it clicked.

That statue wasn't a statue. It was Tabby.

"Ok." Hestia clicked her fingers impatiently to grab the boy's attention, it worked.

"Your friend is suspended in stone." Bryn explained from where he stood next to stone girl. "You can tell us anything now and she will never know you said a word, you two can just go back and she'll be none the wiser."

Alfie blinked as he glanced over at his friend, the four in the thrones leaned forward expectantly. Bryn and Alfie made eye contact; the elemental gave him a calm smile.

"But... I don't know anything..." Alfie pleaded softly, mostly to Bryn. "If I did, I would tell you! Please just listen to us, we know nothing!"

"He's a very convincing liar." Onyx sounded impressed. "I mean... not quite enough but I think he'd manage to fool most simple humans; how does someone learn to trick others so carelessly?"

Alfie gave a bemused frown.

"What do you mean? I'm not lying!" He insisted, keeping his voice strong.

"I'd also like to know how a human gets so... twisted to become so convincing... to find it so easy to lie to the face of others." Azura hummed with a secretive smile, "Makes you wonder what other lies he's told... I wonder if he's ever lied this way to his little friend?"

"Am I crumbling this statue or not?" Bryn asked impatiently, he seemed desperate to get comfortable in his throne again.

"No. Release her." Onyx commanded, their voice dripping with intrigue. "I think Azura may be onto something."

Bryn shrugged as he headed back to his seat, he waved a hand in Tabby's general direction. Alfie watched in relief as the stone crumbled away to reveal his friend, the girl's eyes shot open as she gasped for air.

Alfie suddenly understood his own awakening, he was the second to have been questioned in such a manner. He guessed Tabby hadn't said anything, why else would they have turned to him next.

"Tabitha Murphy!" Azura greeted kindly as she stood from her seat, she strolled over to the girl in question and smiled softly at her. "I'm afraid we have some news... it's rather upsetting but we thought it important that you know the truth."

Tabby glanced between her and Alfie warily, she wasn't quite sure what was going on. Meanwhile, Alfie looked just as confused if not slightly alarmed.

"You see, we've discovered a rather jarring trait of Alfred's." Azura continued, she reached a scaly hand up and used her long, claw like nails to cup Tabby's chin.

The gesture made Alfie's blood boil.

"Did you know he's a fantastic liar?" She asked with a soft giggle, "My goodness, he just cannot stop! I don't think that boy has ever told the truth, not once!"

Tabby didn't look convinced much to Alfie's relief.

Azura leant forward so her mouth was beside Tabby's ear, her watery hair flowed over her shoulder and soaked through her jumpsuit.

"He told us where the dragon is heading." She whispered pityingly, "He betrayed you in return for his freedom... you protected him for nothing."

Tabby shook her head as Azura stepped back, her gaze was so soft and sympathetic – Tabby couldn't bear it.

"I don't believe you." She nodded firmly, Azura sighed sadly and shook her head.

"My, my... you're in so deep you can't even see the surface." Azura pushed, "Your friend is a liar. He has been since day one... I actually wonder if anything he's ever told you is true?"

"Don't listen to her!" Alfie warned, his heated glare on the water element.

The poor boy jumped as a vine crept up from the floor and wrapped around his mouth to silence him, he struggled against it uselessly.

"The fact you're covering his mouth tells me you're the ones who are lying!" Tabby rolled her eyes. She gasped as her legs were finally released from the stone, she stepped forward warily only for Azura to wrap a delicate arm around her shoulders.

"We've covered his mouth so for once you will watch his expression and not listen to his false words." Azura explained in determination, "We are your rulers, we care about you… we only want our city to prosper and stay safe… yes we've done some… heart-breaking things but it's only to keep the population safe."

"Heart-breaking!?" Tabby repeated bewildered. "You've murdered innocent people! You were literally laughing about it earlier!"

"We only did that to antagonise you." Zephyr rolled his eyes from where he was slumped in his throne. "It's called trying to get answers out of our captives by targeting their weak spots, it's a well-known tactic."

Tabby sent the elemental of Air a glare before refocusing on Azura, she still had a soft grip on her and it was starting to make her feel uncomfortable.

She was slowly guided closer to the other elements as they all rose from their seats. Bryn created a soft, mossy stool for her which Azura pushed her onto. Hestia made a warming flame, cool enough to hold in the hand but warm and comforting. Tabby cupped it in amazement, it felt so wrong but it was just so pretty. Zephyr wrapped a wing around the girl, the feathers soft and heavy like a blanket. Azura knelt in front of her, looking up into her face earnestly.

"Tabitha… you are so young yet, you have come so far." She soothed gently, "You have been so brave, so strong… Yet… you have been fooled time and time again by the one person you trust. It breaks our heart to see, we want to free you from his lies."

Tabby couldn't help but stare into her bewitching eyes. She was very aware Onyx was standing behind her, the being was creepily silent.

"Alfred told us what your ability is." Azura continued kindly, "How exciting and interesting it must be to converse with creatures of all shapes and sizes, how fascinating it must be to hear their stories and ways of life."

Tabby stared at the group of elementals completely stunned by their knowledge, she glanced up at Alfie in shock. Her friend was struggling against his binds, his face desperately trying to convey that they were lying.

Tabby wasn't sure anymore.

How did they know her power if Alfie didn't tell them?

"I'm sure you have some wonderful tales to share." Bryn agreed softly. "And we would very much like to hear them but... there is something you should know."

Tabby looked around at the powerful beings curiously.

"Tell me... did Alfred ever tell you why his father was *really* taken away to be executed?" Azura asked, her voice soothing and sad.

Tabby flinched as she heard her friend's frustrated cry muffled by the vine, she looked up at him only for her chin to be pulled by Azura. She blinked as she studied her face.

"No?" She guessed sympathetically.

"He said he didn't know." Tabby answered carefully, "He said his father did nothing wrong, that he was a good man."

The elementals chuckled bitterly, Tabby's eyes widened as she listened.

"I knew it... a liar from the very start." Hestia gave a dark chuckled. "It's impressive."

"I knew you were the good one... the honest one." Azura nodded fondly,

"Of course we did." Zephyr agreed with a proud smile, "The nasty ones always target the kind and gentle. This is why we feel we must intervene, it is not fair of him to continue to drag you down with him. He has not once been honest with you, he is not truly your friend."

Tabby shook her head firmly with disbelief, she refused to believe kind and quiet Alfie was as awful as these five claimed.

"He knows exactly what he is and what his father did." Bryn nodded knowingly, "He knows far more than he lets on. Like we say, he revealed everything about you to us when we were alone... he doesn't care about you."

Alfie growled through his gag as his struggles grew stronger, Tabby could barely hear him through the ringing in her ears.

"Alfred's father was paired with another woman, they had a son together as permitted by us." Azura explained firmly, "But, he snuck out one night to his co-worker's home... you see Mr Knotts was having an affair with Alfred's mother, they were childhood sweethearts but the mother was not permitted marriage or children."

Tabby shook her head numbly.

"Then, she fell pregnant. We demanded the baby be destroyed. Instead, that no good man moved in with his pregnant lover and demanded we take his real family in exchange for this new one." Azura shook her head in disgust. "Well... we decided not to listen. We gave Alfred his name, we even allowed that disgrace to help raise him seeing as the mother was not supposed to be a parent... figured she'd need the help. That miserable man then returned to his previous family to check on his other son, that's the straw that broke the camel's back."

"We decided that there was one clear criminal." Onyx finished, making Tabby startle. "We executed the father for breaking multiple rules... he devastated two families with his crimes. Only the Knotts were aware of his situation, his other family thought he was working overtime. Disgusting."

Tabby gaped at the five in horror, she couldn't believe it was true. There was simply no way.

Then she saw her friend's crumpled and devastated expression. Alfie looked utterly distraught and broken, he couldn't even seem to bear to look in Tabby's direction.

Tabby knew in that instant the elementals were telling the truth.

"Why didn't you tell me?" Tabby asked softly, looking at her friend. Alfie kept his head bowed and his gaze firmly on the ground.

"Because he's a liar." Azura nodded sadly. "He was protecting himself, he knew if you trusted him he'd be able to use you to his advantage."

"Wh-? That doesn't make sense." Tabby stood up suddenly, "He's never used me for anything, why are you telling me this?"

"Because, we're proving to you that we're the ones on your side. Alfred has told us everything, as reward he gets to go free." Onyx grew in size and towered over Tabby, the girl coward under the frightening being. "And he gave us, you."

"M-Me?" Tabby stuttered as she backed away,

"He said you can communicate with creatures, we're gonna need you if we're gonna find that dragon." Onyx laughed, Tabby blinked. The other elementals rolled their eyes at the blunder.

"But... you said-" Tabby didn't get the chance to finish, the dark mauve shadows spilled from Onyx and surrounded the teen.

She choked and coughed as it poured into her nose and mouth. Alfie watched with wide frightened eyes as his struggles intensified, what were they doing now!?

The mist faded to reveal Tabby still standing in the same spot, Alfie stared at her warily – she didn't look any different.

The elementals laughed as they gestured for Tabby to face Alfie, she did as she was told. Alfie gasped and his heart broke when he saw his friend's once golden eyes were now glowing purple.

Did Onyx just brainwash her?

"Ok Tabitha." Onyx announced smugly, Alfie fell to the ground as Bryn was distracted by the show.

It was then Alfie spotted a misty tendril leading from Onyx to Tabby's back, he realised they had to be tethered for Onyx to control her.

So, there were limits to their powers as much as they liked to pretend otherwise.

He hoped his newly hatched plan would work.

"Tell us what we want to know, did you two have something to do with the dragon?" Onyx began as Alfie ran forward, his eyes locked on Tabby. "Where is it going?"

Tabby's mouth opened to answer.

Alfie's full body weight slammed into the smaller girl, effectively winding her and sending them both crashing to the ground. Alfie pushed passed his fear, pain, exhaustion and embarrassment.

A bright, golden, shimmering forcefield spread in a dome around the two.

Tabby fell unconscious as the connection was severed, Alfie's body was still arched over her protectively as his wide eyes stared at the furious elementals.

Hestia screeched as she set the ground aflame, not a spark touched the shield.

Zephyr helped her by creating a hurricane which lifted the fire to surround the bubble, Alfie did not faulter.

Azura filled the room with dark swirling water, still the friends stayed safe and dry.

Bryn growled as he dropped boulders, earth and trees onto the golden light. They simply slid off and lay on the ground, Bryn continued his assault hoping it was at least tiring the boy out.

But, Alfie had never felt so strong.

He watched as the natural debris built up around them, he would keep this shield up as long as he could.

He was angry, furious. Those evil monsters tried to tear their friendship apart, had tried to trick Tabby into no longer trusting him, they had revealed his darkest secret to the one person he truly didn't want to find out.

They had endlessly hurt and tormented them, both hadn't used their powers.

Tabby simply couldn't and she had asked Alfie not to reveal his own.

Turns out, the five already knew what their abilities were because he would never reveal anything about Tabby to those freaks.

Onyx tried to tear the forcefield apart, tried to teleport their self inside it, they even tried to tear the flesh of the two inside. He tore the ground apart only for the shield to turn into some sort of bubble, the two simply floated in the empty space.

The five stared as Alfie glared back at them, his gaze steady, strong and determined.

They had failed.

Onyx let out a deafening scream of furious frustration and suddenly, the five were gone.

Alfie blinked in surprise at the sudden disappearance, the spotlights flickered out leaving the two in darkness. The only light was their glowing protective shield.

The blonde boy looked down at his friend sadly, he hoped that once she woke up she would forgive him for keeping such a big secret from her.

With the absence of the threat, the poor teen became exhausted from holding up his shield against such heavy attacks. His arms shook as he tried to keep it going while holding himself up, he grimaced as his vision narrowed.

The forcefield shattered as Alfie's arms gave out, the poor boy flopped down on top of his friend as he lost his grip on consciousness.

Chapter 26

Alfie took a deep breath as he slowly came too. He was happy to say he didn't really feel very sore or bad in any way, he was even happier that he was lying on his back on something soft. He almost smiled to himself, but this changed as something new registered.

He could feel a light breath on his face.

He slowly blinked his eyes open.

And yelled in surprise.

He flattened himself further into the mattress below him as he placed a hand on his chest, he panted as he tried to catch his breath and keep his heart inside his ribcage.

"Tabby!" He scolded angrily as he stared up into the heated glare of his friend, the girl finally backed off but only marginally. "What the heck!?"

Tabby simply watched in silence as Alfie tried to calm himself, her eyes were hard and her face stony.

He thought his friend would be happy to be back at base, he wondered where the team were.

"What were you doing!?" Alfie demanded grumpily as he sat up, "You nearly gave me a heart attack!"

"What was I doing!?" Tabby snapped back, "What were you doing!?"

Alfie blinked before studying the other's face, he felt very wary at what he saw there.

"Are you mad at me for something?" He probed suspiciously, Tabby threw her hands up in exasperation.

"Funnily enough! Yes!" The girl yelled as if it were obvious – which, to be fair, it was.

"What for?" Alfie tested, still keeping his guard up.

Tabby stared at him, now more concerned than irritated.

"Wait... are you serious?" The girl snapped to attention, leaning forward in worry. "You don't remember?"

Alfie raised a hand placatingly.

"No, no." He soothed carefully, "I remember everything that happened, don't worry... it's just... I can think of a few things that happened that you could be mad about so I kinda need you to narrow it down."

Tabby shook her head in disappointment, she was now looking very serious. Alfie did not like that one bit, he had a feeling he now knew what they were about to talk about.

"Why didn't you tell me?" The smaller murmured gently, her eyes scanning Alfie as if searching for an answer.

"Where is everyone?" Alfie asked hurriedly, trying to change the subject.

"They're fine, Alfie-"

"Is Nova ok? Last we saw she was hurt!" Alfie raised his voice pointedly, clearly this frustrated Tabby.

"She's all good. Alfie-"

"And where did Pokey get to?" Alfie made a move to get off his bed, but Tabby grabbed his arm firmly. Technically Alfie could just push her away and escape, he was definitely more than capable of doing so but he figured that would only make things worse between them.

"Why didn't you tell me?" Tabby pushed, now making her voice stern.

"Why does it matter?" Alfie growled, giving Tabby an annoyed scowl. "It had nothing to do with you! Why did you need to know?"

Tabby's expression fell with hurt.

"Why do you even care?" Alfie continued in frustration as Tabby released his arm, "You have no right to know anything about him, it's none of your business!"

Tabby flinched at that, she even went as far as to shuffle backwards slightly and putting distance between herself and the other teen. Alfie watched her tensely.

"I'm sorry." Tabby apologised openly, keeping a close eye on the other. "I just... When I asked years ago you told me you didn't know why he was taken away... I mean, I get why you wouldn't say much when we first met but... we've known each other for years, we're going through this weird adventure together... I just don't understand why you would hide something like this from me." Alfie deflated in exhaustion, he bowed his head in guilt.

"You're right though..." Tabby nodded, her voice stronger. "It's not for me to know if you don't want to share it, I shouldn't have pushed you or been angry. I guess it was all just a bit of a shock..."

"No." The boy shook his head slowly, looking up at Tabby. "I wanted to tell you but... I was ashamed of it..."

"Ashamed!?" Tabby snorted making the other startle and glare at her, "Sorry but, ashamed of what? Having a father that loved you and your mother so much?"

"No! Having a father that had two separate families, broke the rules and left two single mothers to raise their sons alone!" Alfie snapped back infuriated, Tabby smiled apologetically.

"Your father was open with your mother about everything that was going on and she was ok with it. They were in love from the start and, clearly, your mother wanted a child. They're not in the wrong, The Council are!" Tabby pointed out confidently, "Who are they to say who can and can't have a family? Who are they to tell people who they can love? If they weren't around your father would never have had his forced family, he would've just been with your mother! They pushed him into that position, and he fought back for the life he wanted!"

Alfie blinked tearfully at the powerful speech.

"You should not be ashamed of your father." Tabby nodded kindly, "You should be inspired by him. After all, we're kinda following in his footsteps? We're gonna try and save our whole city so they can make their own choices! He'd be so proud of you for wanting to do this."

Tabby was going to continue, she could have said so much more. She decided to quiet down when Alfie grabbed her and pulled her into a warm, emotional hug.

"Thank you." Alfie mumbled quietly making Tabby smile caringly. They simply held each other for a moment more.

The bedroom door creaked open somewhat, then the scuttling of clawed feet across the ground could be heard getting closer.

Pokey jumped up onto the bed and hurried over to her two humans, she snuffled them both gently which made them chuckle in fond amusement.

"Yes, hello." Tabby smirked as they finally parted to look down at the little marsupial. "We see you."

"Hello big ratty." Alfie petted the possum's head softly, he smirked as he felt Tabby give him an exasperated look.

"You are so mean to her." She huffed but couldn't help but smile.

Pokey clambered onto Alfie's lap and happily sat down so she could stare up into his face with her big, clueless eyes. Alfie grinned and continued petting her, feeling slightly creeped out by the unwavering stare.

"Pokey, stop being weird." Tabby rolled her eyes good-naturedly, "You're making Alfie squirm."

Alfie leaned forward and pointedly stared back at Pokey, they held each other's gazes easily. Tabby glanced between them before chuckling breathily, she found it sweet the two liked each other.

"Stop!" She laughed, "You're both weirdos!"

Alfie laughed as he finally let Pokey win.

He then thought back to the end of the questioning, how Onyx had tried to turn Tabby against him. How he then used his strange power to brainwash her or enslave her – Alfie wasn't entirely sure what it was.

He looked up at Tabby, the girl was patting Pokey silently.

"What did he do to you?" Alfie fussed, his voice almost a whisper.

Tabby looked up at him with a puzzled expression.

"What do you mean?" She asked as she wrinkled her nose, "What did who do to me?"

"Onyx… right after he tried to turn you against me… he…" Alfie struggled to find the right words, "I don't really know what he did to you but, it was like you weren't there anymore…"

Tabby frowned as she wracked her brain.

"Yeah… now that you say it…" Tabby hummed as she squeezed her eyes shut, "I remember seeing a load of shadows and Onyx facing me but… it's all foggy from there to be honest."

"Woah." Alfie's eyes widened. "I think he possessed you or something! Your eyes were glowing purple, you had this thing attached to you that linked you to Onyx and he commanded you to tell him everything!"

"I didn't!" Tabby gasped in dread, "Please tell me I didn't!"

"Oh, don't worry!" Alfie waved her off jokingly. "I saved the day, as usual!"

Tabby laughed at that and gave Alfie a light push against his shoulder, the boy chuckled warmly.

All three glanced round as the door opened fully to reveal Hercules, Oculus, Nova and Vera all smiling at them in giddy relief, the teens grinned back at them.

Without hesitation, the team ran in and leapt onto the far too small bed. Alfie, Tabby and Pokey were pulled into a warm, firm and emotional group hug. They were so pleased to be back, and they were happy their friends were all ok, the team seemed to be relieved to be reunited with their two youngest members.
They were all safe for the time being.

Chapter 27

The six team members snuggled up in their soft, warm sitting area just like they did all those months ago when Alfie and Tabby first set foot in their base. How different it felt now compared to then, how they all had grown and changed. Now, it seemed, their mission had only just begun.

They were all so much more comfortable with each other now, there was a trusting bond that only close calls and battles could form.

Alfie was more calm and relaxed, he seemed to have grown into himself in a way.

Tabby was more confident, stronger. She even had the scars to prove it.

It was finally time for this team to come clean. Everyone needed to be on the same page and up to date on everything that had transpired in such a short time.

After all, Tabby and Alfie had discovered there was a whole world out there, who The Council were and that there was a mystery hovering over simple Slately.

Both teens desperately felt the need to tell their friends everything but, they hesitated.

How could they break it to them that their families were gone? Especially Hercules, he truly believed his two younger brothers were out there living their lives.

There was also the worry of being overheard.

The two teens had possibly convinced The Council that they knew nothing of their dragon, they couldn't now talk about everything they discovered when there may be guards listening in.

"I think it's time you two tell us what happened to you." Hercules nodded, pointedly not looking at the possum that perched on his lap. "Everything. From the Kelpies to when you were dragged unconscious back here."

Tabby and Alfie looked at one another in unease.

How were they going to do this?

"Start with the Kelpies?" Alfie whispered, glancing warily at the door. "How?"

Tabby hummed thoughtfully as her eyes scanned the room, she then had an idea.

"Hey, Oculus?" Tabby smiled at her friend, the man looked up from where he was poking Pokey's side. "Can we borrow a notepad and pencil?"

The four frowned in concerned puzzlement but chose not to comment on the strange request.

Oculus flipped through the many pads he owned, trying to find one with plenty of empty spaces. Eventually he pulled out his cleanest and most intact one, he then flipped to a new page and handed it over along with a very chewed pencil.

"Don't read anything in it." Oculus smirked playfully, "Spoilers."

Tabby and Alfie chuckled as they shuffled closer together.

Alfie took the pencil and pad first.

He wrote out all that had happened until Tabby woke up in that cavern. How he had found the pistol by the opening of the tunnel, and he had risked it by swimming through the darkness and upwards only to find Tabby lying unconscious on the other side.

He then passed it to Tabby.

Tabby wrote about waking up and tried her best to describe what the cavern was like. She wrote about the detailed, labelled and, quite frankly, breath-taking carvings and paintings of animals and mythological beast that covered the walls and ceiling.

She wrote about how they encountered funny little Pokey, her hissing at the slightest thing!

(Alfie snatched the pencil and wrote a very quick note – very much along the lines of 'I told her not to get attached, I told her not to bring her along but she wouldn't listen!')

Tabby snatched the pencil back and stuck her tongue out childishly before she continued their tale.

She described seeing a carving of an ethereal woman – 'Gaia' and how they had found a carved map of their world with all the island regions, she remembered the confusion and surprise when they saw there was a fifth, unnamed island – some kind of mountain stretching up from the ocean.

They worked together, taking it in turns to talk about how knowledgeable Pokey was and how they had found the dragons' lair, the bodies, the eggshells and poor baby Kaida. How Pokey had informed them The Masquerade were behind the culling, but they didn't know why – especially as it seemed the people believed they were sacred and even worshipped them.

Alfie took over to explain how they left the tunnel and why they believed sending Kaida away was the safest option rather than bringing her home. He left out his doubt about whether or not they should come back and instead emphasised how the firebird was a terrible idea and had caused the two to need rescued by the two wolf brothers and Tokka.

They didn't need to write about much more than that.

They finished it by explaining what they felt they needed to do next. They needed to escape The Wall and Slately, they had to find out why the dragons are important, what the other people are like, and they needed to break all the people out of their oppressive city.

With that, they handed back the notebook. They both put fingers to their lips to indicate they were not to read any of the information aloud.

They watched and waited silently as the others gathered around, their faces grave as they read their story.

Apparently, Pokey thought this was all very boring.

She dropped down onto the floor and waddled towards the kitchen, Alfie saw her out the corner of his eye and chuckled in exasperation.

He stomped his foot firmly, Pokey hissed before playing dead.

"Not fooling anyone." Alfie scolded softly, "Get away from the kitchen, you're not allowed in there."

Pokey continued to lie on the floor.

Luckily for her, the two teens' attention were taken away when the others finished reading. She sniffed in their direction before sneaking away into the kitchen.

"Ok." Hercules nodded slowly, "We'll discuss this in a moment… now, tell us about where you were taken."

"We were taken to be questioned by The Council." Alfie answered seriously, the others gasped in amazement.

"You two met The Council!?" Nova's eyes widened as she leant forward, "And you lived!?"

"Yeah." He nodded slightly embarrassed.

"There are five members." Tabby informed them, keeping her voice low. "They are each elementals… I don't know if they actually *are* the elements or if they are just able to control them. So, they're Air, Fire, Water, Earth and Void."

"Void?" Vera repeated, looking unsure. "What's void?"

"You mean ether?" Oculus checked curiously, "Creation and destruction?"

"Pretty much, yeah." Tabby nodded, she knew if anyone had heard of the fifth element it would be Oculus. "Void is made of shadows and they're the one that made The Masquerade."

"They wanted to know where some so-called dragon was going."
Alfie continued pointedly. "Wanted to know if we were somehow involved, of course we told them we had no idea."

"Yeah, this didn't work." Tabby shrugged bitterly, "They kinda... tried to persuade us to give them information. We kept trying to explain to them we knew nothing, we had no idea what they were talking about – we couldn't give them information we didn't have." The two stopped and listened, the other side of the door was silent. They decided to stop milking it.

"Then... they revealed something..." Tabby sighed sadly, her face falling. Alfie bowed his head and looked away – the team became worried.

"They... they uh..." Alfie coughed as Tabby squeezed her eyes shut. "Turns out, when they find those of us who are... gifted, they see it as faulty. They then look to those related to us and... well... just in case they also have some hidden ability, they get rid of them."

"Get rid of them?" Vera repeated hollowly, "How?"

"They... They execute them." Alfie finally confessed, a heavy silence filled the room.

Oculus bowed his head and tucked his hands under his knees, his shoulders tensed and pushed up to make him look smaller. Tabby figured he was just upset like the others were.

Alfie knew better, his heart dropped as he realised.

"You already knew this... didn't you?" Alfie breathed quietly, his voice wobbling slightly.

Oculus' head snapped up and looked at each of his team with wide, scared eyes.

"I didn't know any of it!" He insisted desperately before looking away to the side, "But... I knew our families were dead..."

"Oculus!" Nova gasped as she stared at him in betrayal. "How could you hide this from us!? You really knew all along!?"

Oculus bit his lip nervously.

"I knew…" He admitted, his voice heavy with guilt and regret. Nova shook her head in disgust. "No, Nova! You have to understand! I couldn't tell you! I-I I didn't know how or why I should, isn't it better that you were all happy in thinking your families were ok?"

"Not when it's all a lie!" Nova stood furiously, her face reddening. Hercules had his face in his hands, Tabby stood up and joined his side to rub his back comfortingly.

It was then Vera frowned sadly and looked over at Oculus. She stood up and gently pushed Nova to sit back down, she then knelt in front of the man. He stared at her with a pleading expression.

"You kept it to yourself all of these years?" She asked softly, placing a light hand on his knees. "Oh Oculus… I'm so sorry."

"Sorry!?" Nova gaped, completely lost. "What are *you* sorry for!?"

"Don't you understand?" Vera looked up at her, "Oculus had a vision where he saw all of our families being executed and he said nothing. Think about it, he didn't mourn or act like anything was wrong despite all he saw. He's been carrying this grief and guilt for years just to protect us."

Nova's mouth snapped shut with a click as she thought about Vera's words, Oculus couldn't seem to look up.

"I'm so sorry." He breathed miserably. "I really wanted to tell you I just…"

He startled as the two girls and Alfie enveloped him in a warm embrace, he closed his eyes and hugged them back.

"Hercules?" Tabby checked gently, looking down at the large man. "You ok?"

Hercules took a deep breath before finally sitting up straight.

"I am." He nodded before looking up at Tabby with calm eyes, "I think we all had a suspicion our families were not left unharmed for our differences…"

Tabby gave him a sombre nod, she had definitely thought about it.

"All this does is prove The Council are monsters." Hercules stood up, his team all looked up at him. "We must do something. They've killed our families and hurt our new one, they are keeping us all from the world and the people out there. We make a plan, we're not going to sit here and protect a prison any longer."

The others smiled up at him, all were in agreement.

"So, together we will think up an escape plan!" Hercules nodded in confident determination, too caught up in the moment to realise what he had just done.

The five others stared at him in horror and disbelief, they tensed as they waited to see what would happen next.

There was a clatter as Pokey ran out of the kitchen with a slice of bread in her mouth, they all jumped at the noise but soon laughed as she ran straight through the middle of them and into the bedroom with her stolen treasure.

Suddenly, their door was forced open with a bang and The Masquerade stormed in with arms full of equipment - they headed straight for the door that led to their slope to the outside. The team watched in horror as the beings began boarding up their only escape.

One of them turned to face the group.

"You are all under house arrest. You will be kept here, unable to leave until The Council decide otherwise." They announced in an oily voice. "The Council are forgiving however, if Tabitha Murphy and Alfred Knotts suddenly remember any useful information, they are welcome to inform Our Council and you four can return to your freedom as you had before."

"Wait," Nova glared daringly at the guard, "What do you mean 'you four'?"

"If it is proven Tabitha and/or Alfred were keeping valuable information from our leaders they will be executed for their betrayal." The Mask answered easily, "As per the law."

The team shared a bitter look as their one bit of freedom was snatched from them.

They stayed strong and silent until they were once again alone in the room.

"Nice one, Herc!" Oculus clapped sarcastically, smirking in amusement. "We were doing so well too… shame."

Hercules blushed and glared heatedly at the prophet.

"Makes a change from it being you." Nova pointed out, she felt bad for poor Hercules. "You're the one that normally screws up."

Vera, Tabby and Alfie all nodded in agreement, Oculus put a hand on his chest in mock offense.

"How dare you!" He swooned dramatically, "I've never done a single thing wrong in my life! I've certainly never gotten us locked away, dooming the world in the process!"

"Alright, that's enough!" Hercules griped tiredly, shaking his head. "I'm sorry, ok? I didn't think about it!"

"Ignore him." Vera soothed with a gentle smile, "He's only joking."

"We'll figure this out." Hercules promised them all quietly, "We'll think of something together and we will get out of here, all six of us."

The other five nodded in touched agreement, they believed him.

"For now, we stick to our guns, we stay quiet and submissive." Hercules continued firmly, he then looked at Nova. "I need you to destroy the note."

Everyone looked surprised but Oculus looked horrified, he grabbed his notebook and hugged it to his chest.

"No!" He hushed defensively, "It's useful and informative! What if we need it later?"

"I agree it is informative, that's the issue." Hercules was understanding yet made sure he was clear. "It's also the key to losing everything if it were to fall into the wrong hands. Please Oculus, rip out the note and hand it to Nova so she can make sure no one ever reads it."

Oculus hesitated, he couldn't bear the thought of damaging his beloved notebooks or losing such vital information.

His purple gaze then flicked over to Tabby and Alfie, they gave him soft smiles. Oculus deflated as his grip on his book loosened, if The Council found the note the two kids would be killed.

Oculus couldn't let that happen.

He breathed a sigh as he glumly flicked through his own scribbled notes, he finally found the pages and ripped them out.

He handed the delicate paper over to Nova, she thanked him with an earnest smile.

"You two owe me." Oculus joked weakly at the two sixteen-year-olds, they grinned and hugged him tightly.

Nova held up her hand with the paper, in a matter of seconds it burned up and turned to ash. A wave of her hand and the ashes were transformed into a little potted plant, a single stem stuck up from the soil.

She picked it up and handed it to Oculus with a soft and caring smile.

"This way the information is harmless and gone... but you still get to keep what it was written on."

Oculus took the pot with tender hands and gazed down at it misty-eyed. The others watched him with fond smiles, they thought Nova's gesture was sweet and kind.

"You realise this is gonna die with no sunlight, right?" Oculus smirked cheekily as he ruined the moment.

Nova narrowed her eyes dangerously.

"No! Nova!" Oculus screeched dramatically as he ran around the table, Nova was hot on his heels. "I'm sorry!"

"You're such an asshole!" Nova hollered loudly but her grin was wide and glowing. Her hands were also glowing, but with flames. "I'm gonna burn that nice plant, then your notebooks, then your stupid, pretentious pocket watch thing and then, finally, you!"

"It's a fob watch!" Oculus spluttered as he tripped over the table leg and flopped to the ground gracelessly.

"This is gonna be a long lockdown." Hercules closed his eyes with a long-suffering sigh, Vera giggled but gave him a reassuring pat on the arm.

Tabby and Alfie laughed aloud as Oculus let out another high-pitched scream as Nova lifted him into the air with her magic. They were disappointed their plans had been put on hold, especially when their mission was so important. Being shut in with four big personalities was going to be a challenge within itself but, somehow, they were ok with that.

There was no one else they'd rather be stuck with.

To be continued in…

The Stone Guardians
Book 2: Fleeing for Freedom

Printed in Great Britain
by Amazon

80266297R00150